UNCLE AND ANTS

UNCLE AND ANTS

A Silicon Valley Mystery

Marc Jedel

BGM Press
San Jose, California

Published in the United States by BGM Press.

ISBN 978-1-7327-1640-7 (Paperback edition)

Cover designed by Alchemy Book Covers

Sign up for my mailing list to get free content, learn of new releases and receive special offers:

http://www.marcjedel.com

To my beloved sister: Without you, not only would my whole life have been empty and meaningless, but I also wouldn't have anything funny to say.

(She made me write this.)

1

Monday Afternoon

Be careful what you wish for when you're ten years old because it just might come true. I've had a complicated relationship with my younger sister Laney since we were kids, but I've never wished her hospitalized from a falling drone.

Until the nurse from the ICU called about Laney, my Monday had rocked. Hard to beat clear blue skies and 75 degrees on a beautiful, late August day in Silicon Valley, and if my work kept me stuck inside all day, at least my latest software build appeared bug-free and working well.

I hung up to rush to the hospital, only then realizing I'd forgotten to ask the nurse about Laney's condition. Screwing up phone calls was one of my special skills that only seemed to come in handy with telemarketers.

When I reached the hospital, I hurried into the building, more concerned than I'd want to admit to Laney. Our relationship had survived over the years on a steady diet of teasing and had only begun to deepen in the last few years after her husband died.

She moved to town a few months ago, so I've got her and her two daughters around more often. It seemed like ages since I'd last interacted this much with my sister, or young children. I don't see my own two kids often since they started college across the country, close to where my ex-wife moved. I haven't fully accepted they're old enough for college anyway. I haven't fully accepted that I've crossed forty either.

An unoccupied information kiosk responded to my query for Laney with a map to room 512. Darting through the crowded lobby, I hopped into an elevator right before the doors closed.

The quiet struck me as I got off the elevator and walked to Laney's room. No loud beeping monitors or garbled announcements over the loudspeaker disturbed the floor. An electronic sign reading "L. Tran" glowed next to the door of room 512. Taking a deep breath to slow my rapid heartbeat, I gave a soft knock and said, "Hello?"

No answer. I stepped through the door and peeked around a movable partition that protected the privacy of the patients. To my surprise, I found an elderly Vietnamese woman sleeping in the only bed.

While I like to tease Laney about her advancing years, she doesn't turn thirty-eight until next month. She's also white. About thirteen years ago, Laney married a nice man, Vietnamese-American by background, and took his name. A good guy, he always shared a laugh with Laney about people's reactions when a white woman with long, dark, curly hair and hazel eyes showed up for a dinner reservation in the name of Tran.

Something finally clicked. Why was this old lady in Laney's bed? Had she died since the nurse's call and been replaced already?

I calmed my overactive imagination, took another deep breath and stepped back outside the room to double-check the sign. It definitely listed her name. Someone had made a mistake or the hospital's software had bugs. Annoyed, I rubbed the back of my neck and considered what to do next. Down the hall, past the elevators, a police officer stood talking to a nurse. Perhaps they'd know how to find Laney.

They paused their conversation as I stepped in front of them. The cop stood a few inches taller than me and, although I don't usually notice men, I paused at his Hollywood-style good looks. He held himself erect in a close-fit uniform, crisp, neat, and form-fitting to his muscular body like it came straight from the tailor.

I'd like to think that my clothes fit just as well as his. Other people might comment on some gray in my slowly receding hairline and a tendency toward a dad bod, but I saw none of that when I stepped out of my shower each morning. Self-delusion was another of my skills.

The cop's striking, green eyes stood out from his dark brown skin and closely cropped black hair. Those penetrating eyes watched as I started to fidget from one foot to the other.

I didn't think I'd done anything wrong, at least not that the cop should know about. But he looked like he'd set me straight anyway. A name badge sat level and centered above the pocket on the left side of his chiseled chest. It read "Sergeant Mace Jackson."

His name sounded more like an action movie character than a real person. He even looked like an actor playing the part. If things ever went south in a conflict, I'd want Mace Jackson to take my side. After all, action movie heroes always win.

The nurse wore a standard hospital uniform with sensible shoes. Various medical gadgets hung off her belt. Her badge read "Ruth" and hung slanted, clipped to the untucked top of her uniform.

Under the scrutiny of the Sergeant's gaze, I directed my attention to the nurse. "Excuse me. I think there's something wrong with your directory or door signs. I'm looking for my sister's room. Laney Tran? She's not in room 512. The sign outside the door says it's her room, but some old lady is in there."

Ignoring my helpful assistance with the signs, Nurse Ruth said,

"Oh, you must be Marty. I called you earlier." She pointed behind her to room 518. "This is Laney's room."

"Her name is on the sign by the wrong room." I highlighted the error needing correction.

The cop scowled and looked hard at me. "Your sister is in the hospital and you're worried about a sign?"

I've got a bad habit of obsessing over things that don't work right when I'm nervous or worried. Or when everything was fine. Working to ignore the distraction of the glitch, I said, "Sorry. Is she okay? Can I see her?"

Nurse Ruth answered. "She's stable and should recover just fine in a few days. You can call the doctor for more details or wait for her to come back. I have to check on the other patients. And, yes, you can go see her, but she's not awake." The nurse's warm smile for the cop faded to a forced expression aimed at me before she walked away.

I had more questions and wished she hadn't left me alone with the cop. He might be an action hero but cops have made me nervous ever since a difficult experience with them during my freshman year of high school. Let's just say that I hadn't yet mastered the U.S. postal system.

Squaring my shoulders, I looked up at Sergeant Mace Jackson, standing in the doorway to Laney's room. "Do you know what happened to Laney?"

Instead of answering, he asked, "Can I see your I.D. please?"

"I'm Marty Golden. I'm a software engineer," I said as if that explained everything. Well, it pretty much covered my life. I've got a cool job at a startup. It's not the most successful startup in the world. No big payday yet, but hope can sustain a person for a long time. Even if it meant work consumed all my time. That's life in Silicon Valley.

"Some I.D. please," he repeated with an edge to his voice.

I didn't do it. I fumbled in my front pocket for my wallet as a light sweat prickled on my forehead. When I pulled out the wallet, my badge fell on the floor. Right as I bent down to pick up my badge, Sergeant Jackson reached out his hand for my license, almost smacking me in the head. I stood up holding my license but dropped it when my wrist bumped into his retracting hand. Bending over to pick it up again, I heard his exasperated sigh. When I stood up a second time, I managed to execute a successful handoff. With one fluid motion, he flipped it over, reviewed the information, and returned it to me as smoothly as James Bond handles a martini.

Sergeant Jackson pointed at my shirt. "Did you get called back from vacation?"

"What?" I glanced down. I wore my normal work attire of a Hawaiian shirt and a pair of shorts. Different colors and designs every day, but all Hawaiian-style. Today's was one of my favorite patterns. "No. I came straight from work when the nurse called. How'd her accident happen?"

Sergeant Jackson noted my defensive tone and now raised his eyebrow, but answered, "She was in a pretty unusual accident. Witnesses reported that she was driving through the intersection of Saratoga and Doyle when she tried to avoid an ice cream truck running the red light. The truck was hit by a falling delivery drone and then your sister's car t-boned the truck. She just barely missed getting hit by the drone herself. It would likely have killed her in her little car. It totaled the truck."

I couldn't believe my ears. "A drone?"

"Like I said, it was a pretty unusual accident."

I shook my head in disbelief. Granted, a modern delivery drone was heavy, not one of those lightweight, older generation drones that were only good for taking videos and annoying your neighbors. But, still, this shouldn't have been possible. "That's near her daughters' school. How could a drone hit there? The areas around schools are no-fly zones."

"We're investigating. So, do you —"

My phone buzzed. I held up a finger to Sergeant Jackson to excuse myself. He pressed his lips together but didn't say anything as I stepped away.

"Hello? Marty here."

"Is this Marty Golden?" said a woman in a clipped tone.

"Yes, that's what I said. I'm pretty busy right now. What's this about?"

"Well, now, you don't have to be rude. That's just unnecessary. We teach our children to be polite. It's the right thing to do. Manners start in the home, you know."

I rubbed my nose in confusion. A drone that shouldn't be there had nearly killed my sister and I hadn't even seen her yet. "I'm sorry. Who is this?"

"I'm Mrs. Quarles, school secretary. Skye and Megan are with me in the office. Their mother hasn't picked them up. We're not a babysitting service here at the Discovery School, you know. You're their emergency contact, so please come get them now."

Trying to take care of Laney and her girls was more than I'd signed up for. *Wait, had I signed something?* I couldn't be considered a responsible adult. If someone didn't believe me, they just needed to ask my ex-wife. I wanted to tell her to call another parent. I was going to stick around to talk to Laney's doctor and make sure she was ok. "I'll be there soon" is what I mumbled into the phone, probably not the best way to get across my point.

I turned to see Jackson staring with narrowed eyes at a fixed point on the wall with his hands on his hips.

"I'm sorry. That was my nieces' school. I need to go pick them up since Laney is here."

He took a second slow, deep breath before answering, "Before we're interrupted again, here's my card." He handed me the first paper business card I've seen in years, then continued, "I'd like to talk to her to find out if she saw anything unusual. Tell her to call me when she wakes. But, I won't be back until Thursday because I'm on furlough for the next two days."

"Furlough?" I didn't know that word.

"Unpaid, mandatory time off. All thanks to the city of San Jose not having enough money to pay us." He grumbled at this before striding off to the elevators, chest held high like a champion headed off into the sunset.

I looked around but didn't see the cameras and director following our star. Action heroes in the movies didn't seem to suffer mandatory time off from work because their agency ran out of money to pay salaries for the rest of the year.

I stepped into Laney's room to see her before I left to pick up the girls. Laney looked asleep, with a bunch of tubes and wires running from her to surrounding machines. Bandages covered part of her head. The uncovered portions of her face looked bruised. I moved to her side and squeezed her hand, but she didn't respond.

The nylon satchel, which she used as a catchall briefcase and purse, rested on the chair next to her bed. Her computer, phone, wallet and some papers nearly spilled out. I grimaced as I noticed a splotch of blood on the side. I grabbed it all to take home with me so nothing would happen to her things. I'd bring it back to her after she awoke. Maybe I would even wash her satchel so the blood wouldn't remind her of the accident. Well, I'd think about washing it.

I used the twenty minutes it took to get from the hospital to my nieces' school to check in with her doctor and update my own kids, away at college. To avoid enticing some elementary school hoodlum from breaking into the car, I grabbed Laney's bag as I got out.

The desert landscaping that most in the Valley have adopted to deal with the long-term drought prevailed along the path to the office. Assorted varieties of cacti, succulents, and rocks decorated the red dirt. A creative designer could create an eye-catching display with distinctive colors and textures of plants, but I still pined for green grass.

My nieces sat talking just inside the glass walls of the school office with their backs to me as I approached. Skye, reed thin and pretty with dark hair and glasses was a girl with plans. Twelve, going on thirty, she liked school and read fantasy books all the time. Megan, her younger sister, had her long hair worn up with various colored hairpins sticking every which way. Megan was nine, or eight, or possibly a mature seven. I never could remember. The free spirit of the family, she bounced off the walls with energy.

When I opened the door, Skye noticed me first. She interrupted Megan in mid-sentence. "Hi, Uncle Marty. Did you come with Rover?"

From a side room behind the counter, a disembodied woman's voice called out. "No dogs in here! That's simply not allowed."

Before I could speak, Megan chimed in. "You got a dog?" Without pausing to hear the response, she continued, "Hey, where's Mom?"

"Yes," I answered Skye, as I glanced around and rubbed my chin. What was that voice talking about? There were no dogs in sight.

Megan jumped up and started a little celebration dance at the idea of having an uncle with a dog.

Oops. "No, sorry. I was answering Skye. I didn't get a dog. It's my car, remember?"

Megan's dance ended with a lurch. "Just the dumb car?" She slumped back onto her chair.

"Well, it's not dumb."

A woman walked out of the side office back towards the counter.

She had to be Mrs. Quarles, the school secretary. "You gave your car a dog's name?" she asked in a scornful tone.

I'd never met her before and didn't understand why she felt it was acceptable to judge me. However, my parents had taught me to be polite, even to impolite people, so I answered, "I work for a car service called Rover that drives the cars for you. It's like a taxi, but with no driver. We call all the cars Rover. You know, like 'hey Rover, come —"

Megan interrupted. "Why not Buddy? That's a better dog name. Buddy would always be your best friend ..." Her voice trailed off as she hugged herself, thinking of her imaginary best dog friend, Buddy.

She had me there. "Well, our marketing team decided. Maybe they're not as smart as you and didn't think of Buddy."

Megan looked up at Mrs. Quarles. "Uncle Marty makes the cars go wherever you want."

Skye clarified, "He's an engineer."

I smiled. The girls had paid attention when I'd told them what I did. Turning to Skye, I said, "I think you'll be interested in a new feature we just added."

Skye looked excited and started to ask me about it, but Megan jumped in again. "But, wait. If they all have the same name, how do they know which one should come?"

Can't argue with a child's logic. So, I did the adult thing and ignored her. "Come on girls, get your backpacks and let's go." I turned to shepherd them out the door.

Mrs. Quarles called out, "Excuse me. You need to sign the girls out first."

"I'm Marty Golden, the girls' uncle. You called me."

"Yes, Mr. Golden, I am aware of who you are. You still need to sign the form. It's in THE RULES."

When she spoke of THE RULES, I heard the capitalization.

Mrs. Quarles continued, "We all have to follow THE RULES.

Please show me your I.D. so that I can verify that you are who you say you are and sign this form before the girls can go."

I thought about bolting for the door but didn't think the girls would follow fast enough to make a clean break. And, we had to follow THE RULES. I didn't notice any stone tablets with THE RULES etched in them, but the school might have sent them to the stone mason for cleaning.

After I signed, the girls followed me out the door. I didn't know how to tell them about their mother lying unconscious in the hospital. I didn't even understand how this could have happened in the first place. Drones didn't fall out of the sky nowadays. It's impossible, or at least it should be. Package delivery services had worked out all the bugs years ago. They were safer than driverless cars. Fewer random pedestrians or unexpected street construction projects at a thousand feet in the air.

How did a drone almost hit Laney? This problem with the drone was starting to bug me. I wanted Sergeant Jackson to figure it out now, not waste two days on a silly, mandatory furlough.

2

Monday Late Afternoon

When we got back to the driveway, my Rover car had disappeared.

Sigh. I had more work to do to get my changes working correctly. Turning to Skye, I said, "The new feature I wanted to show you didn't work right. The Rover car was supposed to wait for me." The girls watched as I used the Rover app on my phone. "I'll call for another."

"Don't you mean whistle?" asked Megan.

"Already a smart ass?" I said.

"That's a bad word," said Megan in a sing-song chant.

Ignoring her, Skye asked, "Where's Mom?"

Adroitly changing the subject, I asked Skye, "How was school?" She started talking about her classes and teachers. I didn't pay full attention, but it sounded like she couldn't decide whether she liked pre-Algebra or science the most.

Smart girl. Likes math and science. Maybe she'll be an engineer.

Megan jumped in to inform me that she liked art and lunch. *Well, I like lunch too.*

When the replacement Rover car arrived, we got in to go to the girls' home.

Megan said, "Like wow. You just tell it where to go?" She interrupted herself to add, "Awesome! How does it steer when you're not even in the driver's seat?"

Before I could answer, Skye said, "How does it know the right people got in the car?"

"How does it know where to pick you up?" asked Megan.

"Whoa, let me answer." I broke in to respond before they hyperventilated. "I use my phone to tell it to get me, and having it drive by itself is what I work on with the other engineers."

Megan stuck her chin out. "Betcha we could drive it."

Skye shook her head. "No way. It won't work for little kids."

"Am not little," insisted Megan. She wouldn't let her big sister get away with anything.

"Are too. Betcha got to be authorized?" retorted Skye.

"What's 'authorized'?" Megan pronounced the word carefully.

I jumped in before I got too dizzy watching the back and forth. "It means if you have permission. Skye's right, only adults can have accounts. And it only leaves if the person with the app on their phone is in the car. What's this 'Betcha' all about?"

Skye stuck out her tongue at Megan and then answered while Megan pouted. "It's a new thing, just go with it. She's like always trying to bet on things. Loser pays a buck."

Impressive. Clearly an entrepreneur in the making.

The girls chattered on without me, their little spat forgotten as they had more important school gossip to cover. The car continued driving without hesitation, stopping at stop signs and making the correct turns to get to their house. I smiled with pride. I liked to sit in the front passenger seat so I could watch the surprised looks on other drivers' faces when they noticed we had no driver. Relying on driverless cars might not have reached widespread adoption yet, but this was Silicon Valley after all. People needed to get used to it.

I took a deep breath and turned to the backseat. *Time to stop fooling around.*

"Girls, I have something serious to tell you." Two solemn yet beautiful faces looked at me.

"I had to pick you up today because your mom got hurt. She'll be okay, but she's in the hospital now. She can't come home for a few days so you girls will stay with me."

Silence fell in the car.

"What happened?" asked a subdued Megan.

I explained what I knew. It wasn't much. I didn't mention the drone failure was unusual.

"Is she hurt badly?" Skye's voice trembled.

"I spoke to the doctor on my way here. She told me your mom will be fine but will be out of it until tomorrow."

"Can we go see her?" asked Megan in a plaintive tone.

"Sorry. The doctor wanted us to wait until tomorrow to give your mom a chance to rest. Let's pick up some clothes at your house and you'll go to my place for tonight."

"What about Sunshine?" ventured Skye.

"The car was totaled." Laney's prize possession, her neon yellow, retro style VW Bug, was squashed. She'd spent hours selecting the custom paint job before buying it a few years ago. She and the girls loved it. She said the bright color made her happy every time she saw it.

Silence descended on the car again. The girls huddled together. I didn't speak either, looking out the windows at the passing strip malls while the car drove itself to their house. *The Rover car still drove well.*

Spending a few days at an uncle's place didn't seem like a big deal to me. It takes me about five minutes to pack for a trip. Once you've thrown a few changes of clothes into a bag and grabbed your toothbrush, what else was left? But evidently, I knew nothing of packing for my nieces.

While I waited, I looked around Laney's small three-bedroom home. While she hadn't unpacked all her belongings yet, she'd made the house neat and comfortable. The only decoration on the walls was a large picture of Laney, the girls, and her late husband. Several years after her husband passed away, she'd finally decided to relocate to California and restart her Human Resources career. As much as I wouldn't admit it to her, I liked having her and the girls around.

After a half hour of drawer slamming and consultations between the girls, I grabbed their suitcases and headed out the front door. The Rover car had left again. "Damn it."

"That's a bad word." Megan started her sing-song chant as she monitored my transgression.

"Sorry. I'm frustrated because I told it to wait for us." When the replacement car arrived, I opened the trunk and started loading the girls' bags.

"Oh wait, I have to get my science fair project." Skye dashed off back to the house.

"You won't believe what her science fair project is," said Megan.

Positive that it wasn't smart to ask, I bit, "What?"

"Ants." Megan watched for my reaction with a sly expression on her face.

She got one. "Come on, I'm not stupid. What's her real project?"

"Betcha?"

"Sure." I shook her hand.

Megan called shotgun and climbed into the car's front seat. Probably not entirely legal, but the car drove better than most people so she'd be fine.

Skye walked out of the house carrying what looked like six plastic boxes glued together sitting on a thin wooden board. I started moving things around in the trunk to make room.

"What's in there?" I asked as she approached.

"Dorymyrmex insanus."

"Dory what's it?"

"Dorymyrmex insanus. Their common name is 'crazy ant.' "

"What are you doing with them?"

"My project is testing the effectiveness of different feeding regimens."

"You mean whether the ants need food to live?"

Skye just rolled her eyes at me.

"Where on earth did you get ants?" I asked, not noticing the unintended humor of my question until after I spoke. I chuckled at my own joke.

"Online."

Of course.

She ignored my inadvertent dad humor and turned to put her ant farm into the trunk.

"You're not taking them into my apartment. They'll get all over."

Skye whipped her head back to look at me as tears welled in her eyes. "But, it's my science fair project. I have to keep them with me."

I stood there for a moment as the likely true cause of her tears dawned on me. Well, if some crazy ants would make her feel better while her mother recovered in the hospital, then my apartment would survive. "Oh, okay." *Insane.*

Still teary-eyed, Skye managed a small smile. She wiped her eyes, closed the trunk and we climbed into the car. Megan had her hand outstretched waiting for me to pay my debt for losing the bet. I don't carry old-fashioned paper cash, so I took out my phone and tapped it on her phone to confirm the transfer of a dollar as the car took off for my apartment. "Megan, what's your science fair project?" I held my breath hoping it wasn't worse than ants.

Megan paused, staring back at Skye as if to deliver a telepathic message, and then said, "My science fair project is tasting milkshakes."

"Now you're just pulling my leg. What's it really?"

"Milkshakes. Betcha?" Megan stuck out her chin.

"Sure." My dad didn't raise an idiot. Laney would never permit such poor nutritious choices. Megan couldn't fool me this time. I shook her hand again. I looked at Skye to confirm my victory. She paused, pushed her glasses back up her nose and then rolled her shoulders hesitantly as she nodded toward Megan. I sighed again and brought my phone out to tap against Megan's.

"I really don't like this game." Neither girl seemed interested in my opinion. Before the car dropped us at my apartment building, my phone buzzed with a fraud alert from my bank. I had to confirm that I'd intended to execute two distinct transfers of one dollar each before the bank would unlock my account. The bank didn't know about "Betcha."

As I approached my door, the fob in my pocket released the security system and the door swung open. We walked in without breaking stride. The girls, familiar with my place from previous visits, dropped their backpacks and rushed in.

"I call dibs on this room." Skye's voice rang out.

"Mine," echoed an even louder Megan.

I rounded the corner to see them in the hallway, each standing guard in front of different doors. "You'll both share the guest room. The other room is my home office."

"No fair. Why do I have to sleep in Skye's room?" Megan stood with her arms and legs spread wide apart as she attempted to block the entrance to the double doors of my home office.

"It's not Skye's room," I started.

Skye interrupted from her guard post, where she maintained her protective pose with arms crossed, "Yes, it is. I called dibs on it."

"Look, it's just for a short visit." *I hope Laney's out soon.* "I use my office to work. You both can share this room," I said, gesturing to my spare bedroom behind Skye. "There's a big bed and plenty of space for your suitcases." After some pouting and grumbling, I got them settled.

A diminished supply of groceries and my proposed dinner of peanut butter sandwiches met with a decided lack of enthusiasm. When Skye wanted to know what vegetable they'd need to eat, I tried the hero route. "We can skip vegetables tonight."

"Mom says we have to eat a vegetable every night at dinner," said Skye in a firm voice.

Maybe we're not related. I had only one option to offer. "How about broccoli?" Before I even finished both their faces turned into gargoyles. *Ok, not broccoli fans.*

"Salsa has tomatoes. That's like a vegetable," suggested Skye, sounding as if she's tried this gambit before.

Well, it worked. Gargoyle faces turned back to my beautiful nieces. I'd saved dinner.

When the girls were ready for bed, I went in to turn off the light. "Good night, girls."

"Wait, Uncle Marty." Megan started to sniffle. "What should we dream about? Mom always tells us what to dream about, like unicorns and polka-dotted butterflies."

What? "What?"

I didn't have the energy for this tonight. Laney's situation had me worried too. "Just go to sleep and don't have nightmares."

"You really suck at this." Skye rolled over to hug her sister.

Sigh. "Ok. Dream about puppies," I offered.

"I like puppies." Megan perked up a bit. "What kind?"

"I don't know. What kind of dog do you like?"

"Labradors," said Megan without a second's hesitation.

I suppressed a smile at her decisiveness. "Ok. Dream of Labrador puppies sitting in your lap while you're eating peanut butter sandwiches."

"Gosh, so creative, Uncle Marty," said Skye as I turned off the light and closed the door.

I realized I hadn't updated my own kids, Amanda and Eli, on their Aunt Laney's status since my ride to the girls' school. Working nonstop when they were young, I wouldn't have qualified for the World's Best Father award by a long shot. Now that they were both in college, I was trying to rebuild our relationship. Regular texting made it easier.

GROUP TEXT TO AMANDA, ELI

AMANDA: Glad she'll be ok

ELI: Yea. Good that both will be ok. Truck got what it deserved.

AMANDA: You used to like ice cream trucks ? Best prank ever! #EPIC

ELI: Childhood trauma

AMANDA: Never saw you run so fast

ELI: Thought truck had finally stopped at our stop sign and I could catch it

MARTY: She really got you

ELI: Who knew I had such an evil sibling

AMANDA: *insert evil laugh here*

Amanda had burned Eli with an impressive prank in middle school. Every day that summer, the ice cream truck raced past the house after lunch with the loud, iconic music creating an almost Doppler-like effect as the truck roared past. Ten years old at the time, Eli desired nothing more than to have the experience of buying an ice cream cone from the truck all by himself. He'd rush out the door, cash in hand, whenever he heard the truck, but never managed to flag the guy down. The driver must have used his truck to practice for Nascar.

One July weekend afternoon, Amanda found the ice cream truck music online, then set her speaker in the hallway outside the bathroom door while Eli showered. She hit play just as the shower turned off. He raced out the front door with his towel barely hanging on, only to discover no truck in sight and his sister's riotous laughter thundering from the doorway. She'd pulled a world-class prank on him. Eli got over it, but not the disappointment of his futile endeavors to score an over-priced, freezer-burned Drumstick.

Although his mother and I would never have let him, he would have succeeded if he'd stood in the middle of the street waiting as the truck raced toward him. The truck's automatic emergency braking system would have stopped it without hitting him ... Like Laney's car should have stopped on its own without hitting the truck.

How could Laney have broadsided a truck? Today's cars all have automatic braking systems with advanced, look-ahead and side-to-side radars, not like the early versions when I grew up. Our Rover engineering team spends most of its time programming our controls to deal with various results from the radars so the cars will drive safely. And, for that matter, didn't drones also have autonomous controls to steer them away from collisions? Laney's accident was starting not to feel very accidental.

I scrambled to locate Sergeant Jackson's card and then called him. It went straight to voicemail. I left him a rambling message asking him to check out what went wrong with the drone's collision prevention system. The ice cream truck driver could be a possible suspect too, although this only made sense if Laney inhabited a bizarre conspiracy/thriller movie. In the real world, ice cream trucks didn't target people or have problems driving. Unless they were on a Rocky Road. *Heh heh.*

3

Tuesday Morning

When the alarm woke me, I went into the guest room to wake the girls. Skye lay alone, curled up in the bed. Megan was gone. My adrenaline kicked in. I'd lost Laney's daughter. In my own apartment.

She's going to kill me. Trying to keep the panic out of my voice, I asked Skye, "Where's Megan?"

"Don't know. Don't yell," she mumbled and pulled the blanket over her head.

As I flipped on the light to check if Megan slept in a corner or was waiting to pounce on me, Skye squealed and pulled the blankets even higher over her head. I hurried out of the room, heart pounding, and rushed to the front door to see if she'd sleepwalked. It was still locked.

Where was she? She wasn't in the living room or kitchen. I rushed back down the hall and then finally spied Megan step sleepily out of my office. "Hey! What are you doing in there? You're not supposed to be in that room." I shouldn't have yelled at her, but she'd scared me.

Megan's lip started to tremble and tears formed in her eyes. "But I told you I wanted my own room."

I kneeled beside her. "Look, I'm sorry for yelling. I got scared when I couldn't find you. I thought you might have sleepwalked out of the apartment."

Megan's pressed lips and furrowed brow told me she didn't buy my apology. "I'm not a baby. I haven't done that in years. Besides, Mom told me I'd get my own room in California like back home." Her voice caught on her last words. "I want Mom."

"We'll go see your mom today. You only need to share my guest room for a few more days." *I hope.* I reached out to pat her back.

She stepped back and put her hands on her hips. "That's Skye's room."

Sigh. Time for a tactical retreat. I stood and called out, "Girls, go get ready for school and I'll get your breakfast ready."

When we sat down for breakfast, Skye asked, "When can we see Mom?"

Both girls quieted as they looked for my answer.

"I'll find out today. I'll go see her before work. We'll go after school."

The girls brightened at the thought and ate their cereal.

"I made you peanut butter sandwiches for lunch."

"Again?" asked Skye.

"With Nutella?" Megan hoped.

I shook my head. "But I added an apple." This didn't impress them either. "I'll have some groceries delivered. Just tell my phone what you want to be added to the grocery list." I showed them how to do it by adding bread and more milk to the list. "You can add Nutella or whatever else you want."

Megan grabbed my phone and said, "Add Nutella to the grocery list."

I took advantage of the momentum. "Grab your lunches and

backpacks and let's head out. I'll text Raj and tell him I'll be a little late today."

"Who's Raj?" asked Megan.

"My co-worker."

"That's his nickname. What's it short for?" asked Skye.

"I don't know. I don't think anyone knows his full name. We all just call him Raj."

"Very PC, Uncle Marty," said Megan.

"What do you mean, 'PC'? Do you even know what that means?" I said.

"Do you think I'm four?" Megan tilted her head to the side and threw me a baby face.

"No, I don't think you're four." I imitated her sarcastic whine and head tilt. *Very adult of me.* "But how old are you?"

"Geez, Uncle Marty," said Megan. Skye just gave me another eye roll and walked down the hallway. Perhaps she needed to visit the eye doctor.

⚓ ⚓ ⚓ ⚓ ⚓ ⚓

When I got to the hospital, I went straight to the fifth floor without checking the display to avoid unnecessary frustration. Right off the elevator on the fifth floor, a cop stood in the lobby and, for some reason, wanted to see my I.D.

Twice in as many days, cops have scrutinized my credentials. I was happy to see that Sergeant Jackson must have called in some extra security to protect Laney.

The cop added, "You looking for a luau?"

I didn't answer. Like that was the first time I'd ever heard that line. Years ago, Steve Jobs popularized the concept of wearing the same style of clothes every day. Not having to select and worry about matching clothes every morning simplified an engineer's life. This allowed us to focus on creating genius products. Well, for me at least, it kept me from making major fashion faux pas. I've found it better to ignore skeptics' comments than explain my clothing each time.

The hallway with Laney's room was empty, but a cluster of cops, nurses, and doctors milled around on the other side past the elevators. Compared to yesterday, this felt like rush hour at the hospital, on a Tuesday morning. "What's going on?" I asked the cop, who wore a different uniform from Sergeant Jackson's yesterday. He didn't wear it near as well.

He ignored me and asked again. "Sir, can I please see your I.D.?"

I complied without further questions. Holding my driver's license in one hand, he consulted a list. He handed it back and nodded to me that I could proceed.

Wow, I'd passed. I've never been on an A-list before. I've gone to nightclubs where the bouncers have a list of who's allowed in and only let in a few fancy-dressed people at a time. Ok, I've walked by such nightclubs in the past and seen this in action. Sucked that my sister had to get hospitalized with me listed as next of kin before I made it onto an approved list.

As I'd hoped, Laney's name now appeared on the sign outside her room, next to the number 518. I felt better. It wasn't my software, but I still felt better that it was working. Nurse Ruth, from yesterday, was walking past quickly. I stopped her, gesturing toward the other hallway with all the people. "What's going on?"

Her eyes lit up as she responded, "Oh, it's terrible. A patient died before dawn."

Her reaction puzzled me. People dying don't usually make someone excited. "What's all the fuss?" It was hours later. Why would police show up when a patient dies in a hospital?

"They're searching the room, 512."

"The old lady?"

Nurse Ruth gave an odd, almost eager smirk. "Yes. It's so sad."

Her words didn't match her body language as she seemed almost giddy about the news.

I felt a chill run down my spine. It was creepy that the woman in the room with Laney's name on it died. I double-checked and pointed down the hallway. "Room 512?"

"Yes. It's terrible. Everyone's still shaken." Nurse Ruth's hands both quivered as her eyes gleamed.

The discrepancy between her reactions and words confused me so I pointed to Laney's room. I needed confirmation, even if from this odd nurse. "My sister, Laney Tran. Is she okay?"

Nurse Ruth stepped into Laney's room and beckoned me to follow her. Laney was asleep on the bed. From across the room, she took a quick look at Laney's monitors before walking back to whisper, "Yes. She's fine. We've checked on everyone since ... we discovered her. It's been such an unusual day." Her cheeks flushed.

I followed her out of the room in a daze. Didn't nurses encounter dead people on a regular basis? This shouldn't be so unusual for her. Feeling my stomach churn, I asked, "When did they fix the signs for the patient names?"

"What?" She furrowed her brow as she tried to process my new question.

I pointed to her name on the sign next to room 518.

Nurse Ruth followed my gesture but got distracted again by the noise down the hallway. She didn't look at me as she answered, "I don't know. Maybe when IT started work at eight o'clock? What's that got to do with the murder?"

My head jerked back. "What? What murder?"

Finally looking straight at me, Nurse Ruth said, "The old lady in room 512 was killed sometime last night. We think she was suffocated. We found blood from her mouth and nose on a pillow on the floor."

I hyperventilated a little while I considered her words. At least now I better understood the nurse's odd behavior. An adrenaline junkie, her normal routine at the hospital bored her. She couldn't mask her excitement about having something different and dangerous happen. Dead people didn't surprise a nurse, but murder was a whole new story.

Nurse Ruth watched the hubbub down the hallway with eager anticipation. She ran her fingers through her hair to collect a few strays in a hair clip. "Do you think that good looking cop from yesterday will show up too?"

"I, uh, I have no idea." My sister could have been murdered last night. I wasn't focused on helping Nurse Ruth find a date.

"Sorry, I have to go." She didn't glance at me before striding off to join the crowd on the other side of the floor.

If anything, the hubbub had grown outside room 512. Perhaps Laney's nurse wasn't the only bored person in the hospital. I poked my head back into Laney's room only to find that she was still asleep. I hurried over to room 512. Winding my way through the tittering medical staff, I approached a cop who stood outside the door looking at a small tablet. "Excuse me. Is the officer here from yesterday? Sergeant Mace Jackson?"

The cop eyed me. "That's quite a name." He scratched his head before continuing, "I don't know anyone by that name in the Los Gatos P.D. You sure you're not thinking of a movie?"

Everyone's a comedian. "No. He was investigating an unusual accident in San Jose that my sister was in. Her name was on this door yesterday, but —"

The cop interrupted me, "Sir, you'll need to talk to San Jose police to follow-up on her accident. We're pretty busy here." He looked down at his tablet again.

"Yes, I know. I'm worried whoever killed the old lady made a mistake and was really trying to kill my sister."

The cop's head swiveled up as he eyed me again, this time with suspicion. "What do you know about this?"

"No. Nothing. Not me. I mean the signs were wrong yesterday. Maybe it was just another accident or maybe the software wasn't working right. It's fixed now. But first Sunshine hit the ice cream truck, then the drone, and now this," I babbled nervously.

The cop squinted at me. "Huh?"

"The nurse told me they only fixed the signs at eight o'clock this morning." I emphasized the time.

"So? What do signs have to do with anything?"

"This used to say my sister's name." I pointed to the door sign.

He turned and looked at the door sign, which now read "H. Nguyen." His forehead creased. "What's your sister's name?"

"It's Laney Tran."

His expression turned skeptical. "You're Vietnamese?"

"No. I'm not. She's not either." I continued babbling, "She married a Vietnamese guy."

"Oh. And she's in her late seventies?" he asked, still doubtful.

"No —" I started.

The cop interrupted me. "Look, I'm sorry your sister was in an accident, but this is a murder investigation —"

The noise from a large crowd of people pouring out of the cramped quarters of an elevator caused us both to swivel our heads toward the lobby. The activity resembled the unloading of a clown car. An extended family with multiple generations had all come to visit their hospitalized loved one. I'd heard of families that stuck together, but this defied description. The group bowled over the helpless officer in the lobby who tried to stop them. Three gossiping older ladies in front didn't even notice him as they walked down the hallway toward us.

The cop shot me a quick, impatient glance as his next issue sped closer. "Talk to San Jose police. I'm sure they can help." He turned his head and barked a command into the room.

"But do you think her murder is related to my sister?" I waved in the general direction of the room with the dead woman in it.

Undaunted, but preparing for the oncoming wave, he reached into his pocket and pulled out a business card. "I'm sorry, but I'm very busy. If you think of something else, give me a call."

As the cop stepped away from me, I found myself with a second police officer's business card in two days. *Maybe I win a prize if I collect a whole set.*

The cop planted himself in the middle of the hallway and held up both hands. "Excuse me," he said with his policeman's bellow. The voice of authority worked as the crowd stopped.

I stepped to the side and slid back past the crowd to head to the elevator.

The cop paused for breath, then continued in a softer tone. "You can't go into this room right now. I'm very sorry to have to tell you like this, but Mrs. Nguyen is dead. There are suspicious circumstances and we have to collect evidence from the room."

The news hit with an almost physical impact as a short-lived stillness descended on the crowd. The silence broke as I took a few quick steps to the elevator. The noise and chaos grew as more hospital staff and officers engaged and tried to calm the family.

A slight, thin young woman at the back of the crowd stepped clear of the fray and stood near me as I waited for the elevator. She looked about the age of my kids, perhaps in college. "Did you come to see my Auntie too?"

"No. My sister." I decided not to explain the whole room mix-up situation and finished with a weak, "I'm sorry for your loss."

"Yeah, thanks." Looking at the crowd, the young woman sighed. "They weren't all supposed to come today anyway. My mother messed up and sent the WhatsApp message to the entire family instead of just the smaller group."

Her reaction confused me. "You don't seem too upset by the news?" I edged away in case she turned out to have more worrisome tendencies.

Without looking at me, she responded, "Oh, yeah. It's terrible she died this way. But she had terminal cancer. She was going into hospice care later today."

I felt relieved she'd revealed herself as merely a self-absorbed youth and stopped checking her for psychopathic indicators. I should try not to assume the worst in people. It might serve me better than letting my imagination run wild.

The murder, however, wasn't part of my imagination. Someone had killed this young woman's Auntie in a room with Laney's name on the door.

Sergeant Jackson needed to hear about the murder. He needed to do something to solve this and protect Laney. Another outburst from the crowd made me turn to look. I'd have to call him from the lobby.

The elevator was taking forever. I jabbed at the button again.

I stood watching the crowd. Amidst the noise and chaos, I smelled something new. The elevator had opened and a man in his late thirties stepped out, holding several bags of takeout food. He stopped as he took in the scene. If he were smart, he'd turn and flee. The food smelled terrific and terrible both at the same time.

The young woman turned from her ringside spot as she smelled the newcomer as well. "That's my cousin with lunch." She spoke to him in rapid Vietnamese.

His mouth dropped open. Stunned, he dropped the bags as he burst out wailing and reached to hug her. Out of instinct, I grabbed the bags before they spilled. But not before some smelly fish sauce spilled out and onto my shoes. *Great.*

The young woman looked at me over his shoulder and rolled her eyes.

A new nurse walked up to me. "You can't bring that food in here. Please take it off the floor right away." Instruction delivered, she waded forward into the crowd to tackle the next challenge.

I put the bags down on the ground. The lessons in etiquette that my mother drilled into me did not include how to insert myself into an escalating family crisis conducted in a foreign language while my sister lay injured in the hospital and I was literally left holding the bag.

I rode down, alone and worried. Was someone trying to kill my sister? And why?

The car crash might have been an accident. I could even buy that the drone crash was one too. But I wouldn't betcha that the accident and drone crash plus the murder of someone in a room marked for Laney on the same night all happened by chance. Yogi Berra, the great baseball player who became almost as well-known for his "Yogi-isms", once said, "That's too coincidental to be a coincidence."

4

Tuesday Midday

In the lobby, I found a quiet corner to call Sergeant Jackson.

If this wasn't all just a crazy series of mishaps, I had no idea who might have tried to kill Laney. It could have been someone good with technology like me who tried to get the drone to crash into her. Maybe they'd heard she survived the crash on the news, instead of getting a call from the nurse like me. They could have learned what hospital room Laney was in by checking the directory just like I did.

I put the pieces together. Either this was all a crazy coincidence or someone like me was trying to murder her, possibly more than once already. I knew I hadn't done it so that left a valley full of other techies. Or, my imagination was overheating again.

Sergeant Jackson's voicemail answered my call on the first ring. I hadn't prepared a crisp summary of the situation. I left a lengthy, and likely confusing, message for him.

Perhaps in another lapse in the childhood etiquette lessons from my mother, I'd never practiced crafting a voicemail message to a police officer that someone might have tried to kill my thirty-seven-year-old sister with a rogue drone and had then accidentally

killed a terminally ill, elderly Vietnamese woman in a room that
had my sister's name on the door. Or that the elderly woman, who
wasn't my sister, had a really loud and close family in a different
city, outside of the officer's jurisdiction, and was in the process of
distracting those police from investigating the possible attempted
murder of my sister.

Well, maybe crazy people practice things like that in their head.
My aunt worked as a psychologist at a psychiatric hospital. She'd
know the diagnosis for people like that. When I was a kid, she'd
explain to Laney and me how the brain worked, and how it can
go wacky. Too many people already think I'm wacky. I don't want
anyone thinking I'm paranoid. But as they say, just because you are
paranoid doesn't mean they aren't after you.

Or your sister.

With all the police around Laney's floor, I decided she was
safe for now. As I headed to work, I considered calling 9-1-1.
How would I answer the question, "What is the nature of your
emergency?"

On the other hand, I couldn't just walk away. Crazy as it seemed,
someone seemed to be trying to kill Laney. Like a mantra, the
words "drone", "crash" and "murder" echoed in my head. I needed
help. And not from my aunt. If Sergeant Jackson wasn't available,
I'd have to get someone else to help me.

Had Laney gotten into something dangerous? It didn't seem
possible. She was a human resources consultant with a mere
handful of clients. New to town, she knew so few people that she'd
listed me as the emergency contact for her daughters. That showed
a lack of judgment, not dangerous connections.

Although Laney pissed me off sometimes, I hadn't wanted to kill
her since she threw my car keys down the sewer. On purpose. Of
course, we were teenagers and she'd argue that I provoked her by
tattling to Mom and Dad about her sneaking out of the house.

That was twenty plus years ago. Why would someone want to kill her now?

I set my bag on my desk and dropped with a thud into my chair. In the next cube over, Raj looked up and smiled hello. Raj had moved to the U.S. only a few months ago to start working for Rover. I liked him. Super smart, with degrees in both robotics and computer science, Raj spoke Hindi and some other Indian language I couldn't remember so English was his third language. His English was great, but without meaning to, Raj was sometimes hysterical as he tried out American idioms on me.

"What is it that is wrong?" Raj asked.

Drone, crash, murder. "My sister is in the hospital."

Raj's polite conversational tone shifted to concern. "Hold the horses. What happened? Will she be ok?"

"A car accident. The cop said a delivery drone fell on her car. And, I think so," I said, trying to address his questions.

"My goodness." Raj now sounded confused. "How could that happen?"

Drone, crash, murder. I agreed with his confusion. Drones don't fall on people. At least they haven't in many years. After the "crash" and "drone", "murder" was the only part of the mantra left to explain.

Raj pursed his lips and gave a short shake of his head as he pondered how this could happen. "That is terrible, but perhaps you are mistaken that someone is trying to kill your sister."

"Perhaps. But I'm worried."

"How long will the police stay in the hospital?"

"I don't know."

"You could call the hospital and ask them," Raj said.

"They're not going to tell someone over the phone when the

police will leave a murder scene. They'll be suspicious I'm going to try something."

"Why not ask when your sister's friend, who's not on the approved list, can visit her?"

My mouth dropped open. Raj was clever and sneaky. I admired that about him.

The hospital told me that, due to unforeseen complications surrounding a police investigation, all visitors were banned until tomorrow.

I'd have to break the news to the girls after school. However, with all the police in the hospital, Laney would be safe for now. I'd figure out something to help her later. In the meantime, I took out my things and tried to get some work done.

A few hours after lunch, I looked up. Except for Raj, everyone else listened to music through noise-canceling headphones to blot away the sounds from neighboring phone calls and conversations in the open floor plans that permeated the Valley. Some long-ago misguided consultant must have thought that removing cubicle walls would increase collaboration and productivity. Instead, this despised brainstorm created floors of headphone-wearing zombies trying, in silent desperation, to focus on their work and avoid distractions. Perhaps management used the guise of collaboration to excuse cutting real estate costs by cramming more people closer together.

I found that the trick to listening to baseball games at work, without getting caught, involved the ability to maintain a straight face and not react no matter what happened. After all, not many people cheered in the middle of listening to music. Oh, and make sure to use just the audio broadcast. It's a rookie mistake to have the video playing in the background since the boss might stop by and ask to see something on your screen. With the Giants playing well, I'd struggled to maintain the charade.

Raj looked up from his computer. He never wore headphones.

Perhaps they interfered with the brainwaves from his multi-dimensional thought processes.

I let out a small groan as I stretched. "Hey, I forgot to tell you earlier that new feature we finished for Rover doesn't work. Twice I tried it, and the car left me both times. We've got to pull it out of the beta version before marketing promotes it."

"Most peculiar. I tested it myself this morning and it worked splendidly. What exactly did you tell the car to do?"

"I told it to 'sit.' Stupid marketing guy who thought it would be funny to use dog commands for the car."

Raj did a small head bobble. "Then that is your error. It is 'stay,' not 'sit.' "

"What do I know about dogs?" I complained. "I'm allergic to them, anyway."

"But it is logical. A car cannot sit. A car does not have knees."

"Knees?" I said, perplexed.

Raj added a small finger wag for emphasis. "Yes. You must have knees to sit." Raj was the robotics expert and evidently, he understood canine anatomy better too.

Once started, I continued my list of complaints from this morning. "It was also annoying this morning because my nieces used up my water allowance so I had to shower at the gym." A few years ago, as California's drought extended into our sixth year and counting, the water agency had installed controls that strictly limited water consumption per dwelling, based on the number of occupants and the size of your yard. Since I lived by myself in an apartment, I had a small water allowance. I'd have to call the water agency to get a temporary increase.

"It is very important to conserve water."

"Yes, I know." I'd forgotten about Raj's passion for the subject and braced myself.

"Americans waste too much water. Your farms pump billions of gallons from the ground and the agriculture chemicals pollute the untreated runoff water. This weekend I read about a new plant in California which will distill out the dangerous chemicals and provide clean water to people in the Central Valley. This is good."

"Yes. This is good." Raj tended to go on about water issues. He'd told me his family had owned a farm in India until his grandparents lost their land. Agreeing with him made the water lectures shorter. I enjoyed speaking to him about his family in India as long as we stayed away from rural Indian politics.

I tried to distract him from continuing the lecture. Coming up with an unusual idiom often threw him for a loop. Out of the blue, I said, "I don't think this conversation will cut the mustard."

He laughed out loud at this. "Come, now you are just making them up."

"No. That's a real one." But, I had to leave before this conversation devolved into a contest of silly idioms. "Hey Raj, could you cover for me?"

Raj raised his eyebrows, "What should I cover?"

"If the boss asks, tell him I'm doing some field testing. I'm going to pick up the girls and check on Laney. I'll work from home later."

"Yes, I can do this." Raj gave me a thumbs-up. "I sincerely hope that she is doing better."

We had Rover cars waiting in the parking lot for testing so I jumped in one to head to the girls' school. *Good doggie.*

This time, when I gave the car a firm command to "stay," the Rover car remained where I'd left it. Raj had implemented the new verbal command while I'd integrated the feature into our test version. It felt good to see our software worked as planned. Having code work always felt good. The rush I felt from these successes was the primary reason I became a software engineer. I hadn't realized that engineering would involve working with stupid marketing folks. They dreamed up new ideas attempting to be funny or cute. Who'd remember to tell their car to "stay"?

As soon as she saw me, Megan asked, "Can we go see Mom now?"

Telling them we couldn't see Laney until tomorrow turned hopeful faces into studies in frustration. I told them the latest news from the doctor that Laney was improving while avoiding any mention of why visitors were prohibited.

That good news helped the girls feel better and they chattered about school on the way home again. Years of experience working in an open environment helped me tune them out. Purging the thought of the poor murdered woman out of my head wasn't so easy. I was positive that falling asleep in a hospital room with the wrong name on the door had gotten her killed.

As I thought of Laney asleep in her room, I broke out in a sweat. Sure, the police swarmed the hospital today, but what about tomorrow? Was someone after her? Why would anyone want to hurt her? I needed to look at Laney's computer. Perhaps it had clues that would explain what had happened to her. Maybe Laney had been talking to someone who wanted her dead.

Skye interrupted my thoughts. "Earth to Uncle Marty."

"What? Sorry, I was just thinking."

Megan wrinkled her nose as something caught her attention. "Yuck. What's that smell?"

I didn't want to explain what had happened in the hospital. "It's nothing. I spilled some fish sauce on my shoes earlier today."

Rolling down her window, Skye said, "It smells like a super dead fish."

"Better than dead ants." Uncles don't have to make sense. I take full advantage of this privilege. I'd been practicing since long before the girls were born.

Delivering a well-deserved eye roll, Skye asked, "Oh yeah, that reminds me. Can I use some water for my ants?"

I didn't answer. "What do you call a really big ant?"

Megan blurted out, "Elephant!"

"Oh, did I tell you that joke before?"

"No, we learned lame jokes from Dad." Skye's face fell and she grew quiet.

"I always liked your dad." Noticing that both girls remained silent, I added, "Yes, the water's fine."

My ex-wife would confirm I didn't handle unhappy women well. Looking to distract them, I asked, "What do you call a hundred-year-old ant?" Without waiting for a response, I answered, "Antique" and chuckled at myself.

"Ugh, that's as bad as Dad's jokes used to be," said Skye, without any enthusiasm.

"Well, he had many fine qualities, especially his sense of humor."

But joke time was over, for now. Between their memories of their father and concern for their mother, I wouldn't be able to change their mood. The girls looked out their windows in silence for the rest of the ride.

When we got back to my apartment, the girls started on their homework while I stepped into my office. *Not Megan's room.* I checked in with Raj. Apparently, the boss wasn't pleased that I'd missed our staff meeting. I'd do some extra work tonight after the girls went to sleep so he'd see progress on my project.

I wanted to check out Laney's things and see if something would clue me into what might have happened. Pulling out Laney's computer and phone from her satchel, I examined them. Her phone had one of those retinal eye scanners which prevented me from getting access. But her computer started running as soon as I touched the screen. *Just like Laney. Highest level security on one device and none on the other.*

I searched Laney's calendar. She had only three appointments listed for Monday. One name leaped out at me. Laney had met with Jean Rollag before the accident at nine-thirty on Monday morning.

Jean Rollag's name should leap out to anyone who knew high-tech. He'd co-founded and still acted as Chief Technical Officer of DroneTech. Only hours before a rogue drone almost killed her, Laney had met with the co-founder and CTO of DroneTech. A flush of adrenaline raced through my body. I had to do something. But what could I do?

One of the hottest startups in Silicon Valley in years, DroneTech had grown quickly after the government allowed drone flight testing within the United States. DroneTech's control systems ran most of the commercial drones around the world. Initially, DroneTech built drones before evolving into selling their software and control systems to other drone makers. Now they made even more money managing the commercial flying drone network in a number of countries.

In nearly eleven years, drones had exploded from a hobbyist's toy to serious tools used by businesses globally for all sorts of rolling, walking, and flying purposes. Within the last few months, DroneTech had announced their intention to go public. The news drove anticipation of an astounding wave of money that thousands of DroneTech employees hoped to cash out from their stock options and slosh around the Valley to spend on expensive houses, cars, and other toys.

I wished I worked there. Maybe Laney could get me an interview? *No, wait!* If Rollag is involved in trying to hurt my sister, then I wasn't interested, no matter how many stock options he offered.

Rollag and his co-founder, David Saunders, had started DroneTech while still in school at Stanford. Unlike so many Silicon Valley startup stories, they'd actually both graduated from Stanford, which their public relations people touted as if they were the first Stanford graduates ever to run a successful startup. Saunders turned out to have the business chops to turn their ideas into reality and then to surf the tsunami of success without crashing the company into the rocks. Rollag played the role of technical visionary. He spoke on a regular basis on the TED circuit and appeared on the panel sessions that are such a staple of all the tech industry's many tradeshows. Like too many of the men whose startups had hit it big, his reputation for arrogance was matched only by stories of his womanizing. Perhaps the press hyped that aspect because his French first name sounded exotic, even though he was born in California.

Scared, impressed and more than a little jealous that Laney had met Rollag, I wanted to look him in the eye and see if he knew anything about a drone almost falling on Laney. Rollag had the techie chops to hack into a drone.

It didn't make sense, though. Laney couldn't have posed a threat to Rollag. He was too important for her to affect him. However, he might know who could have done it. Maybe a visit would be just the right personal touch to figure this whole thing out.

If it wasn't him, maybe I could land a plum DroneTech engineering job.

5

Tuesday Evening

Rollag had met with Laney in a nearby Starbucks. Looks like Mr. Big Shot got his caffeine fix same as normal people. Odd that they didn't meet in the DroneTech offices, but I suppose consultants go where they're told.

Most people were creatures of habit. Rollag might have scheduled the meeting with Laney for his usual time to hit that Starbucks on his way to his office. One thing I knew about coffee was how addicted people became to it. I'd go to that Starbucks tomorrow morning at the same time in hopes of encountering him. Talking to him in the coffee line had to be less challenging than breaking through his assistant's protection and penetrating his schedule at the office.

After we cleared up the drone situation, I'd hand him my resume. I liked my job at Rover well enough, but a software engineer would be crazy not to want to work at DroneTech. My folks didn't raise someone that crazy.

The rest of Laney's calendar showed two other, far less interesting, entries for Monday. She'd scheduled a brief call at nine with someone named Fernando Hernandez. His number followed his name on her calendar entry. The last appointment, labeled simply ME, looked like something personal. Laney could have been seeing a therapist, or been taking a personal improvement class, or been seeing an investment counselor. Nah, I knew Laney. She'd scheduled a manicure.

A soft knock sounded on the apartment door. No one had buzzed from outside so it must be someone from the building. Only building maintenance had ever stopped by my apartment unannounced and that knock didn't sound like a maintenance worker. When I opened the door, Mrs. Kim, my nosy, elderly neighbor from down the hall, stood at my door, holding a covered dish that smelled amazing.

"Hello, Mr. Marty. Girls still here?"

"Yes." I hesitated since I hadn't told her about the girls visiting. I've even only spoken to Mrs. Kim a handful of times in the three years I've lived in the apartment. "My sister will be in the hospital for a few days."

She smiled and, bowing slightly with her head tilted down, offered me the covered dish. "Ah, so sorry, but good. Maybe they like special Korean BBQ and rice?"

Her timing was ideal as it dawned on me that I'd forgotten to notify the delivery service to send our grocery order. "Thank you so much. Please, come in."

Drawn by the smell and noise, the girls poked their heads around the corner.

"Girls, Mrs. Kim brought us her special Korean BBQ for dinner. Please set the table."

Even I knew it wouldn't be polite to grab the food and shut the door in Mrs. Kim's face. "Will you join us?"

She smiled and nodded. "Yes. Thank you."

Megan frowned at me. "Do we have to eat salsa as our vegetable again?"

Looking at Megan, Mrs. Kim asked, "What is salsa?"

"Vegetables, chopped up and spicy," answered Skye.

Mrs. Kim gave an enigmatic smile. "I have this. I get." She turned and shuffled back to her apartment.

I left the door ajar and helped the girls get the table ready for dinner. A few minutes later, Mrs. Kim returned with another dish and placed it on the table with a proud flourish. "Kimchee. Vegetables, chopped up and spicy," she announced.

As a general rule, uncles enjoy pushing their nieces' comfort levels. Without saying a word, I spooned some kimchee onto the girls' plates. Despite some wrinkling of noses, they both tried it. I had to give them credit. I'm not sure I'd have tried kimchee at their age. It wasn't a hit.

But the Korean BBQ and rice received rave reviews. Good thing, as peanut butter wouldn't have gone over very well again.

Skye's earlier question about her ants reminded me of some important acting parent responsibilities. As we finished dinner, I asked Megan, "Should we start working on your science fair project?"

Megan squinched up her face in confusion. "What are you talking about?"

"How about if I make milkshakes?" I explained, and then took out ice cream and chocolate syrup. I might not have many food options for dinner or lunch, but I had the essentials. Distracting the girls from Laney's absence could be achieved with dessert as well as bad jokes. Mrs. Kim decided to stick around for dessert as well.

The milkshakes were an even bigger hit than the BBQ. Taking out some paper, I helped Megan organize her notes on vanilla and chocolate milkshakes for her project while Skye supervised our work. We needed to do some extra testing, in the name of science, of course.

"Good night girls," I said as they climbed into their bed.

"Can we go see Mom in the morning?" asked Megan.

"You have school. We'll go later tomorrow to see her."

Megan pouted. "Then, what should we dream about?"

I had completely forgotten about this additional responsibility. Most engineers are not creative in this way by nature. Laney needed to come home soon so she could take back over these duties.

I pondered a bit and latched onto the first idea that wandered past. "How about Labrador puppies sitting in your lap while you eat peanut butter sandwiches?" After a long day, my creativity doesn't quite reach exalted heights.

Megan made a sour face. "That was last night's dream. We need a different one every night."

"Umm …" This had expanded into a bigger challenge than anticipated. While they grew up, children lived at home for thousands of nights. Did Laney really make up a new dream every night? What if one didn't work, could she use it again? Could she repeat dream suggestions every year? Did she use a special dream database to keep track of all the previous dream recommendations? This demanded a careful, systematic approach.

Megan interrupted my deliberations. "Uncle Maarty …"

Startled, I returned to find Megan tugging at my arm and scrambled for an idea. "Okay, okay. How about dreaming of striped horses running in the grass?"

Skye may have damaged her corneas by rolling her eyes so hard. "You mean zebras?" she asked, incredulous, "Do you practice making up bad ones?"

Wow, sarcasm and an eye roll. I was on fire. "How about, um, … you're drinking every kind of milkshake while Labrador puppies try to get some from your cup," I said in a burst of inspiration.

"Ok!" With a huge smile, Megan squeezed her eyes shut, pulled up the blankets, and announced, "Good night." Dream time needed to come right away. Skye looked at me with a surprised look and gave me an approving nod.

Phew. That felt good. I turned off the light and shut the door quickly. With both girls inside their room. Just to be sure, I double-checked that the apartment door chain was in place.

GROUP TEXT TO AMANDA, ELI

...

ELI: Thanks for update on Aunt Laney

AMANDA: And how was tonight?

MARTY: I suck at telling them what to dream but I'm good at milkshakes

ELI: Go with your strengths

Tomorrow I needed to shake loose some answers. I had to figure out what was going on or get Laney more protection. Rollag would be my key.

6

Wednesday Morning

Staying up late to catch up on my work for Rover made the morning arrive that much earlier. I yawned as I walked down the hallway to wake the girls. When I opened the guest room door, I saw Skye, asleep alone in the bed again. Adrenaline slammed into my body. *This works better than caffeine.* At least it was a smaller adrenaline rush than yesterday, so that's progress. Before saying anything, I turned and looked in the office. Sure enough, Megan lay asleep on the floor next to the futon. Regaining my breath, I knelt to touch her head. "Megan, it's time to get up."

Megan woke up bright-eyed and alert like only a child seems capable. "Good morning, Uncle Marty."

I rolled my shoulders to release the tension. I'd lost the battle of the bedrooms once again, but at least Megan remained safe and inside the apartment. I didn't want the girls messing with my stuff in the office. Yet, I had a hard time staying annoyed with Megan for long. Curious about the effect of my suggestion from last night, I asked, "What did you dream about?"

"Milkshakes and Labradors, of course, silly. And that made me starved. What's for breakfast?"

"Cereal again. Remember, I forgot to have the groceries delivered. I'll schedule them to show up for this evening."

Skye, awakened by the talking, wandered out of her room.

No, the guest room. Not as bright-eyed as her younger sister, she bumped into the wall a few times as she made her way down the hallway to the bathroom. Today had gotten off to a better start than yesterday. I walked out to the kitchen to get breakfast and lunches together while the girls got ready for school.

When Megan came to the kitchen for breakfast, she asked, "Do we have to go to school? Can't we go see Mom instead?" She stood with fists clenched and a concerned look on her face.

I turned to face her. "No, we'll go later. She's got a lot of pain medicine so she's very tired and probably still sleeping anyway."

She started to sniffle. "But we didn't get to see her yesterday either."

I stood there for a moment, finally recognizing that she was just a child of eight. Or maybe seven. I bent down closer to her. "I tell you what, I'll call the doctor and make sure she's doing better. Then we'll go see her later."

Skye had come up behind Megan without my noticing. "Yeah, I want to see her too."

Her lip trembled. I looked back and forth between the girls. "I promise. I'll call them this morning. Remember the hospital had an emergency yesterday so we couldn't visit her."

The girls nodded. I left two somber girls eating breakfast while I went to get ready for work. When I got back, they were talking to each other again. Catching their attention at the table, I said "Girls, I've got something important to do this morning. I'm not supposed to do this," I hesitated before committing. "I'd like for you to take the Rover car to school by yourselves. Are you okay doing that?"

A huge grin spread across Megan's face as she gave a vigorous nod and looked over at Skye. "Ha! I win. Told you we'd get to drive Rover." She smirked with her arms crossed over her chest. "Pay up."

Skye made a face at Megan. She didn't like to lose, especially to her sister. Ignoring her debt to Megan in her excitement to use the Rover service, she raced down the hall to grab her phone. "Can you put the app on my phone?" She panted as she handed me her phone.

Megan wasn't so readily dismissed. She shoved her hand toward her sister, making the international "show me the money" sign by rubbing her thumb across her fingers.

Skye dismissed Megan, "I don't have any money."

"You gotta pay up."

Those are THE RULES.

Skye looked up at me as the app downloaded onto her phone. "My money is at our house. Can you give me a dollar?"

I sighed and reached for my phone. "I wasn't even part of this bet and still lost."

Laney had insisted that using paper bills would better teach her girls the value of money. Megan wanted a dollar bill to add to her collection. She held out her phone for the transfer anyway. At this rate, I'd need to find some small bills soon. Old-fashioned cash hadn't yet gone extinct, although almost no adults used it these days.

I still remembered when cash was common. During my college days, my dad would obsess that I needed to carry cash whenever I traveled, in case of emergency. I only needed to use cash once when the gas station credit card machine had broken. I never told him to avoid reinforcing his paranoia. Besides, whenever I mentioned I didn't have any cash, he'd hand over some extra money and I liked that scheme just fine. All I'd needed to do would be to pretend to forget to get money from the ATM and he'd give me some along with a lecture. Cash wasn't critical back in those days and it's even less so now.

Setting up the Rover app and lying about Skye's age didn't feel right, but I had to meet Rollag and discover what he knew about Laney and the drone. Besides our car service worked great now. I'd helped build it so I would know. Our lawyers were overly cautious on things like this. I finished adding the Rover app to Skye's phone under my account and made sure it was connected to the fully working version. I didn't want her running into problems with the beta version.

My petty crime accomplished, I asked, "Ok, everyone ready to leave?"

That set off a last-minute scramble before departing for the day. Locating forgotten items took less time today than yesterday. Pleased with my progress corralling the girls, we headed out of the apartment to wait for the Rover car.

Mrs. Kim opened her door as we walked past. "Good morning, girls." She had impressive psychic skills or she must move like a cheetah when her superhuman hearing noticed someone approaching her door. She had to disguise these skills by walking slowly in public as one would expect from an elderly woman.

They chimed, "Good morning." Nothing else to add this early, so we kept walking.

The car arrived and after the girls were safely on their way, I called another Rover car to take me to the Starbucks to meet Jean Rollag and straighten out Laney's situation.

✦ ✦ ✦ ✦ ✦

The Starbucks buzzed with energy when I walked in. Rollag wasn't there. I'd recognize him on sight from the many stories about him over the years. Despite no Rollag in sight, the place made me a wreck. Like Pavlov's dog, I got nervous every time I walked into a coffee shop. It wasn't just cops that affected me like this.

I didn't drink coffee. Never liked the taste and never got hooked on it. I avoid Starbucks like the plague. Somehow, I'd missed the worldwide training session which explained all the confusing menu options. The rest of the world understood how a cappuccino differed from an espresso, but not me. Once upon a time, coffee came in black or with milk. After those easier days, the choices had expanded to fill the available space on the menu boards and beyond. Everyone in line got antsy if you asked questions, fidgeting, and grumbling as their aggression built while they awaited their latest fix. When my turn came to shuffle to the counter like a good caffeine-seeking robot, I ordered a mere bottle of water and a muffin. Muffins were easy.

Grabbing one of the few open tables, I sat down to wait. Surreptitiously, I scanned the menu board trying to decipher the options. As an engineer, puzzles have always intrigued me. Who knew that Starbucks now sold tea? *I like tea.* Maybe they always had. I didn't understand most of the tea options either. I guess I wasn't on the right email distribution list. Or I'd worked late one evening and missed the training class. Other engineers drank Starbucks. When did they get their training?

My thoughts were interrupted as the door flung open like a tsunami hit it. A tall, trim, good-looking man around thirty entered right as the line disappeared. Dressed in Valley business attire of faded designer jeans, a crisp dress shirt, and loafers, Rollag made his appearance. He strode in with his chest puffed out and strutted over to the counter. His grand entrance wouldn't have looked half as impressive if a line of customers had clogged the path. Perhaps he had an app that notified him of the best time to make his appearance.

Without waiting for the cashier to look at him, he barked, "Get me a Triple, Venti, Half Sweet, Non-Fat, Extra-Hot, Caramel Macchiato. And hurry, I'm late for an important meeting."

I had no idea what all those words meant. It sure didn't sound like coffee. I got up and approached Rollag as he fiddled with his phone. I shifted from foot to foot as I gathered my courage. "Hi, Mr. Rollag. It's nice to meet you. Do you mind if I ask you a few questions about Laney Tran?" I blurted out in a nervous rush.

"Sorry. All interviews need to go through PR." He answered without even looking up from his phone.

Trying again, I said, "No. It's not an interview. I wanted to ask you about Laney Tran."

"Who? I'm pretty busy right now," he said as he flipped through Instagram pictures.

Sure, real busy. "Laney's an HR consultant and had a meeting with you on Monday."

He paused, finally looking at me as he registered her name. "Oh, Laney," he leered. "That hot HR chick? I think she's into me." A rather unpleasant smile broke out on his face.

"She's my sister." I tried to remain calm.

"Cool. You can put in a good word for me." He spoke with confidence as if simply announcing his needs would make them come true.

Unbelievable. "She was hurt badly on Monday. Do you have any idea how it happened?"

Rollag flushed and stepped back as if I'd struck him. His words spilled out. "Not me. I didn't touch her. I barely know her. Why are you asking me about it?"

He slowed as he remembered. "Hey, she blew off our last meeting anyway." Raising his hand as a stop sign in front of my face, he turned away and brought his phone to his face with his other hand. "Remind me to get another HR consultant."

I held it together. "What was your meeting about?"

Putting down his phone, he turned back to me. "Look, our meeting was confidential. I can't talk to you about it. But if your sister wants a good time, tell her to give me a call."

"Don't hold your breath. She doesn't like assholes." I felt like smacking him. He didn't care that she was hurt but he still wanted to see if he had a chance with her. *What an ass.*

Before he could respond and our discussion went even further downhill, a barista bellowed, "John", while holding a large cup as he looked straight at Rollag.

Rollag broke off our conversation but pretended not to hear the barista. He raised his chin and looked off in another direction. Tapping his toes, he shifted his head looking in all directions except the barista holding his coffee. I didn't understand why he ignored his order. No one else waited for their order.

The barista walked around the counter and approached Rollag with a smile. "Hey dude, here's your coffee." He handed over the cup. "John" was written on the side.

Nailing the barista with a poisonous glare, Rollag said, "My name is Jean, not John."

I heard him say both names but couldn't discern any difference between them. Not that there might be two orders as crazy as that today, let alone at the same time.

"Yupsters, that's what I said." The barista maintained his good-natured poise as he handed over the cup. "Have a beautiful day, dude."

Rollag ignored the good wishes, grabbed the coffee and took a sip as the barista turned away. Rollag put the cup down in disgust and sneered, "This isn't what I ordered. It's too sweet and not extra hot."

What an arrogant ass.

The barista turned back with a friendly smile, apologized and promised to make another one right away. He rushed back to the bar to create another drink.

A few beats later, Rollag snorted. "Forget it," he said to no one in particular and strode out.

Rollag's callousness pissed me off, but I had to get to work even though the morning had been a bust. I requested the Rover car but the app showed I'd have to wait a short while before it arrived. Hard to complain that too many customers used the Rover service this morning. I decided to wait inside and sat down.

A minute later the barista walked out from the back with a new cup of whatever Rollag had ordered. He stood in a pleasant manner, searching for his thirsty, demanding customer, but couldn't locate Rollag. He came over to my table. His blond, spiked hair with bright orange tips contrasted with the green apron he wore. On a name tag reading "Brody", he'd added a yellow, smiley face sticker.

Tilting his head as he smiled at me, he said, "Good morning. Here's the coffee for your friend."

"Hi, uh … Brody … He's definitely not my friend. He left."

Unfazed, Brody said, "Well, dude, then I guess it's your lucky day. You can have his drink and have a beautiful day too." His smile was contagious.

I smiled back. As he left the drink on the table and turned back to his hissing, smoking machines, I mumbled, "But I like tea," as I surveyed the steaming drink with suspicion.

An intoxicating scent of caramel wafted over me. Resistance was futile. I finally reached over to the cup and picked it up for a small taste.

Mmm, good. Before I could make sense of that impression, my Rover car arrived.

7

Wednesday Midmorning

I called Laney's doctor on the way to my office. She had good news and bad news. On the positive side, Laney was doing much better and she thought Laney could leave on Friday afternoon, or most likely Saturday morning. On the other hand, the doctor had Laney on pain meds and expected her to drift in and out of sleep all day. The hospital was still restricting visitors on Laney's floor until after dinner tonight. I'd take the girls to go visit her then.

A few hours later, I looked up when Raj showed up. Normally he's so quiet, I don't notice his comings and goings. But today was different. He bounced up and down in his chair and started rearranging everything on his desk.

Surprised by his energy, I asked, "Where were you?"

"Testing with marketing." Raj moved some papers for the third time and accidentally pushed his phone off the desk to the ground. He popped out of his chair and picked it up, holding it high with a triumphant grin on his face.

"What's going on?"

His leg kept jiggling as he answered. "Too much caffeine."

"I thought you don't like caffeinated drinks."

"That is correct. But I cannot tell you more because of top secret."

Raj's attempt at secrecy succeeded only in drawing my complete attention.

"What's the secret? It's okay to tell me. I'm an engineer too."

Buckling under the intense pressure, Raj blurted out, "Marketing has a new idea for Rover cars to get Starbucks coffee for customers automatically."

I scoffed. "That's ridiculous."

Raj nodded in agreement. "Yes, this is true. But our boss told me to be nice to marketing, so I helped them."

I hadn't seen an over-caffeinated Raj before and I struggled to keep a straight face. In his amped-up condition, Raj wouldn't break any productivity records today. I needed a break anyway. Pushing my chair back from my desk, I stretched while I told him about my experience with Rollag at Starbucks.

I realized that Sergeant Jackson hadn't yet returned my call after my Rollag meeting. Thinking I could start checking out Rollag without waiting for the police, I did an online search for Jean Rollag. Reading the first article, I whistled softly.

"What is it?" Raj popped up again and came over to see my screen. He might have actually jumped over the cubicle wall.

"Look at this. DroneTech's now a deca-unicorn," I said.

Raj screwed up his face in confusion, then started babbling as the caffeine boosted him into overdrive. "I do not understand. Are not unicorns imaginary? We believe so in India. Do you have real unicorns here in America? And DroneTech has not one unicorn, but ten?"

Waving at him to calm down before someone noticed us, I said, "No. It's just Valley slang for one of those lucky startups valued at not just one billion dollars, but ten billion dollars. When they go public, Rollag will be rich enough to afford his own vineyard and a house in the hills."

Raj's eyes flashed wide. "I am wishing Rover was a unicorn."

I nodded in agreement with this shared dream of every engineer in Silicon Valley. How amazing it must feel to have options in a company worth a billion dollars. Even a small share would make Raj and me rich. "Right now, I think Rover is far from a unicorn."

Still standing in my cube, Raj looked around and sniffed the air. "Are you smelling something? Something that is rotten?" He moved his head from side to side as he tried to find the source of the offending odor. He was close enough to catch the scent of the fish sauce on my shoes.

I'd meant to clean them last night but got busy working on my software code and then stumbled into bed very late. "Oh, I spilled some fish sauce on my shoes."

Question answered, Raj ignored my shoes and moved on, "Why did your sister is meeting ... No." He gave a frustrated shake of his head and started again. "Why did your sister meet with Jean Rollag?"

I didn't comment on the deterioration of Raj's English skills. The excessive caffeine must have short-circuited some of the neurons in his brain. "Rollag's a pig. He wasn't any help."

Raj grinned broadly. "Unicorns, fish, and pigs, Oh my."

I ignored him and continued, "She's told me before that she helps companies get their HR departments set up, helps others investigate complaints, and sometimes advises the Board of Directors."

Raj leaned over my shoulder. "Maybe you should search for 'DroneTech' and 'investigation'?"

I didn't want him taking away my keyboard so I ran the search. This time the headlines for the top stories highlighted DroneTech's upcoming initial public offering. I clicked on one of the links.

"Let's see ... We knew they've announced they're going public soon. Of course, they hired one of the big investment banks ..." I traced my finger down the screen. "Hey, look at this." I pointed to the screen.

Raj leaned in closer, holding onto my chair for balance.

I continued, "It says DroneTech's venture capitalists are conducting a routine due diligence investigation of the leadership team before they formally file to go public."

Raj shook my chair with both hands. "Is that good? Is that bad? What does that mean?"

He was well into my personal space now and still over-charged. "Raj, chill. I didn't know you got so wound up after you have a lot of caffeine."

Self-conscious now, Raj pulled back a little bit. "So sorry. I do not drink caffeine drinks often."

I hadn't meant to embarrass him. "It's cool, just haven't seen this side of you." Before he would think I was upset, I continued, "That means they're checking out the execs to make sure nothing bad from their background comes out in the press while they are going public. Maybe the venture capitalists hired Laney to help on that project?"

Raj's head bobble appeared with somber resolve. "It is possible. We should look at Laney's computer. Perhaps she was checking out DroneTech?"

We? Raj, robotics expert, ace programmer, and now an amateur private investigator. But it was a great idea so I took Laney's computer out of my backpack. I knew it was unrealistic, but I'd hoped Laney might be doing well enough today that I could bring it home with her, along with her daughters.

When I touched the screen of Laney's computer, it flashed open to her home screen, a picture of Skye and Megan arm in arm at the beach.

"There is no security?" Raj looked scandalized.

"No, can you believe it? Yet her phone has the full retinal security controls activated. She's never been very good with technology. I'm the engineer in the family."

"Sometimes I think we are all engineers in India."

The thought had occurred to me too. Unable to think of an appropriate response, I looked at Laney's recent internet search history. "Yes, she was doing searches on DroneTech. And here," I jabbed at the screen, "she was also researching Jean Rollag."

Opening the last link Laney had clicked, we started reading. It was an old story from the Stanford Daily, the university's student newspaper. I skimmed the story, a typical graduation puff piece. Halfway down the article appeared a picture of a boyish-looking Jean Rollag with his arms around a young man and woman, all dressed in their graduation robes. The caption read: "Graduating seniors Jean Rollag, Howard Thomas, and Sierra Smith enjoy post-ceremony celebration."

Still hovering a bit too close over my shoulder, Raj pointed to the screen. "Your sister highlighted their names in the article."

"I see. I wonder if they were part of her research, too?" Impulsively, I said, "I should contact them and see if they know anything about Rollag and Laney."

Jiggling his leg, Raj shook his head in a different direction. "I do not know if that is a good idea. But I cannot stay. I must visit men's room now." Without waiting for a reply, he hustled away. If this is what he's like with too much coffee, I wondered how getting drunk would affect him.

I didn't know how to contact Rollag's Stanford friends. Scratching my head as I racked my brain, I finally came up with an idea on my own. It was wrong to check the Rover customer database to see if they had joined. I knew it was wrong. However, only last week the boss had told us in a brainstorming session there were no bad ideas. I knew company rules forbid it except in emergencies and it violated customers' privacy. But, surely this counted as a safety emergency. In a narrow, technical interpretation of the rules, I could claim this might keep Laney safe from further harm. That would be my answer if legal asked me and I'd stick to it.

I checked to see if Rollag's former friend, Howard Thomas, had joined Rover. *Yes!* A member in the last year, he lived nearby in Palo Alto.

Before I stopped to think about why I shouldn't do this, I called him.

"Hello," answered a deep voice.

"Hi, uh, my name is Marty. At Stanford, you and Jean Rollag were friends, right?" I should have stopped to think about what to say first.

"What? Where did you say you were from? Stanford?" asked Howard.

Oh, that's a good idea. "Yes, from Stanford."

"And what's this for again?" Howard seemed unconvinced and perhaps a bit confused, but that made two of us.

"Ah… I had some questions for you about that picture of you and Rollag on the cover of the Stanford Daily from your graduation." And a lightning bolt of inspiration struck me. "We're doing a story, sort of a Then and Now-type piece, about friends after graduation." Smug with pride for coming up with that lie on the spot, I leaned back in my chair. Now I'd get to the bottom of this.

"For a story that's eleven years after we graduated and almost three months after graduation?" asked Howard. More than skepticism had crept into his voice.

Sweat broke out on my head as I started to panic. "Ah … Yeah … We're a little late on our ten-year anniversary stories."

"Yeah, right." And he hung up. Not very polite. It's like he thought I was trying to scam him. Stanford graduates are smart. We should hire some at Rover.

"I've got to get better at this," I said to no one while still holding my now-disconnected phone.

Better get my story together if I'm going to help Laney. I still sat there holding my phone and staring into space when, out of the blue, Raj asked, "Did you get an answer?" With his caffeine high dissipating, his silent ways had returned.

I jerked upright in surprise. "No. He thought I was scamming him."

"That is the truth."

The truth hurt. "Yeah, but I'm just trying to help Laney, not steal something. I'm going to try one last time with the woman, Sierra Smith, in the picture with Rollag. But I need to do a better job."

"I wish you good luck." Raj sat at his desk and re-focused on his work.

I sat for a moment collecting my thoughts, then looked up Sierra. My dad liked the old proverb: "in for a penny, in for a pound." It wasn't as if Rover could fire me twice for misuse of the customer database. My luck held, as Sierra also had registered for Rover. If everyone started to use Rover, perhaps we'd become a unicorn company too. Daydreaming about that pleasant thought, I lost a few minutes.

Someone a few cubicles away yelled into their phone and snapped me out of my reflection. I don't know how anyone could work in an open area like this without headphones. I concentrated on Laney's situation and considered what to say. I took a deep breath and then called Sierra.

"Hello, this is Sierra," she answered.

I tried to project confidence as if I cold-called strangers every day and wasn't a scam artist. "Hi. My name is Marty Golden. I'm helping out Laney Tran. I believe she contacted you about Jean Rollag and I wanted to ask you some questions too." I felt pride that I had straddled the line between vagueness and clarity without explicitly lying.

"What?" Sierra spoke with a nervous tremor in her voice. "Are you with the IRS too?"

What?

8

Wednesday Late Morning

What would our mother have thought of Laney pretending that she worked for the IRS? All those crime shows we watched together during childhood must have affected Laney's judgment. Mine too. I didn't pause before answering, "Yes."

Sierra sounded pained. "What else do you need to know?"

As she spoke I saw our boss limping down the hallway toward our area. With a hurt leg that made him grumpy when he had to use it, the boss was on his way to his near-daily check-in of our team around the floor. I had to hurry. A crazy idea popped into my head, probably inspired by my imaginary action movie starring Mace Jackson. "Ms. Smith. Would you meet me at the San Jose IRS office at three p.m.? We can double-check that we have all the facts correct at that time."

Sierra stuttered a little. "Uh. Yes. Okay. I told Ms. Tran that I'd cooperate. I don't want any trouble."

The boss closed in on me. Sweating, I hurried through my confirmation. "Ok. See you at three. Bye."

Our boss reached my cubicle right as I hung up. Raj looked at me with one eyebrow raised. Heart racing, I looked back at him with my eyes wide open, sending telepathic messages imploring him not to say anything until our boss left. Raj must have understood my silent pleas as he pulled the boss' attention away from me and carried the conversation single-handedly, discussing schedules and testing techniques. I managed a few weak comments and after a longer visit than any of us desired, the boss limped away to his next victim.

Raj waited until our boss left earshot. Then, he commented on my conversation with Sierra as if nothing had interrupted us. "I am thinking this is not a good idea."

I understood why he disagreed with my plan to meet Sierra at the IRS office, but I didn't want to hear it. "Laney did it too." I used my best big-boy voice.

"Yes. Now she is in hospital."

Raj, speaker of truth.

"I know." I disliked the truth. "That's why I need to figure out what's going on. I don't want Laney to get killed." Breaking eye contact, I looked down at my computer screen and began searching online. "I think I have an idea how to make this work."

Raj popped over to watch my search. The caffeine high had dissipated, but when he saw the images of IRS badges on my screen, he became agitated again. "I am really thinking this is not a good idea." He shook his hand at me as if to wipe away what I was doing.

Ignoring him, I kept working. Creating a metal badge would be impossible in time for the meeting. Maybe I wouldn't need one. A few clicks later, I'd created an image of a fake IRS employee badge with the IRS logo and added my photo from the Rover employee directory underneath. I sized the image to insert into my Rover employee badge holder attached to my belt. I printed the fake badge and tested it. It fit.

I glanced up to see Raj pressing his lips firmly together. Turning back to my screen, I created a fake business card that could fit into my wallet in place of my driver's license. My excitement built as I realized this would emulate those TV crime shows where the agents flash their credentials and no one scrutinized them. Hopefully, Sierra had seen those shows as well and wouldn't subject my fake credentials to an up-close review either. And with any luck, none of the other workers at the IRS office would see my counterfeit badges either.

Raj reached a definitive conclusion. Pointing at the badge, he said, "This is not a good idea."

I concurred. "Probably not, but I need to do it for Laney. I'll send the boss an email that I'm not feeling well and need to leave early for a doctor's appointment." *My head did hurt.*

"You will put our testing further behind." Raj had given up on a personal appeal and now tried to reason with the engineer in me.

The guilt trip almost worked. "I know. I'm sorry. I'll make it up this weekend and work extra hours next week. Just keep your head down."

"As long as you do not give up your day job."

"What?"

"It is an American saying I have learned. It is true because if you get arrested, you will not be able to work here."

"Ok. Good tip. And, I don't think the boss will come back this direction now that he's finished his drive by." Our boss preferred the "management by walking around" method instead of holding regular one-on-one meetings with us. This way he avoided feeling obligated to help solve any meaningful problems or talking with us about any personal issues.

Raj frowned for a few seconds without moving and then slowly shook his head. "Ok."

"Thanks." I thought I was safe but didn't dare thank him for not ratting me out. That idiom would take too long to explain.

I once read that you build closer relationships by discussing personal topics. "By the way, what's your full name. It's not Raj, right?" That was a personal discussion, right there.

"My first name is Rajendrakumar. In Hindi, it means powerful king. My last name is longer. You should call me Raj, I think."

"Yes. I think I will." *Powerful king of coding, that's for sure.*

I had to leave if I wanted to get to my appointment early to scope out the place. It was time my alter-ego, Marty Golden, fake IRS agent, made his appearance.

9

Wednesday Afternoon

The San Jose IRS office, located downtown just a few short blocks north of Plaza de César Chávez, bore the common government architectural design of concrete and glass from decades ago. I could see only the edge of the grassy park as the Rover car dropped me off at a nearby corner at a quarter to three. Beads of sweat started forming on my forehead as my nerves returned. My idea better work. Getting arrested was not on my to-do list for today.

Sitting quietly in a corner of the IRS lobby, I waited for Sierra Smith to walk in. From LinkedIn, I'd printed a more recent picture of her so I would recognize her as soon as she arrived. My luck held as a lot of pedestrian traffic flowed in and out of the building. The guards looked bored as they sat at the other end of the lobby, scanning people's bags and badges as they passed through the metal detector that led to the elevators. I was counting on them not noticing me.

A few minutes before three, Sierra walked into the lobby and paused to look around. I recognized her from her pictures. A little older than her graduation picture, but she looked pretty much the same.

I jumped up and strode to the lobby entrance. I called, "Ms. Smith? Ms. Sierra Smith?"

She turned her head when she heard her name. A few other people in the lobby looked up at my voice. The guards remained occupied watching people walk through the security scanner and paid no attention to me. I closed the gap to reach Sierra's side before she'd wonder why I recognized her when we'd never met before.

"Yes. I'm Sierra." Speaking with a soft voice, she shifted her weight and hunched her shoulders, not at all the image of the self-confident Stanford student from the long-ago newspaper photo. The IRS was one scary place.

"Good afternoon. I'm Marty Golden." Projecting a confidence I didn't quite feel, I reached out my hand and gave her a firm handshake. Taking out my wallet, I flashed my fake business card resting where my driver's license usually sat. "Our floor is under construction right now and quite noisy, so I thought, since it's a beautiful day, it might be nice to take a short walk and talk in the park nearby?" I held my breath, hoping she'd go for my big plan. I hadn't figured out plan B yet.

"Uh, sure, I guess."

"Great. Well then, I won't be needing my employee badge to go outside." I forced a chuckle as I retracted my hand holding the wallet and moved it down to my side. Her eyes followed as my hand unclipped my fake employee badge from my belt and moved both my wallet and badge into my pocket. I hoped my minor attempt at humor and drawing her attention to my badge, however brief, would suffice to convince her that I worked for the IRS. Not wanting other workers or the armed guards inspecting my fake credentials, I moved toward the door, now eager to get out of here. Holding the door open for her, I said, "After you."

Crime shows must be accurate, or influential. She believed me and headed out the door. *Phew.* Maybe I won't get arrested today. *At least not yet.*

The short walk to the park made me realize I'm glad to be a software engineer rather than a real IRS agent. Although most people don't understand what I do, at least they're not especially awkward around me. As we walked the short block to the park, Sierra's strained face looked like she wished she could be anywhere else but with me. I tried to keep up a steady stream of meaningless small talk, but weather, the Giants, traffic, and weather again used up my entire supply. Sierra had nothing to contribute to the conversation. Even in the best of circumstances, I don't discuss much with strangers besides the Giants and technology.

We sat on a bench at the top of the oval-shaped park. In front of us, several young kids ran back and forth on the grass in the afternoon sun while their parents watched and talked nearby. The burnt orange Tech Museum building and palm trees lining the roadway created an interesting backdrop for the kids. Pedestrians walked along the sidewalk while cars drove around the curving roads alongside the small city park. No one bothered us.

I looked at Sierra and smiled my best, fake agent smile. "Laney, I mean Ms. Tran, is out for a few days so I was told to double-check a few things. Perhaps you could give me a quick summary of what you told her and then I'll see if there were any additional questions we had. Our boss wanted to make sure we had the facts straight. I do apologize for asking you to come down here again."

"Again? I haven't been here before. I just spoke to Ms. Tran on the phone."

Oops. "Oh, of course, I meant to talk to the IRS again."

She bought it. Sierra paused for a moment, hopefully, to gather her thoughts rather than call the cops. "Well, Ms. Tran said the IRS was doing a deep audit on David Saunders and Jean Rollag. She wanted to know if either of them had made any large purchases or suddenly had a lot of money during their last year at college. Something about checking possible discrepancies in their tax returns."

I nodded encouragingly as if I already knew all of this, but Sierra refused to look at me.

"That was such a crazy year. They were working nonstop on DroneTech, finishing their classes, and meeting investors. Those VCs kept them hopping."

I smiled as she mentioned the venture capitalists, or VCs. Perhaps I was right that they'd hired Laney to investigate Rollag.

Sierra continued, "I barely saw Jean or David our senior year. Maybe at a few parties they hit late."

"Sure," I said when she paused. I had no idea where this was headed. Had Laney been checking to see if something fishy happened in the early days of DroneTech? It wouldn't be the first time. I remembered stories about the early days of internet startups. After a company hit the big-time, people would pop up with proof, sometimes real, sometimes fake, that they'd paid the founders and owned the rights to the resulting product, or had loaned them money and owned half the company. If I were a venture capitalist about to see billions, I'd want to know if any skeletons lurked in DroneTech's closet too.

Sierra concluded, "I told her we hadn't been very close in our senior year and I didn't know anything about DroneTech." She stopped and gave me a quick glance before looking away.

That's it? Sierra seemed intensely uncomfortable. She was actually fidgeting on the bench. Unlike Raj, excessive caffeine didn't seem to be the likely cause.

I gazed at her without speaking. After the silence grew uncomfortable, I asked, "Are you sure that's it?" Proud of my superior interrogation technique, I didn't say anything else as I looked at her.

Sierra fidgeted with her purse straps and looked around the park with jerky movements of her head. Letting out a long sigh, she finally spoke. "Well, I was … I mean, I really liked Jean once and … I'm not really sure if I should … I don't know how to say this."

I'd exhausted my supply of techniques so I merely nodded at her.

"It's something I did and I know I shouldn't have done it, but Jean was such a close friend. We'd dated a little off and on … before he took advantage of me." Sierra trailed off.

I leaned forward, trying to show empathy using the lessons from a video I'd watched for work once. I hoped that would help me extract the story from her. Rollag was a scumbag, but I had no idea where this was going. "Go ahead. It'll be okay. I'm sure we can work something out." *Yeah, I'm sure the IRS would approve an agreement she reached with a fake agent.*

Taking a deep breath, Sierra blurted out, "I took a bribe from Jean when I was at Stanford and I didn't report it to the IRS."

Surprised, I jerked my head back. "A bribe? For what?"

With her pronouncement in the open, the rest of Sierra's story spilled out. "I had a work-study job in Stanford's Records Department. Mostly, I just did typing. You know, updating student records and the like. Jean did a semester abroad in Australia during our Junior year. I guess he just partied and didn't go to class much."

Sticking to my successful interrogation technique, I nodded again.

Sierra continued, "When we got back to school after Christmas, Jean got his grades. He'd failed or got incompletes on everything. He wasn't going to graduate and he panicked. He and David had already started their company and the VCs liked the idea of two Stanford grads running the company. They thought it sounded like Google's story. They used that to get other investors. Jean gave me $5,000 to change his grades to C's."

Her voice faltered. "I did it. I needed the money. I'm not proud of it. And I didn't report it on my taxes." With a small sniffle, she finished, "I don't want to go to jail." She slumped down on the bench.

Her revelation stumped me. Not sure what to do next, I looked around the park at the children playing while she collected herself. No IRS agents swooped in to pick me up. Although feeling a bit calmer, I didn't want to go back into the IRS building. What if she wanted to file an official statement? I didn't know how to end this interview without getting caught.

My phone rang. Skye was calling. I excused myself for a moment and answered.

"Uncle Marty?" Skye had a nervous tilt to her voice.

"Hi there. What's going on?"

Skye answered in a rush. "We took the Rover car from school back to your apartment like you told me. But the building door won't let us in and you didn't give us a key."

Oops. "I'm sorry. I forgot." *So much for my great parenting skills.* "Use the intercom to call Mrs. Kim and ask her to let you into the building. You can sit outside my door and I'll come home right away to get you girls into my apartment."

I smiled to myself. This created no real hardship for the girls, yet it solved my problem with Sierra. I walked back to the bench where Sierra still sat silent, looking shell-shocked. Perhaps my superior interrogation skills had surprised her into revealing the bribe after all these years.

"I'm very sorry, but my, um, daughter lost her key and is locked out. I need to go let her in."

This connected. Sierra looked up at me. "I understand. I have two kids myself. Will I need to come back again?"

I hope not. "I think we have all the information we need. Everything else is consistent with Ms. Tran's summary. I appreciate you coming down here. We'll call you if we have any further questions."

"But, is anything going to happen to me?"

"I doubt it." *Truthfully, no idea.* "But, I suspect since it was so long ago and so little that you may just have to pay a small penalty at most. I doubt it will lead to anything serious for you."

Exhaling, Sierra gave me a wan smile and thanked me. I suppose there's nothing like a fake IRS agent telling you not to worry about the consequences of taking an illegal bribe over a decade ago to set one's mind at ease. She turned and walked back to where she must have parked.

While I waited for the Rover car, I decided to leave another voicemail for Mace. I'd made exciting progress in our investigation and needed to catch him up. Clearly, Rollag wanted to kill Laney so she couldn't tell the VCs about the bribe. After I hung up, I realized my message to him might not have been as clear as I wanted. It's not my fault it's hard to explain why impersonating an IRS agent, possibly breaking federal consumer privacy laws, and prying into activities from nearly eleven years ago would help us solve Laney's case. I put aside my doubts as I patted myself on the back for my progress. Mace did need a reliable sidekick for his burgeoning, if yet imaginary, movie career.

Then it dawned on me that Sierra could simply tell her story again. Sierra might be Rollag's next victim and I'd let her go without a warning. I called Mace again.

10

Wednesday Late Afternoon

I rushed home. Ok, the Rover car drove home at its normal, careful pace. For times like this, we needed a special emergency mode that would make the car drive more aggressively. Maybe I could talk to marketing about a new feature. They'd probably call it something silly like "Mush." Of course, everyone would use the feature all the time. Our lawyers would probably not like that. I wonder if we could build it as a special test capability and just keep the feature for the engineering team. We'd leave it in perpetual test mode. Our lawyers probably wouldn't like that either. *Sigh.*

When I got into my apartment building, I didn't see the girls in the lobby or hallway. I walked to Mrs. Kim's apartment and knocked on her door. Uncharacteristically, I had to wait for her to answer.

After a few moments, she opened the door. "Hello, Mr. Marty."

I saw the girls in the room behind her. "Thank you so much for letting the girls in. I didn't mean for you to keep them in your apartment. That was very nice of you."

"No problem. They are pleasure. Come in please."

I walked into her apartment, past a tall stool standing right by the side of the door. The place felt warmer and cozier than mine, even though they'd been built at the same time. The wooden furniture wasn't antique but had experienced a well-lived life. Against the wall rested a bamboo bookshelf filled with various knickknacks, photos, and books. Small lamps sat on side tables next to chairs scattered through the room. Several simple, stylized nature paintings hung on her walls. Although our taste in art didn't match, the paintings complemented her room well.

Both girls sat calmly at a dining table doing homework. They each had a teacup and what looked like a Korean honey sesame cookie by their side. A third teacup and cookie sat on the table by an empty chair. Mrs. Kim had things under control. The girls looked up as I entered and smiled hello, clearly feeling at ease in the comfortable setting.

Skye asked, "Can we go see Mom now?"

"The hospital said they're not allowing visitors until after —"

"What? You promised." Megan's frown threatened to break into tears.

"It's not us. They're not allowing anyone now. We'll go after dinner."

Recovering, Megan said, "Then, can we stay here longer? Mrs. Kim is really nice and she has tea."

"I've got tea —"

"Then can we talk to Mom on the phone?" Skye wasn't so easily distracted.

Reasonable. "Let's call from my apartment. I'm sure Mrs. Kim will let you bring your tea back to my apartment." I looked up to see Mrs. Kim nod. "We'll return her cups later. Let's go."

"The girls are pleasure. They come any time," said Mrs. Kim.

"Thank you."

Ever gracious, she asked me, "Would you like tea and cookies too?"

"No, thank you." But then the proverbial light bulb turned on in my head. "Actually, would you be okay having the girls stay with you after school for the rest of this week, just until I get home from work?"

"And we'd get more tea? And cookies?" Megan jumped in, her excitement growing.

"That is pleasure," Mrs. Kim answered both of us. She poured a little more tea into Megan's cup.

While they balanced their teacups and cookies, I took the girls' backpacks. Together, we made our way down the hall to my apartment. As I entered my apartment, now looking sterile by comparison, my phone's alarm reminded me to have the groceries delivered. I signaled the service to deliver them right away.

I hoped Laney was doing better now than she had looked yesterday. Sitting on the couch, I called the hospital. The girls gathered in front of me, now tense with anticipation. A nurse answered the phone in Laney's room and told me that Laney could talk only for a few minutes before she needed to rest some more. I put the phone on speaker and the girls burst out, at the same time, with pent-up excitement and concern. The girls' animated voices echoed through the room as they took turns asking Laney questions and giving her updates on their day. Laney responded with only a few brief comments. She sounded tired yet upbeat. Long before any of us were ready to stop talking, the nurse took back the phone and told us Laney needed to rest. After the love and energy expressed by the girls, I needed to rest too.

The girls, cheered by talking to their mother, took their conversation to the kitchen table with the intent of finishing their snacks and homework. With their minds still on their mom, I doubted their homework got their full attention.

I went into my home office and shut the door behind me. It was time to confront Rollag, at least virtually. I could be a lot braver over the phone than in person. If Rollag knew his secret bribe was out in the open, then he wouldn't need to kill Laney to keep her quiet. Although, he wouldn't be thrilled to learn his ex-girlfriend Sierra had spilled the beans.

I called Rollag's cell from Laney's contacts. It rang just once before his voicemail answered. I hung up without leaving a message. After all, this hadn't been my best week for voicemail clarity.

Although my idea to confront Rollag had stalled, I was still convinced he'd manipulated the drone to attack Laney. Maybe she'd also learned his Stanford secret and had told him, or she'd damaged his ego by spurning his unwanted advances. Who knew? Any of those could have been his motivation to try to kill her. *The killer was Mr. Rollag, from the air, with a drone.*

Rollag had the skills and DroneTech software powered most of the delivery drones in the country. If Raj and I could add special features into the Rover service at will, I figured that Rollag, or one of his engineering lackeys, could do the same to a drone. If I couldn't get Rollag to talk to me, I'd have to find someone else at DroneTech who would.

Daniel Pope would have to be my ticket into DroneTech. I'd worked in the cube next to Daniel for several years in a previous startup. We'd gotten along well, at first. He had an annoying habit of giving unsolicited life improvement tips to everyone. As a result of his holier-than-thou approach to life, most people in the office avoided him. He seemed like a lonely person. After my divorce, I knew what it was like to be on your own. In a rare moment of inexplicable generosity of spirit, I'd invited him to my monthly poker night.

I wasn't even sure how the monthly poker night with my friends had started. It was probably something my wife made me do years ago, and one of her few good ideas at that. Well, besides my two kids. Calling the poker group my friends overstated things —

perhaps friendly acquaintances were more accurate. We met only on rare occasion outside of our monthly game.

In an experience the group still hasn't let me forget, we held the shortest poker night in history. Daniel walked in, twenty minutes late. *To a poker game!* From that point on, he spouted off a continual stream of advice on everything from hygiene, etiquette, nutrition, and fashion. When he moved to skincare, the game broke up. That experience helped to contain any urges I've had since for random acts of generosity.

Soon after that night, Daniel left to join DroneTech, a new startup at the time. Although we hadn't seen each other in a few years, he nonetheless sustained a steady stream of emails to me containing self-improvement articles. They went straight to my spam folder but I hadn't removed him from my contacts. After all, he worked at DroneTech. *I'm not stupid.* Knowing I'd regret this later, I texted Daniel to see if he could meet for lunch tomorrow.

I sat back, feeling unsatisfied. Mace hadn't returned my many calls. I couldn't reach Rollag to confront him and I had no proof of Rollag's guilt anyway, beyond my gut. Laney would be in danger again once the hospital started allowing visitors later today.

Although I couldn't do anything else about Rollag for now, I wanted to do more on her case. In the time left this afternoon before we could visit Laney, I'd eliminate her other clients from the suspect list. Mace would expect nothing less from his partner when he got back from his furlough and checked his voicemails. *Yeah, right. His partner.*

Pulling out Laney's computer, I wanted to take a look at her other clients in more detail. Working from my home office meant I had more time to look through her files without the possibility of my boss walking by. This wouldn't win me any employee-of-the-month awards, but we didn't have those at Rover. Rummaging through Laney's personal files might not win me the brother-of-the-year award either. On the other hand, I've never seen any of those in stores.

Her calendar listed a meeting with Fernando Hernandez scheduled for this past Monday morning at nine. A phone number was listed underneath, but I wanted to do a little more research before calling him. The IRS angle had worked once, but I couldn't expect my luck to hold.

I looked through Laney's files on her computer. She had a few documents about some of her clients, but her files didn't mention Fernando. My forensic investigation techniques exhausted, I sat back baffled.

As I was pondering, Raj called me. When I answered, he sounded odd, more stilted than normal and he had me on speaker. "Hello, Marty. This is Raj. I am checking if your field test has repeated the bug we found?"

Huh? Then I realized what must be happening. "Not yet. I think I got close. I'm going to try a few more things. Could you let the boss know that I probably won't be back until the morning so I can fix this bug once and for all?"

"Yes. Certainly. He is standing right here. Next to me. I am putting in the updates we discussed now. See you tomorrow." He hung up abruptly without waiting for my response.

Raj was a stand-up guy.

A minute later my phone rang again. "Hello. He is gone," said Raj.

"What happened?"

"I do not know. He is in bad mood. Stomping around and asking everyone what they are doing. I told him I am working to fix bugs. Then he wants to know where Marty is. I tell him we work together to fix bugs. He wants me to call you for update. So, I call."

"Thanks for not letting the cat out of the bag. You were awesome." I appreciated Raj helping me out. I liked my job and was pretty good at it when I spent time on it. However, I hadn't focused on my work much since I'd heard about Laney.

Raj clucked. "It is always better to let a sleeping dog lie."

I was sure he was grinning from ear to ear that he matched my animal idiom. "Touché. Be careful not to let marketing hear you be clever with a dog phrase or it will end up as a future feature we have to code." Rather than continuing to try to one-up him, I switched topics. "I'm stuck. I'm pretty sure Rollag tried to hurt Laney but I also want to cross her other clients off the suspect list. She had this guy, Fernando Hernandez, on her calendar for Monday morning. There's nothing else about him on her computer. Any ideas?"

I heard typing in the background. Raj said, "Oh," his voice edged with apprehension.

"Oh, what?"

"You should not contact him." Raj rarely asserted his opinion with such a definitive statement.

"What? Why? What did you find?" Now he'd succeeded in increasing my anxiety.

"I searched the internet for Fernando Hernandez. There are many articles about him." Raj tried to change the subject back to the safety of engineering. "Let us talk about testing code instead."

"Raj," I insisted, "Read me the articles."

Raj sighed. I could hear the slump in his posture as he realized I wouldn't be dissuaded so easily. "Fernando Hernandez is the son of big Latin American drug lord. One article reports he moved here to start an outpost for their gang. Marty, this is very serious. We should tell police."

I was confused. "Why would Laney be meeting with a drug lord? She's in HR. These articles must be about someone else."

Raj continued, "Here is article claiming he received a college degree in the U.S. and then had a 'falling out' with his father. What is 'falling out'?"

"That means an argument," I answered, distracted. "Still, it's got to be about someone else. Laney's only an HR consultant and she just moved here. She doesn't know any gangs in Silicon Valley."

"In engineering from San Jose State University." Raj stated with conviction.

"Why would my sister meet with this guy?"

"This is very good question. Perhaps he did something inappropriate. Does not HR investigate such problems?"

"Yes, but in a drug gang?"

"Oh, look here." In his excitement, Raj had forgotten I wasn't next to him. "His degree is in software engineering."

"Software?! Maybe Rollag hired him to crash the drone on Laney?"

"Perhaps he works at DroneTech and the drug gang is a side business." Raj must have watched the same shows I'd seen growing up.

"I suppose it's possible she learned that Fernando has a connection to Rollag and wanted to talk to him about Rollag. Maybe she didn't realize he runs a drug gang." What had Laney stumbled into?

The concern in Raj's voice was clear. "You should not talk to him."

This time I agreed. "Yeah. I don't think I could scam a guy who runs a drug gang on the side. I'll call the cop who's investigating Laney's case."

Raj gave smart advice. Drug gangs made me nervous. So did heights, guns, cops, talking to our legal department and, recently added to the list, leaving complicated voicemails.

But, after hanging up with Raj, I faced one of my fears and left another voicemail for Mace. He needed to know that Fernando Hernandez might be working with Rollag to kill Laney. I needed him to check out any possible suspects who were also dangerous drug lords right away. After providing a brief background on Fernando, I made sure to let Mace know that I still believed Rollag was the master villain. I told Mace I would pursue another DroneTech contact, Daniel, to get proof and that I'd keep him updated. I couldn't wait for Mace to get back from furlough tomorrow.

The more I fretted about it, the more Rollag and DroneTech bothered me. If anyone could crash a drone into her car and make it look like an accident, it had to be Rollag. Mace would appreciate my legwork so he could get a jumpstart on his investigation. I know I'd love to have someone find any bugs in my code while I was out of the office. With all my help, Mace would get to the bottom of this in no time.

Daniel Pope finally responded to my text. A whole half hour had passed. My mother wouldn't have been happy if I'd been so rude as to wait thirty minutes before responding to a text from a friend, especially if the friend wanted my help to put my boss in prison for attacking his sister. Daniel seemed eager to have lunch with me and invited me tomorrow to DroneTech. I ignored the link to a self-improvement article that he included and agreed to lunch. If I couldn't get Rollag on the phone, I'd corner him in the lion's den. Now I only had to find some evidence of the lion's guilt.

Before shutting her computer, I looked at Laney's calendar one last time. The last entry on Monday still read "ME." *Me time?* While I understood the concept, my own recent "me-time" consisted of drinking a beer while watching a Giants game from my couch. Laney has talked to me about how tough it's been since her husband died unexpectedly. Mourning him while abruptly becoming a single mother to Megan and Skye would make anyone go at least a little crazy and crave some "me-time."

I looked back at her appointments for last week to see if something else jumped out. Perhaps a previous client had taken a few days to organize the attack on her. Laney's consulting business hasn't reached critical mass yet as she had no other clients scheduled that week. On Friday, just a few days before she got hurt, she had a "Mani-Pedi" appointment listed at a nearby salon. *I knew it.* But if she just had her nails done, then Monday's appointment didn't make sense as a spa trip for "me-time."

Had she scheduled a trip to a financial planner or a lawyer? If so, she'd have no reason to hide their name on her calendar. Had she used "ME" as initials to hide something, or someone, from her girls? I doubted she was ready to date again, but maybe she planned to meet someone and didn't want the girls to see the name by accident. I checked the contacts on her computer. The file was empty. No surprise that Laney hadn't yet figured out how to synchronize her contacts between her phone and her computer.

Oh, Laney. If only she had a tech-savvy relative to help. I needed to figure out what, or who, "ME" was. This could be the person who had tried to kill her. Picking up Laney's phone to look at her contacts, I got frustrated again that it remained locked. In all the excitement of Skye and Megan talking to their mother, I'd forgotten to ask Laney for her phone's password. I'd have to ask her tonight.

11

Wednesday Dinner

Finished with her homework, Skye brought out her science fair project and started taking notes. I wandered over. The plastic boxes of ants all looked pretty similar to me — clumps of ants swarming around as they searched and returning often to touch their antennae to neighbors. These ants looked quite enthusiastic in doing whatever ants do all day.

"So, why ants? What's your project about?"

Without looking up, Skye corrected me. "These are Dorymyrmex insanus."

"Insane dory what?"

"It's a specific kind of ant. They're a vulnerable species, almost on the endangered species list. I'm trying to figure out if they do better with different kinds of nutrients. They do well in very dry conditions."

"Well, we've got a drought here," I added, trying to be helpful.

"Duh. But these come from Texas. Some people call them Texas crazy ants."

"Ha! When your mom and I were growing up, we sure had some crazy Texas aunts. And uncles too." I laughed, remembering the odd assortment of family gathered at my uncle's lake house during the Fourth of July parties.

Skye snorted but didn't look up from taking notes on her project.

I took that as a go-ahead to tell her a story. Never needing much encouragement, I continued, "You know, when I was your age, I started an ant collection in a plastic ant farm that I got for a birthday present from a friend. My mom, your Grandma, told me I couldn't keep it, but I hid it in my closet without anyone knowing. I checked on it every day, but my closet was dark and I didn't notice the ant farm got cracked. But your mother figured out I had a secret ant hideout in my room when she discovered them everywhere in her room. They weren't crazy ants, but your mom sure went crazy."

The twelve-year-old re-emerged from the budding scientist as Skye giggled at me. After that short break, she put her nose back into her journal to finish her notes on her ants.

At least I know the ants are in my apartment. Bored now that Skye had traded my company for science, I pulled out my phone to update my kids.

GROUP TEXT TO AMANDA, ELI

MARTY: Skye thinks ants are cool. Maybe she's not really Aunt Laney's daughter

ELI: Texas crazy ants are cool. They eat electronic stuff and no one knows why

AMANDA: I can't believe I'm related to someone who knows something like that

MARTY: Me either. Gotta go

A call from the building lobby interrupted us. The grocery delivery guy had arrived.

"Hi, I'm here with your order. Most of it anyway. You know we only deliver food." It was my regular grocery delivery guy. He'd never been grumpy before.

Bewildered, I asked, "What do you mean?"

"Your order included a puppy. At first, I thought you meant hushpuppies, but we don't carry those. When I looked at the list again, it clearly showed just 'puppy.' That's not funny, Mr. Golden. We don't deliver live animals, only groceries."

"Sorry for the, uh, misunderstanding. Come on up." I had a good idea who had made the unusual grocery addition. Next time, I'd review the list after the girls added their requests. At least tonight's dinner would be something besides peanut butter.

A short time later, we walked out of the apartment building. Or rather Skye and I walked and Megan skipped ahead as the sugar from tonight's milkshake testing still coursed through her body. We reached the front lobby where Megan waved at us to hurry while she held the door open. A cool breeze blew in from the ocean as the typical Bay Area summer evening cooldown took place. The sky revealed another beautiful sunset, with colors painted across the sky behind the low mountain ranges to our west. Perhaps the only benefit of an extended drought lay in the enhanced beauty of the sunsets.

For once the Rover car pulled up to the door as we arrived. With a short walk from my apartment to the outside, I usually had to wait for the Rover car to show up.

Skye paused in the doorway as the breeze hit her. "I'm cold. I want to go get a sweatshirt." She wasn't yet accustomed to the impact of the Bay breezes, where our summer temperatures could hit the eighties during the day and drop by twenty degrees right after the sunset.

I tossed my apartment key fob to Skye who caught it and pivoted to head back for her sweatshirt.

Seeing the car, Megan said, "Awesome. I like taking Rover." Without skipping a beat, she turned to Skye and yelled, "Fetch my sweatshirt too, please."

The Rover car took off.

By itself.

Without us inside.

"What the hell?" I stared in extreme annoyance at the back bumper of the receding car.

"That's a bad word," came the immediate chant from Megan.

"Yeah, I know," I snapped. "Rover's not working right. I don't know why it just left on its own. Something must be wrong. I need to check with Raj." My mind churned as I tried to think about how this could have happened. The Rover car shouldn't leave without waiting at least five minutes and signaling the customer first. I requested another Rover. While we waited, I called Raj.

"No, it cannot move if you just say 'Fetch,' " said Raj. "I tested this feature very much with marketing this morning, you remember? They had me drink a lot of coffee."

I chuckled. Remembering Raj's caffeine-induced antics from this morning helped take the edge off the moment. "Well, it just left without us."

"What is it that your niece said?"

"Fetch my sweatshirt," I said, still annoyed.

Raj spoke with more confidence about his coding. He knew the strength of his own abilities. "No. The car does not move if you just say 'fetch.' What else is it that she said? "

"I'm not sure. She's a kid. She doesn't stop talking."

Megan stuck her tongue out at me.

"What is it that she said right before 'fetch'?"

I didn't see the point. Talking about Megan wouldn't help us figure out the bug. "I don't know. I think that she was excited we were taking Rover. Then she asked her sister to fetch her sweatshirt."

"This is it." Raj's self-satisfied nod radiated over the line.

That wasn't it for me. "What's it?" How had Megan magically developed the ability to make the Rover car drive off on its own?

Megan misheard me. "We're getting It's-Its?" she asked, referring to the ice cream bar, as a huge smile broke out on her face.

"No," I said to her.

"What?" asked Raj.

I turned away from Megan's disappointed pout so I could answer Raj. "Never mind. What were you saying about Rover?"

"You are to say 'Rover Fetch' and the car goes to get your coffee. Marketing thought that was funny. They think it will be very popular. I do not understand how Starbucks will know what coffee to make for a car."

"Good point. And does the car stand in line to pick up a coffee for 'Rover'? What's their plan?" I asked.

"I do not believe marketing has a plan. You should tell marketing. I do not wish to do more testing. Today was much too difficult for me," said Raj.

The second Rover car dropped us off in front of the hospital just after seven. I patted my pants to make sure Laney's phone hadn't slipped out of my pocket in the car. With the normal medical appointments over and most of the daytime staff gone home, the hospital was less crowded than yesterday. Skye bounded forward through the lobby and pushed the elevator button. Her pre-teen, cool self-image had lost the struggle of competing with her excitement to see her mother.

Megan sulked. "Hey, no fair. I get to push the button in the elevator."

I walked a bit slower as my stomach didn't feel great after our dinner. The girls had talked me into making spaghetti tacos for dinner. *As if that's a real thing.* Who put actual spaghetti into a taco and ate it? They promised me that Laney made it for them. *Yuck.*

We got into the next elevator. I said, "She's on the fifth floor."

Megan pressed the button for five. And then she also pushed the buttons for six and seven. Out of the corner of her eye, she glanced up to check my reaction. I grinned. I'm her uncle, after all, not her mother. A wide smile made her reaction clear.

When we got off the elevator on Laney's floor, there were no cops around. I took a nervous breath. Laney was at risk again.

A different nurse from Tuesday morning sat at the central station idly clicking on her computer. I turned towards room 518 and the girls followed.

"Excuse me, sir," said the nurse.

I paused, pleased that she had stopped me. "Yes? We're going to visit my sister in room 518." Maybe the hospital was still worried about their security after all.

Cocking her head to look at Megan, the nurse said, "Your little one there doesn't look ten."

"No, she's younger," I said, grateful that she hadn't quizzed me on Megan's exact age.

"I'm very sorry, but the hospital only allows children ten and older to go into the patient rooms after hours. She'll have to stay in the waiting area." The nurse pointed to the couches to the side of the desk.

Megan looked crushed. Her eyes welled with tears and she started sniffling. I felt terrible. I'd no idea the hospital wouldn't allow her to see her mother. We'd talked most of the ride over about how much they wanted to tell their mother and how they'd hold her hand gently if she were asleep. I leaned over the counter to appeal our case. The nurse's name badge read "Ellen."

"I didn't know. This is Laney's daughter, Megan. She's wanted to see her mother since her accident on Monday. She's only been able to talk on the phone with Laney once with all the craziness from yesterday's tragedy. I promised her we could go tonight and she's been looking forward to it all day."

A well-timed tear rolled down Megan's cheek.

"Could she, maybe, just go briefly to see her mom, if she promises to be quiet?"

Nurse Ellen wavered. The floor was empty and quiet, quite the contrast from yesterday.

Skye rallied to the cause. "She's super mature and acts like a ten-year-old. Please let us go see our mom together. I'll make sure she's like super quiet."

I don't know where the angelic look on Skye's face came from but was most impressed.

Nurse Ellen caved. "Well ... maybe just this once." Looking at Megan, she said, "Do you think you can be ten for a little while?"

Megan perked up instantly. This demonstration of acting skills by both girls made me nervous for the future. Megan responded to Nurse Ellen, "Sure. I can be ten because then my mom said I can get earrings. Do you think I can get them now? Can nurses pierce ears? I want those circle ones where you can change the colors in the middle ..."

She only trailed off when she noticed Skye making frantic shushing motions from behind Nurse Ellen.

Nurse Ellen glanced past us again, perhaps wondering if someone else had heard Megan's manic display. "Not today sweetie, but I think I'll come with you and then bring you back to the waiting area."

The girls raised their arms to start to cheer, but I hushed them before any noise started.

As Nurse Ellen stepped away from the desk, she frowned as if she was reconsidering. "You know she's asleep? The doctor gave her something for her pain and it put her out."

I slumped. How was I going to unlock her phone now? I needed to figure out if her third appointment on Monday, her "me-time," was as innocent as it appeared. Laney was counting on me. Mace Jackson would need to know tomorrow morning when he came back to work. I needed him to focus his attention on Rollag to save Laney.

When Nurse Ellen reached my side, she wrinkled her nose. "Something stinks. Maybe you stepped in something? Let me grab you some industrial cleaner. I think we still have some on the floor." Without waiting for a response, she walked away. Over her shoulder, she said, "I'd swear it smells just like a spill we had on the floor earlier in the week."

Perhaps my kids could guess their aunt's password.

GROUP TEXT TO AMANDA, ELI

MARTY: I need to get into Laney's phone. Any guess on her passcode?

AMANDA: She's your sister. Her birthdate?

MARTY: Not it

ELI: How about Skye's or Megan's?

MARTY: Both not it. Wait, how many guesses do I get before it erases?

AMANDA: IDK, maybe 5?

MARTY: Any other ideas?

ELI: Her eye

MARTY: What?

ELI: Get it

AMANDA: Ewwww

ELI: I mean put the phone to her eye to unlock it. It's got that retina thing, right? Then add your eye once it's unlocked and you can open it anytime

MARTY: Hmmm. Smart. Gotta go

AMANDA: I don't know you. Either of you. That's what I'm telling the police

12

Wednesday Evening

Nurse Ellen returned empty-handed. "We must have used up the floor's supplies earlier this week."

I gave my best innocent impression as we followed Nurse Ellen down the corridor and then filed into Laney's room.

Laney was out like a light. She had some wires running into her arm and various monitors arrayed behind her with numbers, graphics, and other indicators flashing a dim red. Bandages covered much of her head and face, while the visible parts showed some interesting colored bruising. She looked more alive than when I saw her on Monday, but far from back to normal. The girls stopped in their tracks when they saw Laney's condition.

A movement in the corner of the room startled me. Someone else was in the room.

I breathed a sigh of relief as a nurse stood up from a drawer near the floor. *Only a nurse.*

Then Nurse Ruth turned around. She managed to smile at the girls and ignore me at the same time. I had last seen her heading off to check out the murder scene. Perhaps she felt embarrassed about her unusual reaction to the murder.

The girls were a little freaked out, but I was now a man on a mission and didn't pause to check on their reaction. I stepped around the girls towards Nurse Ruth. "Hi. Remember me? I'm Marty. I'm Laney's brother and these are her girls. How is she tonight?"

Nurse Ruth nodded in acknowledgment. "Hi. She's doing much better." With no murders tonight, Nurse Ruth acted like a normal nurse.

"So pretty much the same as when we called her earlier today?" I said.

Nurse Ruth nodded. "Yes, but the doctor was pleased with her progress when she stopped by earlier this evening. We expect Laney can go home on Saturday."

"Can we talk to her?" Megan's voice trembled a bit as she stood with Skye near the door.

"You can talk to her, but she's out of it tonight. Don't expect her to answer. You can touch her on the arm if you can be gentle. Nurse Ruth stepped back and moved around Laney, tucking in her blanket. She didn't look like she planned to leave the room any time soon. Getting the eye scan on Laney's phone would be tricky.

The girls both moved up the right side of the bed, close enough to touch their mother. Megan stayed close to Skye. With her self-confidence and energy, it's easy to forget that she's a little girl. Careful to avoid any of the wires or sensors, they reached out to stroke Laney's hand and arm. Laney didn't notice. She didn't move and her breathing sounded normal. While the girls talked in soft murmurs to Laney's sleeping form, I wondered how to distract the nurses and get Laney's phone to her eye long enough to unlock it without anyone noticing.

After a few minutes, Nurse Ellen shifted her weight and checked her watch. I walked over to the other side of the bed from the girls with my hand in my pocket holding Laney's phone. Nurse Ruth continued to fiddle with the equipment behind me.

I spoke in a soft tone so I wouldn't startle the girls. "Megan, remember we promised you'd have just a short visit. Say 'goodnight' to your mother and then you need to go back with Nurse Ellen."

Megan leaned over and kissed her mother's hand. She rubbed the kiss in with her cheek and said good night. Then she walked over to Nurse Ellen. "Ok, let's go."

As the two turned to leave, Megan pointed to the wire from Laney's arm to the machines and spoke to Nurse Ellen in a more normal voice. "Is that her power cord?"

Nurse Ellen laughed. "No, dear. That helps make sure she's doing okay."

The two walked out of the room. *One down.* Nurse Ruth continued to putter behind me. As Skye turned to watch Megan and Nurse Ellen leave the room, I pulled my hand from my pocket. Still holding Laney's phone, I reached up to her forehead like I was brushing the hair away from her eyes. As my fingers touched her eyelid, Laney let out a sigh. Spooked, I dropped her phone and clunked her eyebrow with it.

Yikes. Laney moaned. Skye turned quickly and saw my sweaty hand grab the phone off Laney's face. I froze, not sure if Nurse Ruth had seen the phone.

Behind me, I heard Nurse Ruth turn and take a step towards the bed. "It's perfectly normal to make sounds while you're sleeping," she said to us.

I pulled the phone back and moved my hand out of sight. Over my racing heart, I said, "Well, if she snores, I'll have to tease her when she wakes up." I remained near Laney's head in my apparent devotion to my sister. Despite my racing heart, I was poised to try again at the next opportunity.

Skye gave me a stink eye. She'd seen me drop the phone on her mother's face. I shrugged and motioned to the phone in silent pantomime, but successfully communicating "I need to open your mom's phone" in Charades was beyond my skills. Skye squinted at me with her eyebrows scrunched.

Nurse Ruth turned her back to me and started to walk down the side of the bed to cross to the other side. I leaned forward as if I were going to caress Laney's forehead with a kiss. With Skye watching my every move, I raised both my hands so I could get the phone to her eye. I put one hand to her eye to hold her eyelid open while I moved the other hand with the phone closer to her face. And knocked into one of Laney's sensors.

Ugh! A loud beeping noise broke out. The sensor's alarm sounded a warning that a dangerous brother lurked nearby. My elbow must have decided to rat me out. Either that or my coordination had not yet elevated to the super-spy level of my imagination.

Nurse Ruth turned back with a look of mild annoyance on her face now. "Oh goodness, this happens all the time. It looks like one of the alarms has gone off." She took a swift stride back to the headboard and her fingers flashed across the screens as she turned off the beeping alarm. Laney was still out of it.

Skye, however, had an incredulous expression on her face as she gaped at me, clearly amazed at the level of my ineptitude. I've seen that look before from other women in my life.

No, I'm not that stupid. After all, Nurse Ruth hadn't seen me holding Laney's phone or clunking her face with it.

Nurse Ruth waved me away. "It's probably best to stay farther away from her head until she's healed a bit more. Why don't you move a little further down the bed to be safe?"

That's right. Super-agent Marty needed to stand farther away so he didn't do further damage to his sister while she healed from a possible brain injury, and he worked to catch the person who had tried to kill her.

Skye let out a long sigh. One of those why-is-everything-always-up-to-me sighs. I'd heard those before, too. Out of the blue, Skye burst into tears.

Not your mere run-of-the-mill crying, this set a new standard for wailing. Through her sobs, she babbled about whether her mother would be okay, when she'd be able to go home, and whether all the bruising on her face would leave permanent scars. Her words all scrambled together amidst her weeping. Skye had given up on my ability to unlock the phone on my own and had decided to address the situation head-on.

I stood there dumbfounded. This wasn't hard to do. I didn't need to fake my awestruck, frozen-in-place pose. Skye cut an impressive figure as the despondent child. But nurses are made of sterner stuff. Nurse Ruth walked around the bed to Skye to soothe her. After all, we didn't want to disturb the patient's rest.

"Come on dear, let's go sit down outside. Your mom is doing well. She'll be home before you know it." With a cool glance, Nurse Ruth gave me a clear directive. "I think it's time to wrap up your visit."

As Nurse Ruth escorted Skye from Laney's room with her arm around Skye's still shaking shoulders, Skye somehow turned her headback to me. Over a shoulder, without Nurse Ruth noticing, Skye rolled her eyes at me.

How is that even anatomically possible? "Thank you. I'll be right there."

"Don't touch anything," were her parting words.

Which I immediately ignored. I wouldn't touch any of the medical stuff. At least I'd make an effort not to touch them. I moved back closer to Laney's head. The bruises were truly impressive. If I had time, I'd take a picture to show her later. I knew she'd appreciate that. I held Laney's phone in one hand and bent over. I lifted her eyelid and lined up the phone. The retina scan worked and the phone unlocked. *Simple.*

My excitement dampened as a red, angry eye appeared to be looking at me. I let go of her eyelid to make it go away. The drugs kept working and Laney stayed asleep. I turned away with the unlocked phone in my hand. I opened her privacy settings and, without delay, added my own retina to her phone. Now my eye could unlock her phone at any time.

Super-agent Marty is back.

Not feeling especially brave this close to my sister's angry red eye, I decided to follow Nurse Ruth's instructions. Without looking up at Laney's face in case the angry red eye opened on its own, I gave her toes a quick squeeze through the blanket and walked out of the room without looking back.

Flush with success, I hurried down the hallway. I found the girls in the waiting area by the elevators. Nurse Ellen sat next to them while Nurse Ruth stood nearby drinking a cup of coffee. The girls were asking questions about their mother, hospitals, and who knows what else. Skye had made a miraculous, spontaneous recovery. Nurse Ruth told a small joke and both girls cracked smiles.

Nurse Ellen looked up despite my quiet approach. I was pleased she was so observant. I'd have to trust her and Nurse Ruth to protect Laney until Mace got back to work tomorrow.

"Thank you so much," I said to both nurses. Both girls also thanked them, without even needing a prompt. They added cheerful goodbyes as we waited for the elevator.

Riding down in the elevator to the lobby, Megan stood in front pretending to push all the buttons while Skye and I leaned against the back wall. Uncomfortable about what to say, I avoided looking at Skye at first. When I did glance over at her, she shook her head. "Smooth," was all she said.

At first, I looked down at my shoes in embarrassment, but then a whiff of rotten fish wafted my way. I wrinkled my nose before a laugh burst out of me. I turned to Skye, who'd looked over at my laugh, and smirked at her. I held out a closed fist for a moment. After a split second, she grinned and fist-bumped me back. Confused, Megan turned to see what had happened and then decided she wanted in on the action too. We bumped fists as well. I might not always pull off Super-Agent Marty, but at least I could handle my Uncle Marty role well enough. I hoped Skye and I would never have to tell Laney about our little secret.

After the girls went to sleep, I sat down at the table with Laney's phone. I held it to my eye and chuckled when it unlocked. Almost as good as when I picked the lock on her diary in high school.

After the amount of effort I'd exerted to break into her phone, I didn't feel too guilty about reading Laney's text messages. This was all for her own good, after all. Below several texts on Monday afternoon from Skye wondering when Laney would arrive at their school, I saw a text exchange with someone named "Meghan." It looked like they'd planned to meet for lunch on Monday. I searched the contacts on her phone and found a phone number for a Meghan Emerson.

Meghan Emerson had the initials "M.E." Laney hadn't scheduled "me-time." She had a lunch meeting with M.E. It had only taken me three days to crack the code. *Super-agent Marty was back in business.* Tomorrow morning would be time for a certain fake IRS agent to contact Meghan Emerson and find out if she had reason to hurt Laney.

13

Thursday Morning

When my alarm went off, I woke up feeling rested. I'd done well last night. I'd even remembered to have a dream idea ready for Megan. Telling her to dream of playing with Labrador puppies in her backyard with her mother wasn't the most original concept, but it had worked.

Aiming to avoid another spike in my blood pressure this morning, I first opened the door to my home office. As expected, Megan lay asleep on the ground again. I kneeled down and touched her back.

She rolled over and awoke immediately with her mother on her mind. "Hi, Uncle Marty. Is Mom coming home today?"

"Not until Friday or Saturday. I'll get an update later from her doctor," I promised. The hallway bathroom door closed as Skye got herself moving this morning as well.

I paused as conflicting feelings flickered through my head. Surprised that I felt almost sad about the girls going home soon, I shook it off and put on a smile that my apartment would soon be all my own again.

Pulling a box of frozen waffles that arrived with the groceries yesterday out of the freezer, I put some in the oven to toast. Once the maple syrup reached the table, breakfast was ready. Perhaps not the healthiest choice, but a fast one. I needed fast today so the girls would get off to school early and I could contact Meghan Emerson, Laney's third scheduled meeting on Monday. I couldn't call her until official office hours. Not if I wanted to pull off my IRS scam again.

My lunch today with Daniel at DroneTech should give me another chance to exercise my super-agent skills and check into Rollag while Mace did his police thing. I lost a few moments pondering what my super-agent costume should look like. The movie director would appreciate my input.

Skye and Megan interrupted my thoughts when they walked out from their room dressed and ready for school in record time. My parenting skills improved by the day. Pleased with my strong start to the morning, I announced with more pride, "I made waffles and maple syrup for breakfast."

Skye scoffed. "You mean you opened the box of waffles and toasted them, don't you?"

"Exactly." I wouldn't let Skye bring me down. My pride undiminished, I added, "You two have breakfast and I'll get dressed."

When I returned, Skye sat at the table, pounding on the keys of her computer while her breakfast sat untouched to her side.

My approach interrupted her attempts to pulverize her computer. She looked up, did a double take. "Whoa. Who are you and what did you do with Uncle Marty?"

Megan chimed in, "Looking good, Uncle Marty."

I don't understand girls. "What?" Sure, I wear Hawaiian shirts most days to work, but putting on a pair of fitted jeans and a button-down, long sleeve shirt didn't deserve a reaction like that.

"Didn't know you had those sort of clothes," said Skye.

"It's just in case I get an interview today." Self-conscious now, I looked down to double check my clothes. I wanted to make a good impression at DroneTech. I might meet an engineering manager at lunch and, who knows, it could turn into a job interview. With my sparkling personality and superior intellect, I would undoubtedly amaze the management and they'd want me to start immediately. The fancier clothes would help complete the package. *Dress to impress.*

I started to mumble something else but Skye drew my attention with a frustrated wave of her arms. "My computer's not working right."

Computer engineer, Uncle Marty, to the rescue! I threw my arms to the sides with a grand gesture, as if sweeping the crowds aside. "Step back and let the man who fixes everything come through."

"Who's the man and when is he coming over?" Skye had a gleam in her eye and the corners of her mouth quirked up.

"Is Raj here?" Megan looked over her shoulder at the door.

"Very funny girls." They had no faith in their Uncle Marty. "Here, let me take a look at your computer. You need to eat some breakfast so you can get to school."

I tried the basics but couldn't even get her computer to connect to the internet. *Never give up. Never surrender.* Cracking my knuckles and running my fingers through my hair didn't solve anything, although it gave me an extra opportunity to think while Skye smirked at me. Trying an advanced option that one of our network engineers used during a Rover system test didn't solve the problem either. Without pausing for Skye to realize I'd hit a wall, I rebooted her computer, pretending my sophisticated network diagnostics made it happen. The reboot succeeded in getting her Wi-Fi working again even if I had no idea how to fix the rest of her system. "When in doubt, fake it," as my dad always said.

"Here you go." I handed back her computer without any fanfare.

Perhaps I should bring it in to have Raj take a quick look later, after all.

By the time I got my own breakfast and sat down, Skye's eyes were focused intently on her screen again.

"What'cha reading?"

"About my ants," mumbled Skye. Engrossed in her reading, she stuck a fork of waffle against her face. Skye flushed as I chuckled, her face sticky with maple syrup.

I handed her a napkin. "That happens to me whenever I try to eat while I'm coding. It might be better to finish breakfast before doing more research."

Skye dabbed her face with a napkin and then made a more successful attempt to eat her waffle. At the other end of the table, Megan concentrated on her plate as she conducted critical surgery. With careful precision, she removed all the edges of her waffle and swept them with a dismissive wave of her knife to the side of the plate so they wouldn't contaminate the rest of her improved waffle.

"Megan, what are you doing?"

"Cutting off the crusts. I don't like crusts."

"But the whole waffle is made from the same ingredients. It's all good."

"Except the crusts," said Megan with a haughty sniff.

Who was I to argue with such exquisite logic? I reached down to pick up one of the remaining waffles from the plate.

"Megan already licked that one." Skye couldn't hit her mouth with her fork, but nothing would happen to the plate of waffles without her noticing.

"What? No, she didn't. Did you?" I turned to Megan. "Why would you lick a waffle that you're not eating?"

"To make sure no one else eats something I want," said Megan.

In my confusion, it almost sounded logical. "That's gross. You don't lick things to claim them for yourself."

"We do in our family," said Skye and turned back to her reading.

I'm telling on Laney. Giving up on the waffles, I poured some dry Captain Crunch cereal into a mug for myself and sat back down at the table with the girls.

"Oh cool," exclaimed Skye, still looking at her screen as she reached over to grab some cereal from my mug.

"What's cool? Tell me," insisted Megan who held out her hand for some too.

I poured a few into her hand and took a few for myself.

Skye finished chewing. "The Texas crazy ant protects itself against fire ants' venom by squirting a liquid out of its butt into its mouth and then licks its legs to spread the liquid all over its body like a shield."

"Eww." Megan tossed more cereal into her mouth one at a time like popcorn. Fascinated despite the grossness, she asked, "What's in the liquid?"

Nauseated, I put down the mug. No longer hungry, I might not ever eat again. Between the waffles and the ants, I was licked.

GROUP TEXT TO AMANDA, ELI

MARTY: Maybe I've forgotten. Were you two this weird when you were young?

AMANDA: E is still strange

ELI: What are they doing?

MARTY: Megan cuts off crusts from frozen waffles. Skye talks about ant venom

ELI: No fair. You got them frozen waffles?

AMANDA: Could be scarier. Skye could be texting boys

ELI: Or eating ants

MARTY: Thanks for nothing

Skye kept her eyes on her computer until the last second when I told her to grab her stuff for school. While we walked down the hallway, I reminded them to go to Mrs. Kim's apartment after school. Outside, as we waited for their Rover car, I checked on what they wanted for dinner.

With a serious expression on her face, Skye asked, "Can we please go out for dinner?"

Megan chimed in, also looking grim, "Yeah, I don't want peanut butter or spaghetti tacos."

Me neither. "Ok, sure. I'll figure something out."

As the prospect of eating more of my cooking faded, their faces turned to smiles.

They got into the Rover car without a problem before I turned back to my apartment. This morning was "ME" time.

I considered my approach. If Laney had used the IRS angle before, she probably did it again when she reached Meghan Emerson for her investigation. I already had my badge. Plus, the prison term for impersonating an IRS agent twice couldn't be much worse than doing it once. With the fresh new day, I felt more confident about my fake agent skills. Sitting down in my home office, I accessed Laney's phone with my eye to get Meghan Emerson's phone number.

I took a deep breath to get into character and called.

A friendly-sounding voice answered. "Hello, this is Meghan."

"Hi. My name is Marty Golden. I work at the IRS with Laney Tran. I believe she spoke with you recently and I wanted to follow-up on some of your responses."

"What? Why would the IRS be interested in my harassment claim? Is this a scam?"

14

Thursday Midmorning

I*'m really not very good at this.*

Luckily, Meghan Emerson hadn't hung up on me yet. I decided to try something radical. I told the truth. "Wait! Don't hang up on me. I'm really Laney Tran's brother. I'm not with the IRS. Sorry for lying. Laney's been in the hospital since Monday and I'm worried. I think someone might be trying to kill her."

"Those bastards." Meghan's voice turned cold.

Her reaction confused and intrigued me. "What do you mean by that?"

"I'd rather not talk about it."

"Ok, ok. I'm just trying to figure out what happened to Laney. How do you know her?"

Meghan let out a breath I hadn't realized she'd been holding. "She's the HR investigator assigned for my complaint. We were going to meet again on Monday, but she missed our lunch appointment. Is she okay?"

"Yes. She should be home in a day or two. But I'm worried that she's still in danger."

"What about the police?"

"I'm sort of helping them out," I exaggerated.

"Really." Meghan sounded unimpressed. I had long experience recognizing skepticism in voices.

"I can explain. I'm trying to figure out what's happening to Laney. Could we meet somewhere to talk?"

My police connection did the trick. "Well ... I suppose ... But I'd prefer to meet you in a public place."

Now I'm confused, intrigued and apparently potentially dangerous. *That could be super-agent Marty's new tag line.* "Ok, that's fine. You pick the place. Can we meet soon?"

Meghan picked Starbucks, the same one where I had my ill-fated meeting with Rollag yesterday. As I'd caught her on her way out the door to work, she agreed to meet there right away.

A short while later, I walked into the Starbucks and looked around. Like yesterday, the place had a steady flow, but not too many people sat inside at nine in the morning. A couple sat on a couch to one side and a young guy hunkered down over his Mac sat at a corner table. He looked like he was coding up the next big social media craze or just going crazy on his social media.

Waiting awkwardly near the cashier, but not actually placing an order, stood an attractive woman with wavy brown hair and hazel green eyes who looked younger than me, but not too young. As I approached, she threw me a wary look. "Are you Marty?"

I nodded, but before I could say anything, Brody, the barista from yesterday, turned around from the coffee machines and saw me.

"John, dude!" He greeted me with a huge grin on his face. "How 'ya doing? How're the waves out there? Don't want no ankle-busters this afternoon. Don't worry, I'll get your order going." He turned back and started whatever mystical steps are involved in pouring a cup of coffee. I still didn't like coffee, yet now wasn't the time to make a fuss. And I'd hate to dampen Brody's enthusiasm.

Meghan frowned as her suspicions returned. I'd already gotten off to a bad start on the phone with my IRS stunt. I approached her with my friendliest smile, hoping I could still salvage this meeting.

"Hi, I'm Marty Golden. Laney's brother. Thanks for coming," I said before she'd run out the door.

She stepped back a bit and narrowed her eyes. "Didn't he just call you John?"

"Yes. It's a long story. He thinks my name is John, but I'm really Marty." Even I didn't believe myself at this point, so I took out my driver's license and showed it to her. Good thing Meghan didn't notice the fake IRS badge still in there. "Why don't you order something and we can talk. My treat."

Meghan edged back to the counter at an angle and ordered green tea, all without letting me get too close.

We sat down at a table in a corner away from the other guests. As the fishy smell of my shoes wafted up from the ground, Meghan wrinkled her nose and sniffed. Then, a burst of steam gushed out from one of the clanking machines and an overwhelming wave of coffee aroma washed away the rotten fish odor for now.

Gotta clean these shoes. I started speaking in a burst before she could ask about the fish smell. "Thanks again for coming. Laney and I really appreciate it." Laney might not appreciate me meeting her clients though.

The mention of Laney seemed to relax Meghan a little. "Sure. How is Laney?"

"The doctor said she should be able to come home tomorrow or Saturday. Her face is all bruised and she'll be sore for a while. She's lucky it was nothing more than a concussion and some bruising."

Megan's eyes widened and her hand covered her mouth. "How did she get hurt?"

I explained the car accident caused by the dive bombing drone.

Meghan's eyebrows rose higher in surprise. "A drone? I thought that wasn't possible anymore?"

"I didn't think so either. I thought it was something weird that only could happen to Laney. But, later that same night someone tried to kill her in the hospital. I think someone may have hacked into the drone and guided it to hit her." I told her about the elderly woman who'd been killed in the room with Laney's name on the door sign.

Meghan's mouth opened as she gasped. "My goodness. What did the police say?"

"They don't seem to be doing much of anything about Laney. The accident took place in San Jose and the murder happened in Los Gatos."

"You'd think they would cooperate."

"Well, I've left messages for the first cop, the one from San Jose, but he was off for the last two days on furlough. The second cop, from Los Gatos, probably thought I was crazy. After all, an elderly Vietnamese woman doesn't look like she might be my sister and the names on the doors were fixed by the morning."

Intrigued now, Meghan leaned forward. "Didn't the cop understand the names were swapped?"

"Well, to be fair, he got pretty distracted because the old woman's family showed up. Maybe twenty people all at once. It was mayhem. They were angry, in mourning, and shouting at the cop. It reminded me of political rallies I went to in college."

"I remember that kind of mayhem from move-in day in college. Some of the kids brought their whole families to help them move in. Of course, helping might not be the right word to use as it's almost impossible for ten plus people to fit into a college dorm room, let alone do anything helpful." Meghan smiled at the memory.

"Before the family swamped him, he told me to talk to the San Jose police about the accident. I don't think they get a lot of murders in Los Gatos. They were so focused on making sure they got all the evidence from the room, they locked down the whole floor of the hospital." To avoid scaring her, I left out the parts about the drug gang and my secret agent exploits in the hospital to unlock Laney's phone.

"Well, Marty, or John." She paused with a half-smile, as she emphasized the second name. "I can see where you might confuse someone. This story does sound pretty far-fetched."

I smiled at her use of my new Starbucks name. "I guess it does." As I remembered why we were here, the grin left my face. "I just got mad that no one took it seriously that the murder could be connected to Laney. I don't want her hurt again."

"You must be her big brother," said Meghan with a bit of twinkle in her eye.

"Yes, I am. And, sure, I still get a bigger kick out of teasing her than I probably should. She's had a tough time though. Her husband died a few years ago. She and her girls recently moved to California and she's trying to restart her life."

"Oh, I'm so sorry. I didn't realize," Meghan said.

I needed to rein myself in. I was enjoying myself more than I should with someone who might be involved in an attempted murder. Meghan didn't act like someone involved, but I had to be more careful. Switching gears, I asked, "How did you meet Laney?"

"I'm a consultant for the NorCal Water Agency. I do environmental consulting."

I nodded. I'd certainly heard of the NorCal Water Agency. Who hadn't these days? Silicon Valley and Hollywood might get more attention from people around the world, but actual Californians spent more time nowadays complaining about water allocation, prices, and hoping for rain than discussing new gaming apps, electronic gizmos, or reality TV stars.

Over the last few years, the state has forced the merger of the hundreds of water districts and companies across the state into a few big agencies to be more efficient, more consistent, and better manage the limited water for everyone. I don't know if it made things better or worse. In the meantime, the water agencies have become the most powerful organizations on the California political scene in years.

Meghan continued, "I started work on a big project there a few months ago. Their environmental impact analyst left unexpectedly. I don't know if she quit or got fired. Either way, she left in the middle of the project on short notice." She let out a nervous laugh. "And, I found out she wasn't even the first person on this project. I've been picking up the pieces and trying to finish the assessment report on time."

"So, did you meet Laney at work or something?" Impatient to get to the results, I didn't care about her project, just whether she was involved with Laney's case.

Meghan's eyes narrowed. She ignored my interruption and kept going. "Well, recently I started having some problems at work. Not minor stuff, like not getting along with someone or disagreements during a meeting. More serious. It got worse after I talked to my manager."

Pulled into her story despite myself, I asked, "If it were so terrible, why stick around?"

"I can't afford to just quit," Meghan snapped. "Maybe you engineers don't get how hard it is to get a job here."

Clearly not. Her neck reddened, rising up to her ears as she spoke. I hadn't thought about how others don't have it as easy as engineers. Engineers were in high demand. When I got too frustrated with my work, I moved on to another company.

"Having the Water Agency on my resume will help me get other projects. Everyone knows the Water Agency deals with a lot of environmental challenges. They're working on all those new water projects, like the desalination plants and other ideas to increase the water supply. After a project at the Water Agency, I could write my own ticket. All California companies have to complete an environmental impact analysis for their projects. I'd be on the short list for everyone." She ended breathing hard.

"Okay, okay. I'm sorry." I changed my tack so she'd keep talking. "So, what did you do when the problems started?"

"I didn't know what to do. Eventually, I called the employee assistance hotline one evening to make a complaint. Laney called me back to talk about what happened."

Finally. "What happened?"

"She was very nice. She met me for lunch at some El Salvadorian restaurant across town and we talked," said Meghan.

I grew impatient again. Why didn't she get to the important part? "No, I mean what happened at work? Did they hurt you? Do you think they might have tried to hurt Laney too?" Perhaps I came on a bit too strong because Meghan frowned again.

"You have to understand. This is my first consulting gig in a long time." Meghan patted the air with both hands as if telling me to slow down.

"Money is really tight." She hesitated. "I was desperate when the Water Agency called. I don't know why they called me. I'm not well known." Shrugging, she continued, "Who cares? I need the work. I was starting to think about moving out of the area. And I'm good. I can do this. If they'll let me finish my job."

I felt sorry for her. They weren't treating her well.

Unaware that I'd been clenching my jaw, I rubbed it to ease the ache. The stress was getting to me. Maybe Meghan's situation was connected to Laney, but I didn't see how. She hadn't revealed anything that might have put Laney at risk. This was like an elusive computer bug. When I'm tracking down bugs, sometimes I have to give up and start over.

I paused, considering how best to get Meghan to tell me why

her first reaction when I called was that "the bastards" had done something to Laney. "I understand you don't want to go into the details. But, on the phone, you said 'those bastards.' You said that as soon as I told you about Laney being in the hospital. Why?"

Meghan hesitated. "I'm not sure I want to go into the details. I just want to finish my project, get paid, and not have them bad-mouthing me around the Valley."

Brody interrupted our conversation as he walked up with our drinks and a big smile. "Here you go, ma'am. Have a beautiful day." He handed the tea to Meghan. She looked up and returned his smile.

Pretty smile. Brody turned to me. "Yours is one righteous drink, John. Here's your Triple, Venti, Half Sweet, Non-Fat, Extra-Hot, Caramel Macchiato." He only paused for a quick breath before he added, "I can't hit the surf until later, dude, so hang ten for me today. You have a beautiful day, too."

"Thanks, Brody. You too." I shot him a hang ten sign in return.

Meghan and I shared a smile. Brody had cut the tension at our table. Like a puppy, he could brighten up anyone's day. And the caramel did smell enticing.

"Interesting drink. Do you surf?" She still toyed with a half-smile on her lips.

Hey, I'm legit. Or, I used to be. "Some. Never with Brody. Would you believe that I don't like coffee? I'm more a tea drinker myself."

"You seem to have a lot of fake identities. IRS agent, private investigator, and John the coffee drinking, surfer dude. Who is the true you?"

Ouch. "I really am a software engineer for a startup, the Rover car service. I graduated from Stanford. I'm also an uncle to two wonderful, bright girls that are staying with me while Laney's in the hospital. You already figured out that I'm terrible at being a private investigator." This didn't seem like the right time to bring up two kids and an ex-wife. Otherwise, I'd covered all the major bases.

"Well, maybe more crazy than terrible." Meghan's smile faded as she put her elbows on the table and leaned forward. "Look, I can see you're serious about trying to help Laney. I guess I could tell you what happened. But only because of Laney. She was the only one who would help me. You promise not to tell anyone else about this? I mean no one."

"Yes, I promise. No one else. Thank you." I breathed a sigh of relief. I'd have to thank Brody for his help, however inadvertent.

"Ok. If I lose this job, I won't be able to keep my apartment." Meghan took a deep breath. "Those bastards are trying to get me to sign off on their project without finishing the work. After I told the project lead 'no' a few times, they tried to intimidate me. Someone went through all my folders on my desk. They've called me names and yelled at me to sign off on the project and get out. Once, one of the security guys got on an elevator alone with me, squeezed in close and started asking me when I was going to finish and leave the agency."

This time my eyes grew wide. "That's nuts."

"That's not the half of it." Meghan's voice took on a more strident tone. "After that, I found dead rats by my car and then dog shit was smeared on my door handle and left there, on the ground. My car was parked in the lot in front of the building. I complained to my boss. You know what he did?"

"No." I started to feel queasy and a bit unnerved.

"He told me since I was unhappy it would be best if I'd go ahead and sign off on the project. He'd finish and submit it to the state while I took paid time off for the next three months on them."

"He tried to bribe you? You're kidding?"

"No. I was pissed. I didn't want to put my license on the line without doing the work. When I turned him down, he turned cold and told me not to bring my computer or any files out of the office.

Can you believe that crap?" Meghan flushed again, this time with indignation.

"Unbelievable. So, that's when you called the HR helpline and met Laney?"

"Yes. I finally had enough." She rubbed her chin. "Maybe the drone crash was part of threatening Laney?" Her forehead creased. "But for the life of me, I don't know why. Laney doesn't know anything specific about my work. We'd only had one short meeting. I told her pretty much what I've told you and showed her pictures of what they did to my car and desk."

She took a sip of her tea.

This didn't make much sense. Only crazy people would think that public water agency employees would threaten Laney's life, or Meghan's. That had to go against their union rules. I sipped my whatever-it-was.

Mmm. I resolved to drink more tea at work. Healthy antioxidants and all that. I took another sip of the sweet caramel drink.

"So, what's next?" asked Meghan.

"I don't know. I think I'll call the cop who was looking into Laney's accident again."

Meghan's expression hardened. "You promised not to say anything."

"I won't, I won't." I tried to reassure her that I'd keep my promise. "Hopefully, he's made progress. I've left him a bunch of messages already." I focused on Meghan. "What about you? Are you going back to work at the agency?"

"I think so." She hesitated. "I won't stay late tonight and I'm only riding the elevator if no security goons are nearby. Anyway, I've been thinking of calling in sick tomorrow. I've got a busy weekend to get ready for."

"What's going on this weekend?" It was none of my business.

I wanted to know anyway. My earlier commitment to consider Meghan a suspect had fallen by the wayside.

She paused, her cheeks flushing, and then plunged ahead. "I'm into Renaissance Faires. You know those events where people dress up and pretend it's the sixteenth century with food, drink, crafts and entertainment?"

"Sure. I've seen the ads, although I've never been to one. Do you volunteer there?"

Her whole face blushed. "I, um, well, I'm part of the entertainment. I used to be in plays in high school and college. I started going to Faires and got involved setting up plays on weekends." Her hands fiddled with her cup. "Eventually, I got dragged into trying out. Now I'm usually in a few plays every season. I signed up for some this year. With my new project, it's been tough to learn my lines and have time for practices."

I smiled. Not exactly the introverted environmental scientist that I'd presumed. "What are you playing now?"

"I'm Bianca in 'Taming of the Shrew' on Saturday night."

I glanced at the ceiling as my memory for odd trivia kicked in. This, along with the ability to recall most everything I read, had helped me succeed in engineering school. It also came in handy for winning bets. "Isn't that one of the main roles? The younger sister, if I remember correctly?"

She ran her hand through her hair. "That's very good. Most people have heard of the play and some know it's by Shakespeare. How did you remember the character?"

"Well …" This time it was my turn to blush. "Ok, I dated a girl in high school who was into theater and she acted in that play."

Her eyes twinkled. "At least you were paying attention. I don't think any of my high school boyfriends paid much attention to what I did in school."

Lifting my cup to take another sip, I discovered it was empty. *How did that happen?*

Meghan noticed and glanced at her watch. "I should get going." She hesitated and then continued, "Hey, I'm sorry about Laney. But, I don't see how her accident had anything to do with me. I think it was a coincidence that she was going to meet me for lunch on Monday."

My shoulders slumped. "I suppose you're right. I'd hoped there might be a connection and I could figure out what was going on." Although I'd enjoyed meeting Meghan, I hadn't made any headway for Laney.

"It was nice meeting you." Meghan gathered her things. "I hope Laney gets well soon. Give her my best."

I stood as well. "Thanks. Nice meeting you too." Not knowing what else to do, I shook Meghan's hand. Meghan walked out of the Starbucks to her car.

I stayed back to signal for a Rover car. *Maybe I'd go see a play on Saturday.*

Brody walked up to me while I waited. "Dude, she's way better looking than that guy you brought here yesterday. Having coffee with her will make every day a beautiful day, fer sure."

Maybe a beautiful day, yet I was no closer to figuring out what was going on. I'd met "ME" and learned that she was good looking, liked tea and acted part-time. Nothing that helped Laney's case.

15

Thursday Late Morning

While I waited, I called Mace to give him the update on Meghan and see if he'd made any progress after all my helpful voicemails.

"Hello," came the deep, calm voice of Sergeant Mace Jackson.

Surprised to catch him live, my voice cracked. "Hi," I croaked. I cleared my throat. "This is Marty Golden, Laney Tran's brother. I've left you some messages and wanted to see if you've made any progress with the investigation."

"Oh yeah, you're that guy." Mace's voice rasped. "What is your problem?"

"What do you mean? I'm just trying to help you figure out what happened to Laney."

"You're nuts. You've left me like four messages in two days, each crazier than the next."

Five. I tried to explain. "Maybe, I, uh …"

Mace rolled on, "Look, she was in a car accident, not a rogue drone attack targeting her. The founder of DroneTech and the IRS are not out to get her."

"But … I …"

He continued, "There are no South American drug lords after

Laney. Or whatever other crazy conspiracy theories you might cook up next. You've got to stop wasting my time."

I tried to explain again. "I ... I'm just trying to help —"

Mace interrupted my bumbling, "You can help by leaving me alone. Go visit your sister and bother the doctors at the hospital."

He hung up the phone before I could respond again. Not that my responses had been all that coherent so far. Good thing he didn't seem to understand my message about impersonating an IRS agent. That one was best left unexplained.

I'd learned that Mace liked to fly solo, handling his action hero duties without a sidekick. He took his time to warm up to new partners. Good thing my status as his partner remained only a part of my imagination, so far. As I headed to work in the Rover car, I took the opportunity to update my kids.

GROUP TEXT TO AMANDA, ELI

MARTY: Found 'ME'. You won't believe it but her name is Meghan

ELI: Did she hurt Aunt Laney?

MARTY: I can't imagine she did anything to Laney, but they worked together. Maybe there's a connection

AMANDA: Wait, another Megan?

MARTY: with an 'H'

ELI: What's next?

MARTY: I don't know

I plopped my stuff down in my office and let out a sigh. My work didn't magically finish itself simply because I had to take care of the girls and help with Laney's investigation. It was almost ten. Time for hyper-efficient coding man. Not my most impressive super-hero tagline, but I had a ton of work to catch up on before my lunch today with Daniel Pope at DroneTech. I pulled my keyboard closer and connected my computer to my screens.

Raj walked up. "Good morning. You are lucky you did not miss the mandatory HR training."

"What training? It's not on my calendar. I'm too busy for training today." I panicked and started checking the calendars on my phone and computer.

"We received an email after nine from the boss. Did you not check your email for the last hour? This is mandatory training. It is about harassment in the workplace. We should go. It begins in two minutes."

I groaned as I found the email. Even though our boss had forgotten to tell us until the last minute and he would miss it for an important meeting, he still expected all of us to attend.

Raj had remained calm through my temporary panic. He didn't have nieces staying with him, requiring dinners and dream advice, or a sister in danger, lying in the hospital with her phone needing an emergency retina unlock, or an action movie hero cop depending on my assistance. *Well, I didn't have that last part either.*

Raj interrupted my thoughts. "I do not understand this class. They are going to train us how to harass people at work?"

His question brought me back to reality. "No. They're going to harass us for ninety minutes so they can say they trained us on how to avoid bothering other people in the office." Snarkiness remained my go-to sentiment in the workplace.

As we walked to the room, Raj cocked his head to the side. "Do not American parents teach their children to be nice to others? That is what parents in India do."

I had no answer as we walked into the largest conference room on our floor.

We took a seat around a large table. About twenty people had already crowded into a room that normally held twelve chairs. Our engineering team plus some of the finance and operations folks filled the rest of the chairs. Perhaps a quarter of the company had joined today's class. Of course, no one from management attended. They needed no extra training in how to harass people at work.

A young woman I didn't recognize with straight blond hair strode into the room with shoulders thrown back. She stood at the front of the room to catch everyone's attention. Beaming at us, she spoke in a perky tone. "Good morning everyone. I'm so excited to be here today. My name is Emily and I'm the HR consultant for Rover. This morning I took my first Rover car ride to get here. It was so exciting."

I hoped Emily didn't consult for Rollag. I was curious to see what an HR consultant did as I've never seen Laney in action. Laney wouldn't have been silly enough to describe a Rover car ride as exciting. Our cars drove conservatively on purpose to reduce the risk of accidents. Other drivers seemed to delight in darting around self-driving cars with dangerous, aggressive moves. Perhaps it's some underlying aspect of human psychology that resists getting replaced by automation.

Emily continued, "Today's training covers workplace harassment. Before we get started, I want us all to get to know each other. So, we'll do a fun, icebreaker exercise."

Raj looked puzzled.

I leaned over and whispered, "We're not really going to break any ice. Just get everyone warmed up."

"I understand. We break the ice so people get warm. Warm people talk more." Raj winked. "And you think I speak funny?"

Cassandra, a saleswoman, raised her hand. Cassandra spoke so loudly on the phone that we could hear her sales calls from across the floor. Lucky for the whole office, she traveled often so she only disrupted us once in a while. Emily pointed at her.

"What do we get if we win?"

"It's not a competition," said Emily.

One of the finance women who I didn't know raised her hand. Emily called on her.

"Since we all know everyone but you, wouldn't it be more efficient if you just started the training?"

Emily's smile wavered as she eyed the finance woman. "Let's try this exercise. It's an important part of the training."

Emily turned back to the room. "Before we start the exercise, it's important that we all consider ourselves part of a circle of trust. That means …"

Although she kept talking, I had stopped listening. *Aha!* I smiled to myself. I loved these "aha!" moments when the solution to one of the bugs in my code pops into my brain all of a sudden. I looked down at my phone to make a few notes before I forgot my idea. This could save me hours of time later if it worked.

At some point, it dawned on me that the room had gone quiet. Raj's foot nudging mine further helped me recognize the change in the room. I glanced up and realized that everyone was looking at me. I've always hated getting called upon by the teacher. "I'm sorry. I got distracted."

Emily's smile seemed more forced now. She repeated her question. "Will you be able to agree that this is a safe place and whatever people say won't leave this room?"

Now the thin chorus of agreement from the room that I'd heard earlier made sense. "Oh, yes, yes, sure, sure," I agreed. Putting my phone down, I nodded my thanks to Raj. He raised his eyebrows and opened his mouth in mock horror at my transgression before smiling at me.

Emily clapped her hands in pleasure. "Good. Now, if everyone else could please put away your phones too, our icebreaker exercise is called 'Two Truths and a Lie.' I'll call on people to tell us three things about themselves. Two of these should be truths and one should be a lie. Mix it up and don't tell us which one is which, at first. Then, the rest of the group will try to guess which is the lie. You can say boring things, but it's more fun if you have more outrageous statements."

I hated these sorts of games. I could never think of anything to say that didn't sound stupid or obvious. Desperately casting about for ideas, I tried to remember anything remotely interesting about myself. My brain went blank. Beyond my name, I had nothing. I might have remembered my name wrong.

Pausing to make sure everyone understood the game, Emily looked around the room. She gestured to one of the young engineers. "If you could go first. Tell us your name and then your three statements and we'll try to guess which is the lie." With a satisfied smile, Emily sat down.

The engineer didn't pause a beat. Perhaps she had advance warning of what game we'd play. "Hi, I'm Suzy. I was part of a group that danced a jig at an Irish pub on St. Patrick's Day. I can burp the alphabet. And I've been in the studio audience to watch the filming of the TV show, Jeopardy."

No one spoke after she finished. A chair squeaked as we waited and looked at each other. I wondered if Mace had arrested Rollag yet.

After a moment of silence, Emily jumped up and reminded us how the game worked. "Remember, you're supposed to guess which one of those statements was a lie. Someone guess." She dropped back down to her chair.

The finance woman I didn't know said, "Burping is your lie. You told us about the jig and Jeopardy at the last monthly office birthday party."

"Oh, that's right, I did," said Suzy with an embarrassed giggle.

Who knew we had monthly office birthday parties? When did this start? I can't believe I'd missed cake every month and no one told me. This training had already proven more valuable than I'd expected. I needed to find out when the next cake party would take place.

Emily popped up from her chair, gave a broad smile and applauded Suzy. "That was great, Suzy. Thanks for starting us off. Okay, how about if you go next." She pointed at Cassandra, the saleswoman. Emily lowered herself into her seat again.

Cassandra stood to deliver her sales pitch. "I'm Cassandra. Let's see ... how about ... I have 59 rose bushes in my yard. I have 3 drawers of socks. And, I dance nude on stage."

That last statement made the whole room pause. Then someone shouted, "The dancing part is the lie because she's a numbers person and that's the only one without a number." Others murmured hopeful agreement because no one wanted to speculate about Cassandra's naked dancing exploits.

Cassandra smirked as she realized everyone had succumbed. "Ha! I won! I tricked you all. My lie was the first sentence. I only have 42 rose bushes in my yard, not 59." She turned to a neighbor to attempt a high five. The effort wasn't reciprocated as the person shrank away from touching her. Cassandra didn't seem to mind and settled for turning the abortive movement into a fist pump as she congratulated herself on her success.

I'll never understand salespeople.

Raj leaned over to whisper, "Is this what your sister does?"

I whispered back, "I hope not." Did Laney do an HR training that had upset someone? I could see someone getting annoyed at Emily for being too perky. Laney, however, had never been perky. Anyway, why would someone try to kill their HR trainer for being annoying?

The room fell into uncomfortable silence other than Cassandra's continued, self-satisfied hoots. She hadn't grasped that there were no winners in this exercise. After her oversharing, Cassandra certainly hadn't won anything from this crowd today.

Emily pushed herself up from her chair and made a game attempt to move on. With a brittle smile pasted on her face, she looked around the room trying to pick someone very different from Cassandra. She picked me. "Why don't you go ahead?" This time she perched on the edge of her seat.

I started to sweat because I'd only come up with two of the three required statements. "Ok. I'm Marty. Let's see ..." I considered announcing that Sergeant Mace Jackson needed my help to solve a case, but I didn't want to explain everything. "I ate spaghetti tacos for dinner last night. I met Jean Rollag, the founder of DroneTech, yesterday. And, um, I like romance novels." I'd admit my third statement wasn't the best lie in the world, but it was the first thing that came to my mind at the moment. Although I might not win the exercise, at least I wouldn't be embarrassed.

My feeling of minor accomplishment and lack of embarrassment lasted for about a second.

"Why would an engineer meet with the founder of DroneTech unless he's trying to get a job there? Are you leaving Rover, Marty?" challenged someone I didn't know.

"Hey, Marty's not wearing a Hawaiian shirt and shorts. Maybe he really is interviewing," said another person.

The whole reason for wearing the same outfit every day was to avoid the challenge of figuring out what to wear. Ever since Steve Jobs, the co-founder of Apple, had popularized the concept, lots of engineers, at least male engineers, had followed suit. Preferring cheerful, bright colors to his all-black, I kept a closet full of Hawaiian shirts that I wore most days.

Another person at the end of the table spoke. "No, that's not it. He paused before the last sentence because he needed to make up something. No way a guy likes romance novels."

The woman to my left asked, "What's wrong with a man liking romance novels?"

"What's a spaghetti taco?" came another voice.

Distracted by thinking about Laney and Meghan, I'd been foolish. If I admitted I'd really met Rollag, everyone would think I had interviewed at DroneTech. I needed to claim my lie as the truth and fast before this spiraled any further out of control.

I fake laughed. "I guess I won too. I only read an interview about Rollag. That was my lie."

Small titters sounded across the room. I caught some odd looks thrown my way. The woman sitting to my left leaned over. "So, what's your favorite romance novel?"

Oh, great. Not quite as embarrassing as Cassandra, but I hadn't won this exercise either.

Emily interrupted with a polite clap as she stood. "Ok. Thank you, Marty, for playing." Her smile had returned now that we'd started playing her game properly. "For our last one, how about you go next?" She pointed at Bruce.

Bruce barely fit between the armrests of his chair. His upper body overflowed onto the chairs of the people next to him. Bruce spent his day on the phone handling customer support calls and snacking. We didn't talk much beyond the occasional passing courtesies. I was impressed I'd remembered his name.

"Everything I say is protected, right?"

"Why, yes." Emily nodded. She continued nodding, making meaningful eye contact with everyone as she looked around the room, pausing and doing a double nod to me. "Remember we all agreed that this would be a safe place. Go ahead. Tell us your three statements." Emily sat again.

I wondered when we would get to the actual training so we could get back to work. Work didn't usually take second place to other activities during my week and I needed to catch up. I needed to call Mace too. I'd forgotten to ask him to increase security for Laney. Sneaking a glance around the room, I saw quite a few people glancing at their phones or gazing off into space. Only a handful appeared engaged, looking attentively at Bruce.

Bruce settled himself. "Hi, I'm Bruce and I'm an alcoholic. And a drug addict. And a compulsive overeater." He paused like he was waiting for the ritualistic response from the room.

Startled, everyone jerked to attention. We weren't a twelve-step support group and no one had expected this.

Emily leaned forward in her chair. "I'm not sure if this is the right place for —"

"Oh, I'm sorry if I didn't play the game right," interrupted Bruce. "My therapist told me I should never lie while I'm in recovery."

Awkward silence again. Emily's mouth was open, but no words came out.

Bruce plowed ahead with a nervous tic that caused his left eye to twitch. "Well, the Overeaters Anonymous part would technically be a lie. I did try it for a while. Then I had to drop out. Is that considered a lie or not?"

It was like sitting back and eating popcorn while watching a movie with an out-of-control freight train. Weird that I thought I could actually smell the popcorn.

Bruce didn't wait for a response. "All three programs have twelve steps to remember. It's crazy hard to keep track of all of them. That's like, twenty-eight steps to remember."

Raj and I exchanged glances. I'm sure we'd be discussing the poor math skills of American students sometime soon. I realized that I did smell popcorn, coming from the break room next door. Who'd want to microwave popcorn at ten thirty in the morning?

"It was so hard to stop. I met my drug dealer next to this awesome place, Restaurante El Salvador." Bruce was building up steam and continued, "Their chicken special is to die for."

I recognized the restaurant name from Meghan Emerson this morning. She'd planned to meet Laney there for lunch. Was Fernando the drug dealer that Bruce met? Why would Laney get involved with a drug dealer in the first place? Maybe she liked the chicken special too. Or, maybe Bruce wasn't kidding when he said it was to die for.

Bruce was so absorbed in his own story that he didn't notice the room's reaction. "That made the food and the drugs part of the same trip. I'd eat there all the time. It's a really popular place —"

Emily found her tongue. "Bruce, this might not be the best time —"

The freight train chugged on, unstoppable. "It's not my fault I dropped out. It's my mother's."

Sucked into Bruce's vortex, Cassandra couldn't help herself. "Your mother's?"

Emily tried again to interrupt, however, Bruce's momentum rolled on. "Yea. I live with my mom. Well, technically, I guess I don't. I mean I have my own door now that we converted the garage into my room. She cooks for me though."

Watching this unfold, I felt like I was at a theater. Bruce's emotional outburst had captivated this audience like any award-winning drama. It even smelled like one. Movie theaters sometimes have that rancid, burnt smell from overcooked popcorn. Sniffing, I thought I smelled that odor here as well. Then, the woman next to me sniffed a few times also, so I knew it wasn't my fanciful imagination.

Bruce powered on, "I can come and go as I like. Well, I guess as long as I let my mom know … And she doesn't need me for anything … And I won't be out too late."

Emily's smile had disappeared, frightened away by the onrushing train. She took a step toward Bruce. "We should —"

The fire alarm blared. That stopped Bruce.

Saved by the bell.

Awakened from Bruce's theatrical spell, everyone stood and started streaming out the door. The woman to my left leaned in and whispered, "I had no idea you liked romance novels also. You should join our office book club."

"Ah, sure, that sounds fun." Like hitting my head against the wall. Maybe she'd forget. With a gentlemanly nod, I waved her ahead of me. I decided to be extra courteous and allowed more people to get between her and me.

As Raj and I jostled down the stairs, he asked, "That was very interesting. Do you think your sister did any training for her clients?"

"I hope not."

As we emerged outside into the parking lot, Raj asked, "Do you want to know what I would say for my two truths and a lie?"

"I don't think so. Not after those others."

He ignored me. "I speak three languages. I acted in a Bollywood movie. I am traveling home to India next month to get married."

Despite not wanting to play, I paused to consider. I already knew he spoke three languages. He had also told me he had a trip home to India planned for next month. Although he hadn't mentioned anything about getting married, that did happen on a regular basis with single Indian men in the Valley. They'd go home to India on a vacation after living in the U.S. for a while and return with a wife, arranged by their families. I've worked with three or four other engineers who'd gotten married this way. The Bollywood line had to be the lie. Raj designed code, not acted.

"Should I say congratulations on your upcoming wedding?" I reached out to shake his hand, feeling clever for outguessing Raj.

Raj chortled. "You silly Americans. You always think Indians get married when they go home for a visit. That is my lie. When I was a kid, I was an extra in a crowd scene in a Bollywood movie. I appeared in the movie, although you can barely see me."

I had to laugh. "Yes, I guess I am a silly American." In the distance, I heard fire truck sirens approaching. *Ridiculous.* We had a little smoke from some idiot putting their popcorn in the microwave for too long. Now we'd have to wait forever for the firefighters to tromp through the building and confirm that nothing had happened, except we employed an idiot. I wouldn't get anything done the rest of this morning before I needed to leave for my lunch at DroneTech.

Today's training had been an even bigger waste than I'd expected. At least I got a good idea of where to take the girls for dinner tonight.

16

Thursday Lunch

The Rover car made it to DroneTech in near-record time during the late morning time period after rush hour and let me out right in front of their huge headquarters. After explosive growth for the last decade, DroneTech had built a new campus after tearing down an older complex of buildings from another tech company that had missed the next technology wave and gotten swamped into bankruptcy.

After I texted Daniel, he met me in the lobby. He came out the elevator rather than using the curving yellow slide from the third floor. Ironically for a company famous for rigorous protection of their own intellectual property, they'd stolen the slide design idea from an earlier startup in the Valley.

All around us, fresh-faced and nimble employees whooped as they flew down the slide and connected with co-workers to head for lunch. What happens to older workers in the Valley has started to perplex me in recent years. Tech company employees seem to get younger and younger every year. Perhaps the secret society of middle-aged software engineers will soon contact me and let me know where I'm supposed to report for duty.

Daniel's lush, brown hair, smooth skin, and fashionable outfit, which my kids called metro chic, proved that he did more than merely forward all those self-improvement articles. He walked with the erect, strong gait of an athlete, although he spent his days peering at a computer screen. Perhaps I'd have to go back and read those articles he sent me after all.

Daniel gave a wide smile which revealed bright white teeth as he approached and shook my hand. "Marty. It's been a long time. How are you doing?" He paused to consider my appearance more closely. "Are you exercising? It looks like you need to follow that skin care regimen I recommended."

I remembered why it had been a long time. In light of my priorities to dig up dirt on Rollag and get a job at DroneTech, I ignored his last comment. "Fine. I'm glad you could make lunch."

Daniel clapped me on the back. "Come on, you'll like our cafeteria. Everyone does." He signed me in and handed me a badge that I clipped to the belt on my jeans under my untucked dress shirt. The long sleeve shirt had better impress any potential DroneTech hiring manager. It was most uncomfortable compared to my normal Hawaiian shirts. Although I liked my job at Rover well enough, I'd have to be crazy not to accept an offer at a hot company like DroneTech.

I followed him past security into a long hallway crowded with people heading in both directions. Along the way, we passed a door on the right with a sign reading "Meditation." Across the hall was a door with the sign "Yoga." The label on next door down read "Bikram Yoga."

"Wow, you have a meditation room and two dedicated yoga rooms?"

Daniel's chin lifted as he started to lecture. "DroneTech believes a healthy body and spirit make for a better employee. That's why I love working here."

And those stock options.

He seemed to wait for a follow-up question. I let out a silent sigh. "Do you do yoga?"

"All the time. It's a great way to strengthen your core. I alternate between the hot and regular yoga. How about you?"

"I yogurt often."

Daniel looked bewildered before becoming distracted as we dodged the growing crowd flowing back and forth from the cafeteria. A sign above the door read, "Bistro Tech." Fancy names for company cafeterias in Silicon Valley satisfied the egos of the employees, or the executives. The one near our office had some odd name too. Maybe the marketing and HR people needed something to do while they waited for the engineers to finish the next product.

Daniel badged into the cafeteria and held the door for me. I never quite understood why companies put badge access controls on their cafeteria doors. You never have to badge out so it's not like the company is keeping track of how long their employees spent at lunch. Perhaps DroneTech docked the pay of employees who visited their cafeteria too often during the day.

We walked inside. A huge colored banner with sparkling LED lights around the edges hung across the extra high ceiling. I had arrived in time to celebrate "Pecan Month." Pecans weren't my thing, yet I could eat pistachios every day for a whole month.

Different food serving areas dotted the massive room. Large monitors above each area announced the food served at each station, including Asian, Indian, Latin, Southern, Salad, and others I couldn't see from the entrance.

"Here we are." Daniel swept his arm out in a dramatic move that almost hit several co-workers carrying plates of food.

"Wow. You sure have a lot of choices. I'll bet you still get bored though, with the same choices every day."

"The options change daily. Although salad's always an option.

Oh, look, they have the chicken tortilla soup at the Latin station. I'm going to get that. It's awesome. Want to join me?"

"No thanks. You go ahead. I'll wander around and pick something. Meet you at the cashiers?" I looked around for the cashiers.

"There aren't any cashiers. Everything's free here."

"Wow. I should come back for dinner."

He gave me another odd look and headed off to the Latin station. Despite the stories I'd heard about DroneTech's cafeteria, this blew me away. Rover's too little to have our own cafeteria, but the building next door to us had a small one with a few pre-made sandwiches and salads. I felt fortunate if I got one of the sandwiches before they sold out.

A printed page in an acrylic stand stood at the end of the Indian line like a menu. Except this page took two paragraphs to explain the one option at this station. These were squash, corn, and pecan dumplings with lavender floral notes that blended the sweet flavor with the earthy vegetable tones into an autumnal homage, yet without foliage. It took me longer to read the description than eating the food would take.

I walked over to the Southern station expecting to find fried chicken or barbecue ribs. *Nope.* Nothing would be simple at Bistro Tech. According to the menu, the Southern lunch option included basil-infused, pecan cornbread with honey from DroneTech's own beehives. I hoped the bees were kept outside the building. The cornbread accompanied a beautiful rockfish with a textured crust formed by crushed, mixed pecans, walnuts, and almonds. The description took so long to read that I had to start over to remember what it was.

I glanced up and saw Daniel waiting for me, shifting from one foot to the other, with his hot soup and a side salad already in hand. Browsing time was over. Even though I'm not sure how they knew a beautiful rockfish from an ugly one, I took what the guy handed me. Carefully plated with a swirl of some decorative, green oil, the fish looked a lot better than my normal lunch of tuna salad on stale sourdough wrapped in plastic.

I'd have to suffer for the sake of the investigation.

We grabbed an open table overlooking a patio full of more tables. On the patio, a small waterfall ran into a pond filled with lily pads and surrounded by colorful flowers. Little LED lights ran up the sides of the waterfall and changed colors in rhythm with the mood music.

I pointed to the waterfall with a question on my lips.

Daniel knew what I was thinking. "Oh, it's not wasting water. They ran a whole story about it on our internal homepage. We're using recycled gray water from the bathroom sinks that are filtered on site and stored in an underground cistern. The water recirculates and the waterfall and solar panels generate enough electricity to run the pond off the grid." The pride in his company flowed through his words and left me feeling saturated.

"Wow." As this had been my main contribution to our conversation today, I started eating instead of repeating myself again.

A few minutes later, I asked, "What's Rollag like?"

Daniel flinched. Perhaps I hadn't interjected that question into the conversational flow as smoothly as I'd thought.

"I guess he's a typical startup founder. He can be inspirational, and also sometimes a jerk. The company wouldn't have made it to this point without him and Saunders. I don't see them too often."

"Can drones be crashed?"

Daniel opened his eyes wide. "Crashes are extremely rare."

I watched to see if he knew anything. "No, I mean on purpose."

Daniel rocked back in his seat and darted his head from side to side to check if anyone had overheard me. "Why would someone intentionally crash a drone?" He put down his fork. "We shouldn't talk about crashing drones here. I like my job. It's like talking about bombs in front of a TSA agent. You can attract unwanted attention." He no longer seemed so pleased that I'd come for lunch.

We fell into silence as the hubbub of the cafeteria flowed around us. A few people interrupted the tension when they stopped by our table to ask Daniel about various projects. I tried to get back into his good graces by talking about former colleagues and my own work. By the time we got into a technical argument about programming languages, he seemed to have forgotten my earlier questions. All in all, it was a fairly typical social gathering of engineers.

After a while, Daniel said, "I'll show you the view of the Bay from the top floor." He stood up without waiting for my response.

"Sure." Although I wasn't all that interested in looking out a window, I hoped to encounter Rollag so I could ask him more questions. Plus, I've learned it's worthwhile to spend the effort networking with colleagues at high-value companies. Perhaps Daniel would help me get a job here. Or at least invite me to eat in the cafeteria again.

As we collected our lunch trash, Daniel's phone buzzed. He requested I take his things while he responded to a message. He pointed me toward the recycling area and told me he'd join me in a minute.

Choosing my lunch paled in comparison to the difficulty in figuring out how to get rid of our trash. Four different trash cans sat under four holes in a countertop next to a long container for used silverware. Above the holes, signs with pictures depicted what to put in each can. I put the silverware in their container. That was simple. I stood looking at the pictures above the other containers while DroneTech employees swirled around me, putting their trash into different containers without any hesitation.

Despite the elaborate pictures, I didn't understand what to do. I approved of composting in theory. Distinguishing a brown versus a green from our lunches was an entirely different thing. The napkins were dirty from food so I didn't think they should go into the paper recycling can with the photo of clean napkins above it. Sure, the salad was green, but Daniel's leftover carrots were orange. I didn't see any pecans in the pictures. The pictures didn't match what I held. After looking around to make sure no one noticed, I dropped everything in the nearest can and walked away before anyone could comment.

Daniel led the way down the hallway and continued past the elevators. "You should see our gym first. Maybe it would inspire you to go more often."

Keeping my eye roll in check, I looked through the glass door leading to the gym. The room was all white — floors, walls, ceiling and even white leather couches on the sides. The equipment was all silver and black. The gym looked nicer than most homes. I'd never seen a gym designed by a decorator before.

Once again, "Wow," was all I could manage.

As we walked back to the elevators, I saw a short line of people leading to an open door. As we walked past, I saw four chair massage stations in use. I wondered if Daniel would notice if I stood in line as well.

But I followed Daniel to go see the view. I kept my eyes open for Rollag since Daniel hadn't yielded anything useful. If I ever got hired, I could return for a chair massage. I'd need one to handle the stress of figuring out what's happening with Laney.

In the enclosed space of the elevator, Daniel wrinkled his nose. "I think you spilled some of the fish."

I sighed. "It's my shoes, not the fish."

Looking puzzled, Daniel didn't ask for more details. Probably for the best.

On the sixth floor, we walked to an open room with a few small tables, chairs and a refrigerator next to a microwave. Floor to ceiling windows looked out north over the Bay for a beautiful view. Boats sailed in the Bay and marsh grasses waved in a light breeze closer to shore, with the Dumbarton Bridge in the distance.

Daniel puffed out his chest. "Quite a view, huh?"

"Nice break room." The vintage Rover building, squashed behind a crappy hotel next to the highway, overlooks the next office building across the parking lot from our second-floor vantage point.

"Come on, I'll show you my office." As we left the breakroom, he pointed to the left. "That's the Operations Center. Takes up the other half of the floor."

I saw a door with a badge reader, but no sign, past the bathrooms. "What's in there?"

"I'm not entirely certain. It's a secure room that I'm not allowed in. Rumor has it they track all our drones from there. No one knows for sure."

His answer made me twitch. I wanted to get in to see if Rollag guided a drone to hit Laney from there.

Instead, Daniel turned to the right, past several conference rooms into a large, open area. Large windows kept the area bright even with all the chest-high cubicles. Daniel's cube contained a desk with two large monitors connected to his laptop and a comfortable chair. A few knickknacks and photos on the desk completed his typical, modern engineer's office.

"Nice," I said to be polite. His cubicle contained no anti-gravity zone, lounge chairs, or even a stand-sit electric desk. Not that I expected such exotic office furnishings, but all bets were off after the cafeteria and lobby slide from the third floor.

Daniel's phone rang. He glanced at it and sighed. "Shoot, I have to take this call."

I held out my hand. "I can find the elevators. Thanks for lunch. Let's do it again."

He shook my hand as he looked helplessly between me and his ringing phone. He answered. Putting the phone to his chest, he said, "I'm supposed to escort you out. You can make it without any trouble, right?"

"Sure." If I ran into Rollag, I'd ask him some more questions. I didn't expect trouble unless I saw someone holding a big sign reading "Kill Laney."

He nodded goodbye and turned to his phone.

I kept my eyes open for Rollag as I walked back to the elevators. Today's research had been tasty, but otherwise useless. DroneTech had much better food and perks than Rover and nothing to implicate Rollag, yet.

Before heading back to work, I stopped at the restroom. By the time I came out, my inner map had gotten muddled. Like most men, I believed my sense of direction is better than average. Like most, it's probably average at best. As I left the restroom, I turned to the left. After a few steps, I realized my mistake and turned around before reaching the Operations Center door.

A short, heavyset man carrying several boxes, as well as a bag of apples tucked under his arm, turned the corner, hurrying toward me from the elevators. Out of nowhere, everything went flying as he tripped over an invisible bump in the carpet. The boxes made a loud metallic noise as they hit the ground. Equipment and apples scattered across the floor as he flung his arms out to break his fall.

Slowed by the sudden spray of debris, I halted. "Are you okay?"

"Thanks. I'm fine. Just clumsy and late." The man scrambled on the ground collecting his things. Sweat dripped down his face as he hurried to organize his mess.

I bent down to help. Collecting some unusual pieces of equipment behind the kneeling man, I saw his DroneTech badge on the ground nearby.

Inspiration struck.

17

Thursday After Lunch

If the man was rushing toward the Operations Center, then he must be able to get inside. My pulse rate accelerated as my thoughts raced. Here was my ticket. If I wasn't meant to go inside, then why had a badge been delivered to me? It's not like I could knock on the door to ask if they'd committed a felony there on Monday.

I palmed the badge and continued helping him straighten out his mess. After all, my mother had raised a well-mannered boy. Temporarily borrowing a badge didn't mean I couldn't help a stranger.

I handed him some apples and picked up one of the boxes as we stood up. "You like apples?" I wanted to keep him distracted.

"Oh absolutely. I eat a few in the morning and a few more in the afternoon." He put the apples back into his bag.

"Here let me help you get this stuff inside." My mother would have been proud of my helpfulness. *Yeah, I'll keep telling myself that.* Covering his picture on the badge, I swiped the reader by the Operations Center door and it clicked open. I pulled it open like I'd done this a million times and held it for the sweating man. "Go ahead, you're carrying the big load and we wouldn't want it to spill again."

"Thanks. Thanks for your help. Just set that box down on the left and I'll come back to get it." He gave me a grateful smile as he slid through the door.

I followed him into a dark entranceway. I'd penetrated the top-secret DroneTech Operations Center. The site where evil drone controller minions led by Rollag, their dark overlord, had steered the flying drone of death that barely missed Laney's car and destroyed the ice cream truck.

Well, maybe. Ok, so I enjoyed science fiction a little too much. But I was inside.

So cool! The D.O.C. — what we regulars called the DroneTech Operations Center — looked like N.A.S.A. Space Control or a huge air traffic control room almost the size of the cafeteria on the ground floor. The ceiling extended up almost twice as high as it did on Daniel's side of the floor. Huge screens mounted on the back wall contained thousands of colored dots. The dots moved slowly across a map of the U.S. pulsing in every direction in a rhythmic dance. Some dots flashed red or yellow, while most remained a steady green.

A semi-circular array of desks and tables faced the screens. Smaller screens to the sides of the huge map displayed scrolling lists of text, colored graphs, and close-up maps with moving dots all over them. At least a hundred people filled the room. Most sat at the desks wearing headsets in front of their own computers and large displays. Several small groups of people stood by different desks or to one side of the room talking and gesturing at the displays. The room buzzed with quiet conversation and electronic beeps. The room must have had great noise-canceling materials because it sounded no louder than a typical office floor despite more people and equipment.

I stood in silence to the side while my eyes adjusted to the dim light in the room. The moving dots must be the drones run by various delivery companies and controlled by DroneTech software. Some of the side screens showed detailed status updates for drones with red and yellow lights.

Despite the thrill of entering the secret room, I felt frustrated at the same time as it became clear that Rollag couldn't have crashed the drone on Laney from here. I'd envisioned Rollag, perhaps with one or two trusted lackeys, directing a drone onto Laney from his computer and then producing an evil laugh. If he'd tried that here, someone would have noticed and reported it. After all, engineers followed safety protocols. There was no way so many people could be involved in an attack on Laney without someone reporting it.

Demoralized, I set the box down on one of the empty desks near me and turned to slink out of the room before I got caught. Across the entrance hallway, I spotted another door. This one had a small sign that read: "Lab. Do Not Enter."

Something must be wrong with me. "Do Not Enter" signs have always been an aphrodisiac for my curiosity. When I was young and our family went on vacations, I'd often gotten in trouble by sneaking into rooms or hallways labeled like that. I always figured that the museums stored their best stuff in secret rooms for special people like me to view. However, I never found the right secret rooms when I was young. Maybe this was my lucky day and this door wouldn't lead to a boring office or storage room. My overactive imagination demanded confirmation. Rollag might have worked his devious deeds from this secret room.

My body moved as if on autopilot. I had no choice. Stepping across to the lab door, I put the borrowed badge to the reader. If it worked, I'd take a quick peek inside to make sure this wasn't their secret, death drone control room.

The door clicked open.

I edged into a fairly empty room with some large mounted

displays and a variety of mechanical equipment laying around the sides. In the middle of the room, a man lay on a hammock held up by four, small, hovering drones with a controller in one hand and a sandwich in the other.

Awesome. A test room. I wanted a cool hammock like that for my office.

That's when the klaxons sounded. I hadn't known that a klaxon made an "ah-oo-gah" sound until that moment. Imagining the loudest fire alarm ever, combined with two more at different frequencies, along with flashing red lights, would approach the reality of DroneTech's klaxons.

Out of the corner of my eye, I saw the massive monitor screens flashed red in place of their normal displays. Frozen in shock by the noise and light, I failed to notice the two security guards until they tackled me.

Really. Not. Necessary. Thanks to the guards' assistance, my body stung from the accelerated impact of my up close and personal investigation of the floor. The two, rather large, guards yanked me up. Each held me by an arm as they turned me around to leave. My legs might have touched the ground, but it didn't matter. The bruising would come later.

The whole control room stood to look my way. Quite a few of the technicians held their hands over their ears to protect against the unnecessarily loud, klaxon noise. Most of the techs were too far away for me to see their faces, however, the ones nearby made their displeasure plain with clenched jaws and glaring eyes. One slight, older technician even shook a raised fist at me. I missed my chance to apologize for disrupting their day as I struggled to catch my breath from hitting the ground.

The guards growled something and yanked me out of the lab, made sure the door closed behind us and took three quick steps out of the Operations Center. I don't think they were pleased that I'd interrupted their low stress, security guard positions. Smacking my head on the way out of the Operations Center might have been an accidental byproduct of their lack of recent training, or perhaps as a sign that they'd realized my actions had endangered their gravy train.

They half-dragged, half-marched me to the elevators. I saw workers from the other side of the floor stepping into the aisles to gape down the hallway to see what disaster had struck their Operations Center.

Nothing to see here. Go back to work.

As the guards pulled me into the elevator lobby, I saw Daniel standing by some co-workers. His mouth agape and eyes wide, he stared at me from down the hall. He seemed in shock that I hadn't followed his simple request to leave the building without incident.

Maybe, I'd need to wait a few weeks before asking him to recommend me for a DroneTech position or visit for lunch again. Shame, I'd miss the rest of Pecan Month.

The guards hustled me across the lobby, yanked the temporary badge off my belt and the stolen badge out of my hands. They deposited me on the sidewalk with a warning not to come back. Probably they just meant not today.

Brushing myself off, I regained my composure and tried to ignore the stares of the people around the driveway. Although embarrassed, I'd made some progress in my investigation. There was no way a rogue controller could have attempted to crash a drone onto Laney undetected by the other workers in that crowded Operations Center. However, as co-founder and CTO, Rollag had access to any secret labs. He and his evil minions might have used secret controller access from within a secret lab to crash the drone while hovering in the hammock eating any number of pecan delicacies.

Well, it's possible.

Why was Rollag trying to kill Laney? He didn't seem the sort to suffocate an old lady in the hospital in the middle of the night, even if by mistake. However, if Rollag hadn't done it, then who did?

Fresh out of answers, I brought up the Rover app to request a car to take me back to work. It looked like I'd be working there for a while at least.

The Rover service was down.

Getting stranded during a Rover engineering crisis wouldn't endear me to my current boss. Hanging around while DroneTech's security guards watched me suspiciously and talked on their walkie-talkies from inside the lobby doors wouldn't endear me to a future DroneTech boss.

Great.

18

Thursday Early Afternoon

I rebooted my phone and tried again. The Rover app wouldn't connect to our servers to locate a car for me. The whole service had crashed.

I called Raj to check in. The call went to voicemail. Not a good sign. I'll bet it was an all hands on deck situation at the office to get the service running again. And here I was, out of the office. Again.

My boss would notice my absence during the emergency. I called his phone to tell him that I'm on my way. Voicemail as well. I left him a message that I'd left at lunch for a doctor's appointment and noticed the service was down when I tried to get back to the office. Better that than tell him I was calling from DroneTech, where I definitely wasn't going to get a job today. My parents raised me to tell the truth, but they also raised a smart boy.

I refused to get dropped off at work from a competing rideshare car. With my luck, I'd show up at work in a non-Rover car only to meet my boss standing outside. I called a taxi, one of those old-fashioned kinds with the light on top and a human driver inside. The only remaining taxi company in the area quoted me thirty minutes for pickup. Perhaps they knew where I worked. I walked a little farther away from the DroneTech building in case their security people decided they didn't like me hanging around.

My phone rang and I answered it quickly, hoping Raj had called me back.

"Hello, this is Sergeant Mace Jackson." His deep voice sounded different from before, not annoyed, perhaps even neutral.

Instinctively, I ducked and looked around. No cops with drawn guns were visible. "Hi … What? … They called the police?" I couldn't believe the DroneTech security had called the police that fast. And how had they reached the one cop with my number?

"What are you talking about? Who called the police?" The familiar irritation returned to Mace's voice as it rumbled across the line.

I realized DroneTech couldn't have reached him and I didn't know why he'd called. "Wait. No, I'm sorry. What's going on?"

"Well, maybe you aren't totally crazy after all." Mace's almost-apology sounded good to me. He continued, "I'm at your sister's house right now. Someone broke into her house last night."

The hairs on the back of my neck stood up. "What?" Burglars creeped me out even without my family involved. One moment you're asleep and the next, they were standing over your bed with a knife in their hands …

Mace broke my train of thought. "Her place got tossed. The thief, or thieves, were clearly looking for something. They didn't take the TV and we don't think they took any jewelry or other valuables. I'd like you to come over here to figure out if anything's missing."

"Oh, my god. Okay. I'll come over as soon as my ride shows up." I reached up, trying to massage out the tension in my neck.

"Ride?" Observant like most successful cops, Mace latched onto the unusual comment.

"I don't have a car. I'm an engineer for the Rover car service so I use our driverless car service to go everywhere."

"Interesting. I don't know if I could give up my car. Doesn't it get annoying to wait whenever you want to go somewhere?" Mace paused to consider this possibility.

I ran my hand through my hair as I paced back and forth. "I save a ton of money. No car payments, no insurance, no gas. And normally we have enough cars floating around that I never wait more than a few minutes. But the service is down right now so I'm waiting for a taxi."

I wasn't about to use one of our driverless car service competitors. But, we'd gotten sidetracked. This happened every time people found out that I don't own a car. Many people in crowded cities managed without a car for part of the week and even more were considering it, but car-crazy Americans would take a lot longer to fully switch gears. *Ha. Car joke.* Hopefully, my job at Rover would last long enough for that to happen. It would help if I didn't lose my job for not showing up during a crisis.

Still discombobulated by the idea of giving up his car, Mace could only grunt.

My mind spun. *Drone, crash, murder.* Drones were falling, an old woman got murdered in a hospital, bribes paid at Stanford, dead rats left by a car in a parking lot, and incredibly loud klaxons activated. They didn't seem connected. What if they were? Mace needed to get moving on Laney's case.

Trying to pull his attention back to more important issues than driverless cars, I blurted out, "I'm worried that someone's trying to kill Laney."

Nothing like the prospect of murder to catch the attention of a police officer. Mace woke from his reverie. "What?"

Now I got annoyed. "Didn't you even listen to my messages?" Not waiting for a response, I continued, "I don't think the drone dropping on her was an accident. And remember that Laney's hospital room didn't have her name on the outside sign? Well, on

Monday night, an old lady in the room with Laney's name on it was murdered."

"I didn't hear about a murder." Jackson hadn't listened to my messages. He didn't treat prospective partners well. "Why would anyone want to kill your sister? What does she do again?"

I clenched my fist and my voice rose along with my frustration. "She's an HR consultant. It's a totally boring job. I don't know why anyone would want to hurt her."

My phone buzzed, breaking into my rant. Probably a good thing. I needed Jackson to focus on Laney's attacker, not get angry and ignore me. The screen showed the other call was from the girls' school. "I'm sorry. I need to put you on hold. My nieces' school is calling." I switched over without waiting for a reply.

"Hello, Mr. Golden? This is the Discovery School." Mrs. Quarles, the school secretary who had called me on Monday, sounded annoyed. I pictured her with a prim, disappointed scowl on the other end of the line.

"Yes. Is everything ok?"

"No, it is not." Mrs. Quarles launched into a lecture. "You should know that all school absences need to be called in before noon or the student gets an unexcused absence on their record."

"What? Who's absent from school? Skye and Megan both went to school today." I did not need this extra aggravation today.

"Megan is present today. Skye was marked absent in her class this morning. Rule 17 clearly states that if a student is sick or has a doctor's appointment and does not attend school for any reason at all, including all religious or spiritual observations, you need to call before noon. We explained all this in the guidelines that we sent home on the first day of school."

"Okay, okay. But she should be at school. Where did she go?" Sweat broke out on my head as I started hyperventilating.

Mrs. Quarles harrumphed. "Well then, that is definitely not an excused absence. Truancy is a serious situation. Skye will need to come to the office to meet with Principal McCarreon when she returns to school."

"We'll deal with the principal later. Where is she?" I looked around the DroneTech driveway and parking lot. Skye wasn't here either.

Mrs. Quarles had a one-track mind. She continued with bruised indignation, "Well, she's certainly not in her classroom or she would have been marked present, wouldn't she? Did you see her walk into her classroom when you dropped her off this morning?"

Oops. I couldn't tell her that I let the girls go on their own to school in a driverless car. She'd probably make me go to the principal's office too. But, that gave me an idea. "I've got to go so I can find her."

"Yes. I would think so. It is important that she not miss school. Be certain to sign the Unexcused Absence form and —"

I hung up on her and called Raj again, hoping he would answer this time. He did.

"Raj! Hi, it's Marty. I've got an emergency."

"Yes. The Rover service is down. All the teams have gathered to fix the problem. We are needing you, but you are not here. Where are you?"

"I don't have time to explain. Could you please track my account to see where I went?"

Raj called me out. "Why? Do you not know where you are?"

"No, I know where I am. But, my niece, Skye, used my Rover account and I don't know where she went."

"She is too young to be an authorized user."

He was right and I knew it. I begged. "I know, but I needed to get them to school and also go talk to someone about Laney. I sent the girls to school by themselves in a Rover car. Could you please check my account?"

"Now I am understanding. I can't right now as the system is

down. I will look as soon as we get it working again. Oh, and the boss came to look for you."

"Thanks. I left the boss a voicemail that I went to a doctor's appointment during lunch today. Please cover for me."

"Sure."

I switched back to Sergeant Jackson. The line was dead. I'd hung up on him by accident. I called him again.

"Don't hang up on me again. I'm too busy to hold for your nonsense," answered Jackson, without even a greeting. I could feel his displeasure radiating through the phone. Although he might be my imaginary action movie star partner, politeness wasn't his strong suit.

"I'm sorry, but Laney's daughter, Skye, is missing from school. They just called. I don't know where she is. She should be at school with her younger sister, but she's not there." My heart raced as I paced along the sidewalk.

"You're sure it was the school that called you?" asked Jackson, skepticism tinging his words.

I ran my hand through my hair again. "Yes. The school's secretary called to lecture me for not notifying them of her absence on time. Do you think someone took her? Like whoever broke into Laney's house?"

Jackson had no problem believing that Mrs. Quarles called to yell at me. His voice changed in an instant to concern for Skye. "I don't know. There are too many coincidences all at once. The girl's missing, her mom's in the hospital and someone broke into their house."

"You think I'm right?"

"I wouldn't go that far." To Jackson, once a flake, always a flake. "But, I'm going to assign an officer to guard Laney's hospital room and start an Amber Alert for your niece. There's too much going on with that family right now."

I took a breath. At least Laney would be safe while the Amber

Alert notified other police officers and citizens around the state to keep an eye out for Skye.

Jackson collected the basic info about Skye and told me he would grab a picture of her right there from Laney's house. Jackson hung up to start the process while I continued to panic and wait for my taxi.

My phone rang again. I answered it, hoping it was Raj even though it wasn't his phone.

"Hello, is this Marty Golden?" asked an unfamiliar male voice.

"Yes. I'm pretty busy right now."

"I've got your niece, Skye Tran, here with me," said the voice.

My heart rate spiked so high it almost pushed out through my chest. *Oh, my god! Is this what a kidnapper sounds like?* "Who is this? Is she ok?" I stammered.

19

Thursday Afternoon

"**S**he's quite the special young lady," said the voice.

I fumbled with my phone, looking for some app to record the call. Why didn't I have an app that could trace calls and send in a special police SWAT team?

The voice continued, "I'm Dr. Nathan Mahowald. I'm a professor in the biology department at Santa Clara University."

Although still flummoxed, my heart rate slowed. I didn't think normal kidnappers gave their full names or worked as a professor at a prestigious university. "Why do you have her? What's she doing?"

"Skye showed up a little while ago for an appointment she'd requested. I was startled when I saw how young she was. I told her that she needed to go to school," said Dr. Mahowald.

Now confused, I stopped pacing along the sidewalk. "Why did she meet with you?"

"We've been corresponding for a while. She had questions about a project she's doing on Dorymyrmex insanus."

"What?" I couldn't help myself.

"They're commonly called crazy ants."

"You're kidding?" With everything else going on, I couldn't believe he was talking about ants.

The professor continued, "Based on her questions and the depth of her research, I assumed she was in a community college or at least high school."

"That's Skye for you. But it's only a seventh-grade science fair project." The DroneTech security guards might have seen the steam coming out of my ears. Skye hijacked Rover, put my career in jeopardy and interrupted the search for Laney's attacker all for some crazy ants. It wasn't the professor's fault, but I was going insane.

"You have a budding scientist on your hands." Dr. Mahowald sounded impressed.

If I don't kill her first. "Could you put her on the phone?"

Skye spoke with an unsteady voice. "Uncle Marty? I'm sorry I skipped school. Dr. Mahowald is like an expert on endangered ants. I couldn't get the Rover car to respond. Mom was going to take me and I didn't know what to do." Skye started crying.

I'd never known how to handle people when they cry. I took a deep breath and told her to stop. "Ok. Don't cry. We'll talk more later. I'll take a taxi to come get you."

"Thanks." She sniffed and, with her voice steadying, asked, "Could you not tell Mom about skipping?"

"We'll talk later," I said, careful not to promise anything. At this point, I'd ground her myself. I gulped as I remembered the Amber Alert.

"Skye, I've got to go. I'll be there soon." I hung up.

I called Sergeant Jackson again.

No greeting again. "Now what? Pretty busy here."

Although I could feel Jackson's lack of love, I needed to give him the update. "Yes, sorry, it's Marty again. I just heard from Skye. She's okay after all."

"What?" Jackson's voice raised from his normal low rumble. "I thought she was missing and you didn't know what happened to her?" He didn't sound pleased.

I babbled, "It's … um … because of her ants. I mean, her science fair."

"What?" Jackson's voice grew more curt and annoyed. "I just put out an Amber Alert."

My nervousness increased. "Stupid science fair. I mean, she's talking to a professor. And Rover's not working."

"What? I started an Amber Alert because of ants? That's crazy." Jackson cursed.

He had no idea. He intimidated me, even when I hadn't done anything wrong. I'd hate to see his reaction if he knew about my fake IRS agent gambit. In a weak voice, I mumbled, "Good news is she's okay after all."

Jackson continued, "I've got to stop it before it goes state-wide. I'll keep the officer on Laney's hospital floor until we can figure out what's going on. But, Golden, get your act together. Let me know right away if anything was taken from Ms. Tran's house."

Yes, sir! I'd better get my act together before Sergeant Jackson got it together for me.

As Jackson hung up, Raj finally called me back. "Hello, Marty. Rover is now working again. I tracked your account. You had a car that went to DroneTech and another that went to Santa Clara University. Why are you at DroneTech? Is it true you are interviewing for another job? You told us that you are not."

"No, no, no. I had lunch there with a friend I used to work with before Rover. Well, he was a friend until security threw me out. Did you know they have flying hammocks in a lab here?" I was still flustered by Jackson.

"Is your niece ok?" A smart man, Raj ignored me when I got too crazy.

"Never mind. Yes, I just heard from her. She's safe. It was a wild goose chase after all."

I'd managed to puzzle Raj more than usual.

"She went to chase geese? I do not think our Rover car would be good at chasing geese. Do not tell marketing. I do not think they need more ideas."

"No, Skye's fine. She went to go talk to a professor. I'm going to go get her."

As we hung up, my taxi arrived. I stepped inside and told the driver to take me to Santa Clara University. I leaned back in the seat and closed my eyes. My heart still raced. Who needed exercise when you could get your blood pumping merely by hanging out with Laney and her daughters?

I found Skye waiting in the biology professor's office at Santa Clara University. When I walked in, she hugged me. I paused to enjoy the moment instead of yelling at her right away. We thanked the professor and left. With Rover working again, I requested a car.

While we waited for it to arrive, I turned to Skye. "What were you thinking? You're only in seventh grade. It's not okay to skip school and bother a college professor for a mere middle school science fair project."

Skye didn't agree with my assessment of her project's lack of importance. "But Dr. Mahowald is an expert in ants and his name kept coming up during my research. He studies the effects of drought and agriculture on ant behavior. I sent him an email with some questions. He answered and I sent him some more questions. He offered to meet to talk more. I had to go."

"School is more important than a science fair project." I adjusted as I noticed her reaction. "It's great you did all that research, but you didn't ask me for permission."

"Mom was going to take me, except she's in the hospital. I didn't think you'd take me and the only time he could meet was at lunch."

Although I respected her philosophy of begging forgiveness

rather than asking permission, I needed Laney back, safe and sound. It was her job to manage the chaos that came with Skye and Megan, not mine. I had to figure out what was going on.

Skye's contrite attitude lasted approximately ten seconds before she got excited again. "You wouldn't believe what we talked about while we waited for you to come get me."

From there on, I didn't understand her rapid-fire, science-geek speech. Although her passion impressed me, it didn't diminish my annoyance that she had gone without permission. Did I need to discipline her? An uncle can't punish his niece and still remain the cool uncle. *Was I even considered the cool uncle?* As Laney's only brother, I had limited competition for the title. In the meantime, I needed to get to her house. Later, I'd have to ponder what to tell Laney about today. Weighing my potential cool factor versus getting in trouble if Laney found out would take some consideration. I'd deal with it after she was safe.

Skye interrupted herself when she noticed that the Rover car approached her school. "Wait, you're not taking me back to school today, are you?" She had a panicked look on her face.

"Why?"

She hadn't looked this scared when I arrived at the university to pick her up. "If I have to go back to school in the middle of the day, then I'll have to talk to Mrs. Quarles."

I remembered my own challenging conversation with her earlier. She'd seemed less concerned about Skye's whereabouts than whether she had an accurate attendance report.

"Yeah. You're not going to make me talk to her, are you?" Skye's eyes nearly bugged out and her face grew pale.

"No, that's okay. I figured I'd pick up Megan a little early today and then I don't have to go back to pick her up again later."

Skye breathed a heavy sigh of relief. "Good luck with that,

Uncle Marty." Her anxiety dispelled, she picked up her phone and ignored me.

I smiled quietly to myself. Kids always seem to fear school officials. Mrs. Quarles had seemed a little prickly, but school administrators could overwhelm a young student not used to dealing with other adults in positions of power. Skye's absence had undoubtedly worried Mrs. Quarles, too.

When we pulled up to the school, Skye shrank into her seat hoping her disappearance would go unnoticed. I let her wait in the car and this time I remembered to tell the Rover car to "stay." Maybe marketing had a good idea after all.

I opened the door to the school office and saw the school secretary standing guard behind the counter. "Hello, Mrs. Quarles. Good to see you again. I'm Megan Tran's uncle and I'm here to pick her up early today."

Mrs. Quarles sniffed. "School is not yet over." She looked down at her papers as if that ended the discussion.

"Yes, I know. Like I said, I need to get her early today." I started to get annoyed. I had to get to Laney's house, help Mace with his investigation, and hadn't received a job offer at DroneTech today. Megan could survive missing an hour of elementary school so I didn't have to return in a few hours to pick her up.

Mrs. Quarles frowned. "This is highly irregular."

"What? Having a student leave a little early?"

"Students need to stay in school until they are dismissed. That's not for another hour and fifty-two minutes." Mrs. Quarles checked the clock on the wall to confirm. Without further consideration, her eyes moved back to her papers.

"I understand, but today I need to take her out early."

"Why?" Rather than wait for my response, she found a piece of paper urgently in need of filing. She turned her back to me and walked across the room to deal with it.

Why? "I am on her pickup list. I am here to pick her up now." I spoke in a loud voice with careful enunciation to make sure she heard and followed my line of logic despite having her back turned to me.

"No need to yell. It is not yet time to pick up students. School is still in session." Mrs. Quarles had not followed. She huffed loudly and walked back to the counter where I stood. Recognizing that her tactics of mystifying and evading the foolish uncle hadn't driven me from the building, she faced me head on.

I hoped she didn't have a secret room with bright lights and a hard chair for a more intensive grilling. Seeing her frown deepen, I didn't want to find out what might be hiding behind the closed doors in the office.

"Look." I sighed, not knowing how to resolve this. Sergeant Jackson told me to get to Laney's house right away and I was wasting time arguing with a school secretary. A metal nameplate reading "Irene Quarles, Secretary" faced me on the counter. "Irene, right?"

"Mrs. Quarles," she corrected with a fastidious sniff. She tilted her head to the side as she squinted at me through her thick, black plastic glasses.

"Ok, sorry, Mrs. Quarles," I said, careful to pronounce her name just as she had, before continuing, "I need to get Megan early today because of my schedule. I can't take the time to bring Skye home and then come back in an hour for Megan. I just want to pick up Megan a little early today. Could you please call her to the office?" Telling Mrs. Quarles that I'd left work early myself didn't seem like my best path forward. I might learn which room hid the interrogation chamber after all.

Mrs. Quarles' eyes narrowed at Skye's name. "You have Skye? She should be in school too. Are you turning in a signed

Unexcused Absence form for her now?" Mrs. Quarles stretched out her bony arm in anticipation.

"No. Sorry, I'll have to do that later. But I'd really like to get Megan now." *Pretty please.*

"This is highly irregular," she repeated. Her voice got shriller and more staccato with each syllable. "Students may only leave early for doctor's appointments or if they get sick in school. Otherwise, it is an unexcused absence."

I didn't know what else to do.

I got flustered.

My options extinguished, I lied. "Um, sure. Well, I should have told you that I need to pick up Megan to take to her doctor's appointment. And Skye turned out to be sick today too. I had forgotten earlier. I'm also bringing her to the doctor." Not my best moment, but no one was there except for the two of us.

Mrs. Quarles stared at me without speaking for several long breaths.

I could feel the disapproval crackling through the air. I squirmed and started sweating.

Finally, she harrumphed. "Are you a regular rule violator, Mr. Golden?"

Shocked that she remembered my name, I didn't answer her hopefully rhetorical question. Telling the truth now wouldn't help me get out of here and over to Laney's house any faster.

Mrs. Quarles huffed. "If you don't follow the school guidelines properly, then we will have to remove you from the approved pickup list."

Can I be removed? I hadn't even known I'd made the list before this week. Now I didn't want to lose my privileges, such as they were. I doubled down on my lie. "I'm sorry for the confusion. I do need to get Megan to her doctor's appointment soon. Could you please call her?"

Again, the long stare. With a little muttering under her breath, Mrs. Quarles turned and picked up an old-fashioned, handheld microphone wired into an old-fashioned switchboard, flicked a switch on the switchboard, and announced, "This is the school office. Please send Megan Tran to the office right away. Thank you." The microphone's feedback screech as she signed off may have woken the dead. At least it should bring Megan to me.

She turned back to me with an imperious glare. "Be certain to send a copy of the Excused Absence form, signed by a doctor to school tomorrow." Wiping her hands of me, she returned to her filing.

Relief poured through my body. I had successfully extracted Megan from school a whole hour and fifty-two minutes early. Only one slight hitch. I had to get a doctor to sign the girls' forms before tomorrow morning without Laney finding out. Detention seemed like a distinct possibility for me. Could I get expelled from a school that I didn't attend? Maybe Sergeant Jackson could sign my excuse form after I checked out Laney's house.

A few minutes later, Megan peeked apprehensively through the office glass door. Her worried face turned into a smile when she saw me in the office. I wondered what she'd done in the first few weeks of a new school that had garnered her an opportunity for an up-close-and-personal interaction with Mrs. Quarles.

When I told Megan we were leaving early, she took my hand, rushing me out of the office with a quick backward glance over her shoulder. As we speed-walked back to the car, I asked, "Why did you look worried when you first came to the office to see Mrs. Quarles?"

"I didn't do it," said Megan.

"Do what?"

"Nothing." She ran and jumped into the car while I decided to let our conversation end there. I had enough to worry about with Laney without delving into Megan's shenanigans.

At least the Rover hadn't disappeared. And neither had Skye. When we got in, Skye looked expectantly at me. "How was Mrs. Quarles?"

"Let's just say I'm surprised she's not named Mrs. Torture."

20

Thursday Midafternoon

Mrs. Kim clapped her hands gleefully when I brought the girls to her apartment a little earlier than planned. Despite our early arrival, she'd already set out teacups and cookies neatly on plates on her table. No one noticed when I took my leave to head over to Laney's house.

The cops had departed from Laney's house and no fancy crime scene tape blocked the door. Vaguely disappointed about not getting to slip past police tape, I stopped dead in my tracks as soon as I walked in her door. I've never pondered the phrase, "getting tossed," but Laney's house defined it at a glance. Clothes from the dressers had been thrown on the floor, drawers were pulled out, and everything in her closets had been shoved to a side or the floors. The bookcase had been pulled over with the books strewn on the floor. The kitchen cabinets were open but nothing looked broken. Fortunately, most of her stuff still sat in sealed boxes in her garage or her house could have been much worse.

I hated to think of her walking into this mess. This week added to her pain. Laney had suffered enough with her husband dying a slow, painful death from cancer when they lived in Spokane.

She'd had to get the girls to school, make sure they had food, and keep them positive, all while taking care of her husband. She even managed to come up with new dream ideas for Megan each night. At least she hadn't needed to deal with Mrs. Quarles at the same time.

Although it went against a long-established, ingrained habit from my childhood, I began to clean up. I couldn't put everything back where it belonged, however, I could get things generally in the right place and not looking like the aftermath of a burglary. I kept an eye open for any clues that could help Mace and me figure this out.

As a child, I'd mastered the concept of cleaning barely enough to pass my mother's muster. It's all about the small details that catch the eye when you walk into a room. Moving messy papers into a drawer, placing the blanket neatly over an unmade bed, and straightening items on top of all surfaces were all secrets to my success in avoiding parental complaints of untidiness.

Now that Mace had told me that he'd have extra security guarding her room, my fears had calmed a bit. Besides, what older brother wouldn't enjoy messing with his younger sister a little? If a sweater ended up in her sock drawer or a book of Megan's landed on Laney's nightstand, I considered that simple payback for something Laney must have done in the past. It kept me alert while I tried to remember if anything was missing in the mess.

While straightening up some papers on a side table in her living room, I got a paper cut. I've never been big on pain, even small pain, so I looked for a Band-Aid to put on it. Laney's bathroom didn't have any or at least none I could locate. Perhaps the thief had stolen her supply of medical basics. It didn't make any sense that a thief would steal only her Band-Aids.

The girls' bathroom looked like a disaster zone with hair doodads and other unknowable supplies strewn everywhere. It hadn't improved at all since I'd last seen it on Monday afternoon when the girls packed to come with me. Opening drawer after drawer, I finally found the only Band-Aid in Laney's house.

Pink. Careful not to ruin it, I placed the pink, yellow, and purple Princess Band-Aid over my cut on my pinkie finger. The girlie Band-Aid wouldn't bother me. I was no longer in elementary school. My coworkers wouldn't make fun of me, or at least not too much. A pink Band-Aid worked fine.

Returning to the living room to continue cleaning, I sighed. Laney had so many paper files laying around. She was so old-fashioned. Keeping all your bills and records electronically takes up no physical space and was so much more logical. Now that Laney had moved to Silicon Valley, I'd have to show her how to enter the modern age and eliminate the dangers of paper cuts forever.

When I moved into Laney's bedroom, I picked up a picture from the floor in her closet. I had no idea why she had this particular framed picture of both of us from high school. Perhaps she kept it so she could secretly laugh at my frosted tips and Birkenstock-covered feet every night. Of course, Laney's own outfit, including a plaid flannel shirt, smiley face slap bracelets, sparkly hair scrunchie, and Doc Martens shoes looked no less ridiculous to modern eyes. I didn't remember any of these fashion trends even surviving past our high school years. I almost threw it away. I could have blamed it on the burglary. But I decided to set the picture in a prominent position on the shelf in their living room. I hoped to see Skye's reaction when she saw it.

After a while, an odd regularity of the mess in the rooms struck me. Almost everything I picked up from the floor belonged to someplace clockwise along the room. It was as if the burglar had trashed her place room by room, methodically tossing items on the floor to their left, leaving space for the thief to rotate clockwise to the right through each room. The thief had been meticulous in trashing her place in a circular pattern. That didn't sound like any normal thief, at least from my vast experience watching thieves on television.

The break-in didn't make any sense to me. Mace was right that the thief hadn't taken Laney's jewelry or valuables. An emergency cash supply even lay untouched in a drawer. I didn't remember anything else expensive that Laney owned. Unless the burglars had stolen her bandages or an old, plaid, vintage shirt from her closet, I discovered nothing missing. It looked like whoever had broken in had gone through all the rooms systematically searching for something. Since all the rooms had a similar clockwise pattern of disarray, it didn't look like they'd found what they were after.

I stretched for a bit and scratched my head.

Then it struck me. Laney's briefcase lay under my desk in my apartment, not here. Maybe the thief was looking for something important in her briefcase. I needed to get home to search through it.

21

Thursday Late Afternoon

Eager to take a closer look at her satchel, I locked up Laney's house and took a Rover car back to my place. When I got back to the building, I picked up the girls from Mrs. Kim's apartment. Although it was already late afternoon, she was reluctant for me to take them. Again, the girls brought their teacups and an extra cookie back to my place. I'd have to remember to return Mrs. Kim's teacups before they all migrated down the hallway to my apartment.

Once in my apartment, the girls sat at the table while I went into my home office and pulled out Laney's satchel. I'd looked in her computer before, to no avail. As an engineer, if something's not on my computer, then it doesn't exist. Maybe HR consultants don't live and die by their computers.

Her briefcase contained almost nothing, perhaps a sign of a new consultant with only a handful of clients. One pocket contained a small box of unopened Milk Duds. Next to them rested their friend, a package of emergency cashews. Another pocket held a few receipts. They seemed to have no value other than for Laney to use in her expense reports.

The main section of her satchel held a notebook and some old newspapers from Spokane. Laney and her husband had lived in Spokane for fifteen years before she'd moved to the Bay Area a few months ago. I set the old newspapers aside and picked up her notebook.

Rifling through her notebook uncovered one startling fact. Laney kept notes for work. *By hand.* She must have started this notebook when she moved here a few months ago and returned to her HR career. One page listed the companies where she'd wanted to contact their HR departments. I wondered if any of these needed a good software engineer. I'd come back and look at her list again later.

Laney had a few sparsely filled pages for several clients. I flipped through, searching for notes on the clients she had scheduled for Monday. The page on Jean Rollag listed his phone number and several questions to ask him about David Saunders. A page mentioned the NorCal Water Agency, but only listed last Friday's date and "Exec Meet and Greet." Underneath that, she'd written "Gonzaga." Nothing else. No mention of Meghan, her harassment complaint, or anything else useful. Laney hadn't taken detailed notes from any of her client meetings.

Fernando got his own page. A small shudder ran down my spine when I saw she had written "drugs?" on the page. Raj had cautioned me about Fernando's relationship with his drug lord father. I hadn't believed him. Laney didn't list any more details on Fernando, with the rest of the page filled with oddly shaped, repeating doodles.

More of Laney's doodling splattered across other pages, but none that I'd deem worthy of calling a drawing. Clearly, our mother's artistic skills had skipped a generation and landed in Laney's girls. Neither Laney nor I could sketch anything more complex than stick figures. Skye and Megan, on the other hand, exhibited far superior skills. Several impressive pictures by the girls decorated the walls in their bedrooms and their refrigerator. Perhaps they'd craft a special picture to thank their Uncle Marty for staying at his apartment for a week? *Well, an uncle can always hope.*

Frustrated by not finding anything useful, I put down the notebook. My fifteen minutes of wasted time had only earned me an encounter with lots of bad doodles and a few meaningless notes on Laney's clients. I didn't find anything that would make her a target.

Idly, I picked up and flipped through the newspaper clippings. Although not usually a packrat, Laney had twenty-year-old copies of the Gonzaga Bulletin, the university newspaper, in her satchel. First, she'd written Gonzaga in her notebook and then these old newspapers. She probably felt homesick for Spokane.

She'd circled articles with a marker. *Pink.* Why is everything in their house pink? The stories read like the typical collegiate newspaper articles I remembered from my day, with complaints about the administration and stories about the sports teams. One article focused on an underground Greek fraternity that had gotten into trouble for a wild party, which the cops had to break up. *What a shocker.* The school couldn't ban an already-banned fraternity so they'd resolved their dilemma by expelling a dozen students.

The final paper's front page highlighted a large fire in the Bulletin building caused by a spark in the printing machines. The fire had destroyed much of the printing equipment and supplies. That explained the sparseness of this edition. Although most of the staff had escaped unharmed, the editor-in-chief had rescued a female student trapped under a fallen roof beam. Laney had circled this story also. An accompanying picture showed the heroic editor, with heavily wrapped hand, his arm around a pretty girl and her arm in a sling. Dazed and disheveled, both kids looked quite the worse for wear. The caption read "Editor William Robert

Allen saves colleague, Nancy Trumbull; loses part of right thumb."
Whoever had managed to publish this paper after that fire must
have some pretty impressive crisis management skills.

Twenty years ago, drones and self-driving cars were still in early
testing stages and Laney hadn't been hospitalized. I needed to stop
wasting time reading old college newspapers and update Sergeant
Jackson about the circular patterns left by the thief in Laney's
house. I returned the papers to her briefcase.

After I left Mace a message, I heard the television turn on in
the living room. The girls must have finished their homework, or
given up. Much earlier today, I'd also given up on getting any of
my Rover work done during daylight hours. I walked to my room
to change out of my interview clothes into a more comfortable pair
of shorts and a Hawaiian shirt. Then I went to check if the girls
had found anything good to watch. "Hey girls, I have an idea for
dinner tonight."

Skye's left eyebrow raised as she looked up with a skeptical
expression on her face. Megan seemed to hunch lower in the
couch.

My cooking's not that bad. "A guy at work talked about a good
restaurant with Mexican-style food." After all, spaghetti tacos don't
qualify as Mexican, nor Italian.

The girls cheered. I cheered too.

At my joining their cheer, Megan started giggling, which
became contagious. After my ill-advised attempt at doing the
chicken dance landed me sprawled on the couch, we settled in and
watched some stupid cartoon. Megan lay her head on my chest and
Skye lay her head on the other end of the couch with her legs on
top of Megan.

Tonight, I'd have an El Salvadorian chicken special for dinner. I
also needed to look into Fernando Hernandez so it would be like
killing two birds with one stone.

⸎ ⸎ ⸎ ⸎ ⸎ ⸎

After a long ride to dinner, our Rover car dropped us in front of Restaurante El Salvador. The restaurant on San Jose's East Side sat on a small street next to a church and a small food market with window signs all in Spanish. I could see small houses and duplexes on the cross streets and a liquor store several buildings down. A group of young men, ranging from high school to the late twenties, loitered smoking outside the liquor store. Across the street, an older couple strolled down the street while two young kids jumped and played around them. While not the best neighborhood in the city, it also didn't look like the home of a Latin American drug lord's son. Perhaps Fernando had some connection to the restaurant and I'd learn something else to report to Mace.

Megan bounced as we walked along the sidewalk. She pulled my arm. "I love Mexican food. I want a bean and cheese burrito."

A typical taqueria-style restaurant greeted us as we entered, with inexpensive plastic furnishings, posters with Latin American scenes on the walls, and a phenomenal aroma. A young waitress waved us to a table.

The menus were all in Spanish. Worse, they contained no obvious section of burritos or tacos. I knew a few Spanish words — it's impossible to survive in California otherwise. None of these words looked familiar. I mentally kicked my high school self. Studying Spanish in high school, instead of French, would have been much more useful later in life, like right now. Of course, there were quite a few things I'd do differently from then, given a second chance.

At least, I'd chosen to study French for an excellent reason. My high school girlfriend at the time registered for French, so I followed along. Show me any sixteen-year-old boy whose brain functions weren't impacted by similar hormonal logic.

Pursing her lips and squinting, Skye scanned her menu before putting it down on the table. "This is all in Spanish. I can't read it."

"You'll need to study Spanish when you get to high school." *Uncles truly add value.*

Skye scoffed. "Well, that doesn't help me now."

"It smells like bean and cheese burritos so that's ok." Megan's one-track mind had clamped down hard on her dinner plans.

The waitress came over to our table with three glasses of water. She started in Spanish before switching to English. "Welcome. How can I help you?"

I'd never understood why everyone took one look at me and automatically assumed I spoke only English. Hawaiian shirts, shorts, and flip-flops were sold worldwide. The same thing had happened when I'd traveled to France once years ago. Everyone had taken one look at me and then spoken in English. Before I'd left America, people had warned me to speak French while in France to avoid rude reactions. I'd tried, but the instant I spoke in French, the locals answered me in English. It was as if I offended their sensitivities and they couldn't bear to hear their blessed language besmirched by my horrid accent.

Finally remembering to answer the waitress, I confirmed her guess. "Hello. Do you have any menus in English?"

"Just Spanish. Our customers usually speak Spanish." The waitress paused, her English held just a hint of an unexpected accent, which must have been El Salvadorian. "Have you had traditional food from El Salvador before?"

Skye answered first. "No. Is it like Mexican?"

"A little, but also different," said the waitress. "Maybe you want to start with some yucca frita? It's a very popular appetizer."

Megan jumped on this. "No, we don't want yucky fruit." She wrinkled her nose. While Skye didn't respond, she also looked rather dubious about the suggestion.

"Yucca frita is fried yucca," said the waitress, trying to be helpful.

"We don't want anything yucky." Megan pounded her small fist on the table for emphasis.

Case closed. I shot the waitress an apologetic look. "I think we'll skip the appetizers for tonight."

Megan spoke up again to avoid the risk of getting anything yucky. "I want a bean and cheese burrito for dinner." She crossed her arms and sat back smiling, satisfied with her order.

The waitress winced. "I'm sorry. We don't have burritos." She rallied, "But we do have pupusa." She smiled at Megan.

Megan recoiled and her face screwed up into a grimace. "I don't want to eat poo-poo for dinner either." Although still silent, Skye turned a bit green.

My throat had gone dry. I might have looked a bit green, too. I took a quick sip of water. The positive vibes I'd been feeling from the girls earlier in the apartment just got mired in yucky poo-poo. Bruce's enthusiasm for this restaurant had convinced me to bring the girls and I'd figured I could take the chance to ask about Fernando without causing a stir. With the girls along for dinner, we looked like a normal family.

Now, this restaurant seemed like a terrible idea and I was in a pickle. "I'm sorry. The girls aren't very adventurous eaters yet. Is there something basic that you'd suggest?"

The waitress thought before asking the girls, "Do you like black beans and rice?"

Still wary, both girls gave small nods.

Phew. Not the most fervent response that I'd ever seen, but I'd take it.

"Ok, I'll bring you some." With a relieved smile, she turned to me. "And you, sir?"

"I'd like your chicken special, pollo." I think I pronounced it correctly and didn't further insult the waitress. Sometimes my

Spanish comes out sounding more like I have a Bulgarian accent. Of course, I'm not quite sure since I'd never met anyone from Bulgaria. In any case, my Spanish accent definitely doesn't sound like I'd immigrated from a native Spanish-speaking country.

The waitress pondered, probably trying to translate my words. "I think you mean "Pollo encebollado." That's very popular here. It's a traditional El Salvadorian pollo dish with onions and sauce that we eat growing up." She pointed helpfully to the item on the menu with a description that I couldn't read.

"Yes, that must be it. I'll have that." I wanted to get the order out of the way without starting an international incident. The waitress nodded and escaped to the kitchen.

Megan crossed her arms and glared at me. "I thought we were going to Mexican for dinner. Why would you take us to a place where they eat poo-poo and yucky stuff?"

Massaging my temples to keep a headache from starting, I shrugged. I'd forgotten how annoying it could be to take kids out to dinner. I tried to appease her. "Everything smells great here. Why don't we wait and see what it tastes like?" It's not like I could tell her that I'd dragged them into the middle of a potentially dangerous drug lord's den because I'd heard they had a great chicken special from a colleague in three separate twelve-step programs who couldn't resist over-sharing at work.

Megan frowned, slumped in her chair with her arms still crossed and pretended to read the menu. Skye looked around at the posters and other patrons in the restaurant, anywhere except at me and Megan. Another delightful family dinner brought to you by Uncle Marty.

The waitress returned a short time later carrying two identical, bright red plates. She put them down in front of the girls. A sphere of black beans about the size of a golf ball rested carefully in the middle of a bed of aromatic white rice. Black sauce from the warm black beans oozed down into the steaming rice.

Both girls leaned forward with renewed excitement.

"Awesome. It looks like a black bean volcano," said Megan.

The red plate enhanced the perception of a lava flow across the mountainous field of white rice. I'd never seen these two ingredients served together in this way.

Skye used her fork to dig exploratory lava tunnels for the black bean sauce to escape out of the surrounding white rice mountain. Megan expanded on her sister's idea by reenacting a black bean lava eruption. She flicked small bits of her black beans across her plate and onto the table.

Before the eruptions got too dangerous to the surrounding community, I suggested, "How about eating your food instead of playing with it?"

Small sulks of disappointment greeted my buzzkill comment. But, as they tasted their food, contented smiles quickly spread across their faces. The waitress soon returned with my plate. She looked at the girls but they were too busy eating to notice. She nodded at me with satisfaction and left again.

I dug in. *Delicious.* The whole plate of chicken with sautéed onions, garlic, and some tomatoes over rice made me reminisce about the El Salvadorian countryside. Quite an accomplishment delivered by a chicken dish considering that I'd never traveled south of Houston.

We ate for a few minutes, enjoying the food in silence. Sensing my opportunity would vanish soon, I reached over to Megan's plate and scooped up a forkful of her food.

"Hey! That's mine," said Megan. Black beans and rice had risen to her "Do Not Touch" level. The waitress had pulled off a hit for the girls.

I tasted it. The chef must have added some secret herbs and spices to make the black beans so superb. "That's really good." I restrained myself from taking more and sparking a bigger argument.

Eventually, we slowed down. The waitress returned to our table. "Did you like the pollo encebollado?"

"Delicious. And thank you for the recommendation for the girls." I pointed to their nearly empty plates as proof.

She nodded, with a small smile on her face, and started to move away.

I raised a hand to stop her. "Excuse me. I was wondering if you know someone named Fernando Hernandez?"

She froze, her smile immediately disappearing as her eyes widened and her mouth opened. "I'm sorry. I have to go." She bolted back to the kitchen.

Skye looked at me. I could feel the eye roll getting queued up. "Why did you scare away the waitress?"

"I just asked her if she knew someone who your mom was going to talk to on Monday."

Before Skye could reply, a stocky, older lady stalked out of the kitchen carrying an industrial-sized, wooden stirring spoon in her hand like a sword. She advanced on our table. In what felt like an instant, she stood in front of me with a stern look on her face and her weapon pointed right at my face.

"Why you talk about Señor Hernandez? You scare Gabriela." She spoke with a thick accent.

Surprised, I was more than a little concerned that her stirring spoon might have a hidden sword blade ready to flick open. "I'm sorry. My sister was going to meet Fernando Hernandez but she wasn't able to keep her appointment because she got hurt."

"She hurt? You should learn not to talk about him here." She leaned in closer until I could smell the garlic on her breath. She lowered her voice as she spoke again in a voice roughened by smoking or, perhaps swordplay. "Do you want girls to get hurt, too?"

At this threat, the girls paled and huddled together. None of us had expected to be accosted by an intimidating chef wielding a scary wooden spoon with unknown, possibly dangerous properties that could hurt us.

I tried to keep my voice from squeaking. "I only wanted to find out if he was a frequent customer here or, maybe, owned the restaurant?"

"Stop foolish questions. You leave now and don't come back." Even though she spoke in a low voice, her command struck me like a blow.

Megan overcame her fear. "What? But, Uncle Marty … I like the black bean volcano." Her voice came out with an odd combination of anger and whimper.

The chef calmed a bit as she glanced at the girls. "Girls. You come back another time. Maybe when your mother is better. Do not bring him." She thrust the spoon at me to make sure everyone understood who she meant.

But, I liked the volcano too.

Concerned and chastened, I requested the check. Without another word, she glared at me and backed into the kitchen to sheathe her weapon. Seconds later, our waitress scurried out of the kitchen with downcast eyes, holding the check.

I took out my credit card and handed it over. "Do you have a bathroom?"

Instinctively, she half-pointed at a small swinging door that led to a corridor running alongside the kitchen. Then she yanked her hand back to her side as if it had been burned and clasped it with her other hand. "But, sir …" Helplessly, she looked over her shoulder at the kitchen and then back at me.

"Yes. Yes. We're leaving. I need to go to the restroom first." Annoyed, I strode off. Scary stirring spoon or not, some chef couldn't stop me from going to the bathroom. We had a long ride back home.

I pushed through the wooden, swinging door into a dimly lit

corridor. The corridor ran deeper into the building than I had expected from the dining room. Beyond a few closed doors, signs for the men's and women's bathrooms glowed with a barely visible, green light. I walked down an old, creaking wood floor to the men's room.

I put my hand on the knob. As I pushed the door open, someone grabbed me from behind. "Hey!" I said, alarmed as two large men yanked me back down the corridor and thrust me through a now-open door into a back room.

22

Thursday Evening

The men shoved me into the room and took up positions by the door. I stumbled forward but caught myself before I fell. I looked up to see three men in their thirties and forties sitting behind a long table set for eight. Shadows lurked in the corners while two younger men in their twenties stood to the sides of the table, in addition to the two behind me. Somehow, I didn't think I had been selected as the lucky, eighth person to complete their dinner party, or that ordering the chicken special came with a surprise trip to this private dining room. Perhaps the security team from DroneTech had notified the restaurant of my visit.

The Latino men didn't look friendly. In fact, one of the seated men scowled at me. "Who are you and why are you here?" His accent sounded authentic, with no hint of Bulgarian.

I decided not to point this out and simply answered, "I'm Marty Golden. I came here for dinner."

His face twisted. "Then why are you asking questions about Fernando Hernandez?"

"Uh ... my sister, Laney Tran, was going to meet with him and I wanted to talk to him too."

His scowl deepened as he studied me. I didn't even believe myself. I'd never been very good at lying. Perhaps the man could read my mind and knew that I wanted to find Hernandez so Mace could investigate him. The man shifted his eyes briefly to the two young men standing at the sides of the table. "Search him," he commanded.

One of the men grabbed my arms while the other one patted me down. I had no weapons, not even a stirring spoon. The man pulled my wallet out of my back pocket. He flipped it open and saw the fake IRS badge where my driver's license usually sat. I hadn't removed it from yesterday's adventures.

"Federales!" shouted the man.

The room erupted in turmoil. Chairs flew in all directions as six of the men pulled guns from beneath their shirts or behind their backs and pointed them at me.

"No, no. No federales," I yelled back. "Me engineer. I work for Rover, not government." I couldn't even speak English at that moment. I didn't care as long as they understood I wasn't a threat. My hands shook in the air as I held my breath.

Everyone stood still. Before I passed out, the man who seemed to be in charge, still seated at the table, asked, "I have not heard of Rover. Are they another gang?" He gestured with a beer in his hand, which I much preferred to his colleagues' guns.

One of the younger men puffed out his chest. "We will take care of this Rover gang." He kept eyeing me for target practice.

I answered before they tested their weapons on me. "No, no! Rover isn't a gang. It's a company that drives people around. I'm an engineer there. I help make it work."

The man next to me kept flipping through my wallet. He pulled out one of my business cards. This one had Rover's logo on it and my name and email. *Whew.* He stepped over to the table and showed it to the man in charge.

When the man in charge reached for the card, I saw he had a tattoo near his wrist of a hula dancer. He threw a quick glance at the card before dismissing it. "Rover? Like the dog? Why such a stupid name for your company?"

I took a small, shaky breath. Until that point, I hadn't realized that you could actually hear your own heartbeat if it's pumping fast enough. "I don't know. Maybe marketing thought it would be funny to say 'Come Rover' and our car would show up."

The tattooed man pursed his lips and gave a slow nod as he pondered this marketing strategy. "Sí. That could make a funny ad on social media." Everyone's an advertising expert nowadays. He continued, "So, you're a driver?"

"I'm a software engineer. It's a driverless car service."

"You can order a car that drives people around without a driver?"

Off to the side, one of the young men looked stricken by the concept.

I didn't want to confirm that my work might put the young man out of a job while he still pointed a gun in my direction. "Sort of."

The tattooed man made a small waving gesture with his hands. The guns went down but still stayed in their hands. Software engineers don't scare normal people, let alone gangs.

After taking a deeper breath, I could no longer hear my heart beating in my ears. If I hadn't needed to go to the bathroom before, I definitely needed to go now. Maybe I'd live long enough to get to one.

The tattooed man chuckled to himself. "I have an idea."

Any idea that didn't involve gunfire was fine with me.

"Can you order a driverless car sent to the boss?" he asked.

"Who is the boss?" I asked without thinking.

He grunted. "Fernando."

So, tattooed man was only in charge when Fernando isn't around. "Yes. Sure." I paused before adding, "But only from my office." My own inspiration surprised me.

The tattooed man believed me this time. Maybe everyone's an advertising expert, but not everyone's an expert software engineer. He didn't stop to consider that a car service wouldn't be much use if it could only be ordered from your office. He took out a pen and wrote on the back of my business card. "Here, you call this number and you will find out where to send the car to him tomorrow." He hesitated. "The boss, he is staying at a friend's house tonight."

The other men snickered at this but stopped when the tattooed man glared at them.

His dark eyes glittered when he turned back to me. "You don't tell anyone and make sure you get it to him tomorrow or we will come find you at Rover. And your sister. You won't like that if we have to come find you. Understand?"

I nodded as my heartbeat sped up again. I stuffed the card he handed me into my pocket.

He set his beer down on the table and pointed a stubby, scarred finger at me. "Tomorrow, I want you to send a red Land Rover to Fernando. He will like a big, big one. With armor plating. And champagne. Yes, he likes champagne. You will do this." He squinted at me with beady eyes, checking to make sure I understood.

It wasn't a question.

"Uh …," I stammered. "I'm really sorry, but we only have small, electric cars. Good mileage and they're cheap."

"You think I am cheap?" The guns went back up. "You think Fernando wants cheap?" The tattooed man was not amused.

I stopped breathing again. Sweat poured down my sides. "No, no. We are cheap. Not you. It is us. Rover. It is marketing that is cheap."

The tattooed man waited for what felt like an eternity. I held my breath while he glowered at me.

Finally, he spoke. "The boss does not want a cheap car. You bring him a red Land Rover tomorrow for a test drive if you know what's good for you." He took a swig of his beer. "Now get out of here with your cheap cars and don't come back."

I let out my breath. My wallet was thrust back into my hands and I was shoved out the door into the corridor before I could blink. I decided I didn't need to go to the bathroom as much as I had thought. I scampered back down the corridor to the restaurant, away from the now-closed door of the private dining room.

When I came back through the swinging door, the young waitress sat at the table talking to the girls. I'd been gone for longer than expected.

"You took a long time," complained Megan.

I could only manage, "Let's go." Paying with my phone took mere seconds before we walked out into the street. I didn't stop looking over my shoulders until we were safely in the Rover car on our way back to my apartment. The girls didn't seem to notice my silence as they planned what they would tell their mother about yucky poo-poo and delicious, black bean volcanoes. No one had ever pointed a gun at me, let alone six. At least, not since some water guns during hot summer days growing up.

Later that evening, Megan asked, "What should we dream about tonight?"

"I don't really feel up to a new idea —" I started, still shaken from the restaurant.

Megan interrupted, "You have to. You promised. Mom always gives me ideas. I want Mom to come home." Her eyes welled up and she started to sniffle.

I couldn't let this get out of hand. Laney was safe, protected by a police officer, and she'd be home any day now. Without pausing to think, I proposed the first idea that popped into my head, combining a previous, award-winning concept with tonight's successful dinner. "How about dreaming of dogs and volcanos?"

This earned me a full eye roll from Skye.

"No, that's scary. Do you want me to have a nightmare?" Megan's tears dried up as she gave me a look filled with horror.

"Sorry. How about dreaming of Labrador puppies eating black beans?"

Skye snorted. "Wouldn't that make a dog sick? My friend's dog ate some human food and he threw up all over the house."

"How would I know? I've never had a dog before." Maybe only movie dogs ate food from the table. It's probably from their specialized actor training.

Both girls turned their heads to watch me, with their dark hair spread all over their faces. How did girls with long hair avoid pulling their own hair and waking themselves up when they sleep? I thought it would bother me to have hair in my face while I slept. Of course, plenty of men with beards slept perfectly well.

I'd rarely seen my own daughter, Amanda, sleep when she was this age. My kids had lived with their mother since our divorce soon after Eli's birth. In any case, long hair had never interrupted my own sleep, and with each passing year, it seemed less and less likely to affect me. If I asked Amanda to explain, my text messages would either go ignored or she'd send me links to hair restoration websites. This had to remain just another great, unsolved mystery of the world.

"Earth to Uncle Marty?" Megan brought me back to my current dilemma.

The girls stared at me now, patience waning, curious to see what crazy idea would pop out next. The pressure grew. I'd wasted time getting sidetracked rather than brainstorming for brilliant ideas. Needing to avoid my third strike, I proposed another idea based on my previous successes.

"Dream about a Labrador puppy playing with you and your

mom in a park." *Ka-boom. Nailed it!* Anticipating my congratulatory high-five, I put out my hand.

Megan squirmed a little on her pillow. "That's kinda boring. And you shouldn't use the same dream every night." She ignored my hand.

Didn't nail it. "Well, sleep is supposed to be boring … so you can fall asleep."

With only a little grumbling they accepted my excuse after I promised to do better tomorrow. I turned out the light and stood up from the side of their bed. Maybe Laney didn't invent new ideas every night and simply used something that happened earlier in her day? However, after leaving out any mention of drones holding up floating hammocks, security guards tackling you, klaxons, worldwide drone tracking control centers, Amber Alerts, South American drug gangs and weapon carrying chefs, I didn't have any more creativity left tonight. I wanted the girls to sleep through the night rather than causing them new nightmares.

As I closed the bedroom door and left the girls' room, Megan's sleepwalking gave me an idea. From the front closet, I took some string. To double-check, I opened the office doors and confirmed the room was empty. Pulling the doors shut, I tied and knotted the string tightly around the handles of the two office doors. I pulled on the handles but couldn't budge the doors without serious effort. No one could get inside without taking off the string. That should keep a sleep-walking Megan out of the office and in the right bed.

Finally triumphant, I high-fived myself before crawling into bed too. Tomorrow, I had to locate a red Land Rover.

23

Friday Morning

I walked out of my bedroom in the morning dressed and ready in my normal work attire. Working in Silicon Valley had its perks. Seeing that my office doors still had the string tied around them made me smile. I'd finally stopped Megan's sleepwalking, or her defiance.

I opened the door to the girls' room and discovered that only Skye lay there. "What? Where's Megan?"

Mumbling greeted me. Not a morning person, Skye buried her head under her pillow.

Pulse accelerating, I hurried out to check my apartment's entrance door. The door indicator showed that it hadn't been opened since we got home from the restaurant. I didn't find Megan hiding in the kitchen, closet, or living room. I walked back to check the bathroom or if I had missed her in my room.

As I passed, the office doors started shaking. "Hey, let me out of here," yelled Megan.

"Megan? What are you doing in there? I'm right here. Let me get these strings off the door." I couldn't untie the taut string wrapped around the door knobs. I went back to the kitchen, grabbed a pair of scissors, and cut through the string.

Megan burst out of the room into the hall as both doors swung open and banged into the opposite wall. "Uncle Marty, that's mean. I'm going to tell Mommy that you locked me inside." She stormed off to the bathroom and slammed the door.

Skye stood staring at me from her doorway and shook her head. "Geez, Uncle Marty. That's dangerous. What if there was a fire?" She too slammed the door, leaving me alone in the hallway, rubbing my head, bewildered. *But ... how'd that happen?*

Today hadn't gotten off to a good start. I had to find a way to dig myself out of this hole. Somehow, I didn't think frozen waffles or peanut butter sandwiches would save the day for Uncle Marty. Uncles were supposed to be heroes, not villains. Besides, I didn't want to get in trouble with Laney. Not on a day when I had to find a red Land Rover and watch Mace arrest Rollag.

I shouted down the hallway. "Hey girls! Get ready for school quickly and we can go out for a fast breakfast before I drop you off."

Cheering broke out, which saved my hero self-image, for today.

In record time, we made it into a Rover car. Yesterday morning, I'd noticed that Starbucks served veggie smoothies and some healthy breakfast options, as well as coffee. *Who knew?* The girls could get some healthy vegetables and, hopefully, would forget this morning's little incident.

As I got out of the car, I told it to "Stay." I'd started to appreciate the value of this idea from the marketing team. Although, I'd avoid telling them so we didn't have more crazy ideas thrown at the engineers under ridiculously short timelines.

My shoelace flopped on the ground. As I knelt to tie my shoes, I got a good whiff of fish sauce and my hands felt sticky from the laces that I hadn't cleaned.

"My hands got dirty," I told the girls. "Go order one of the smoothies and something small, like a yogurt, if you want. I'll run to the restroom first to wash my hands."

When I came out, Skye gestured for me to hurry up. The cashier stood waiting impatiently while a short line had formed behind the girls. I walked up and ordered. "Strawberry yogurt, please. And Tea. Earl Grey. Hot."

The cashier didn't find my Trekkie humor amusing. "How else would tea be served?"

"Is Brody here?" I asked while I paid for our order.

The cashier tilted her head and glanced skeptically at me, not believing me cool enough to associate with Brody. "No, he works later today."

I might not look like Brody's friends, but the girls would have gotten a kick out of meeting him. We moved to the side to wait for our order.

Skye gave me a full report about her order. "I ordered a small, Sweet Greens smoothie. It has green juice from celery, cucumber, and spinach. Then they add Greek yogurt, banana, and a little mango juice. And you can even add fresh kale to it. So, I did that too. And I got a spinach, egg wrap. I hope that's ok, Uncle Marty?"

No complaints from me. She'd ordered four green vegetables. "Sure." I didn't even know that cucumber and spinach could be made into juice. Grinding up spinach made pesto, not juice, or was that basil? I wouldn't know as my pesto came pre-made in a jar. The English habit of eating cucumber sandwiches had always sounded odd to me. An occasional cucumber might not ruin a salad, but you needed to add more substantial fillings to create a complete sandwich.

"Yeah, I wanted to eat healthy like Mom does."

Her words reminded me how much the girls missed their mother. I needed to help Mace figure out what was going on before Laney came home from the hospital and she lost her police protection. "I'll check with your mom's doctor again. She'll come home soon. Maybe we'll call her again after school." Mace had to wrap up this case soon.

Both girls grinned. Skye might have done a little happy dance, even if she would never admit it.

I turned to ask Megan about her order, but the exciting news had turned her helpful.

"I'll go get some napkins." Megan darted off and grabbed enough napkins for an army. This reminded me again of Laney. She always grabbed an excessive number of napkins, whether she was eating ice cream or crackers.

The barista called our order and we went to pick it up at the counter. Skye grabbed a green drink and a wrap that looked like it had spinach, tomatoes, and eggs inside. Next to it, along with my yogurt and tea was a tall chocolate-colored drink with a big topping of whipped cream with sprinkles and a croissant.

I squinted at the food. "Megan, what did you order?"

"I ordered a smoothie and a croissant like you told me." She grabbed the chocolate smoothie and licked her croissant. She must have felt a safety precaution was in order.

Still confused, I asked, "But, what is it? It looks like a milkshake."

"It's a chocolate smoothie with extra whipped cream, sprinkles, and a chocolate croissant. It's on the menu." Megan took a big bite of the croissant and, as chocolate spread across her face, demonstrated that Starbucks hadn't skimped on their croissant filling.

"Um," I didn't know where to start. "That's not very healthy."

"Chocolate is a bean and beans are vegetables, right? And there's a banana in my smoothie so I even have fruit too." The whipped cream spread across Megan's face as she took a big sip.

I grinned. How could I complain when she used her brains to outsmart me? I'd need to remember the bit about chocolate being a bean to use some other time myself. The girls made quite the dynamic duo — each clever in her own way.

We got back into the Rover car to take the girls to school and me to work. When we pulled up to the school, I saw that my favorite school secretary, Mrs. Quarles, directed the drop-off lane flow on Fridays with paramilitary precision. *Uh-oh.*

The car pulled into the driveway and stopped. Mrs. Quarles opened the back door. "Everybody out. We have lots of students who need to get to school today."

The girls grabbed their backpacks and scrambled out the door.

Mrs. Quarles stopped them. "Skye and Megan Tran. Do you have your signed Excused Absence Forms?"

They stood mute, frozen in place. I hollered through the back door, "I forgot them this morning, Mrs. Quarles. I'll make sure they bring them on Monday."

"Yes, that is quite important. We need to have all forms returned in a timely manner or the girls will have to stay late on detention." She trailed off as she took a closer look at both girls. "What's that on your faces? Is that whipped cream?" She turned to look at me with her mouth open and horror filling her eyes.

Both girls also turned back to look at me, eyes wide with scared expressions on their faces. During the ride, Skye must have decided she needed to share some of Megan's smoothie.

"Yes, it was a special morning so I got a smoothie for the girls."

The girls exhaled as I threw myself under the bus. The girls made their escape to their classrooms as Mrs. Quarles' hawklike attention shifted fully to me. *Go, girls, go!*

Her vision honed in on the cup lying discarded on the backseat. "A chocolate smoothie with whipped cream and sprinkles? Highly irregular and extremely unhealthy."

Idly, I wondered how Mrs. Quarles knew the Starbucks

chocolate smoothies came with sprinkles as none were left by now. I decided not to probe.

She continued her diatribe. "You are aware that's a milkshake, are you not? It's not a proper breakfast for students. Rule 24 reminds parents that eating a healthy breakfast is the foundation of a good education. We sent home flyers outlining healthy eating choices to get signed at the beginning of this year. Obviously, you did not read it. I'll send another home with the girls for you to sign tonight."

"It had a banana …" I tried Megan's excuse before my voice trailed off.

"Indeed." Mrs. Quarles stood, her head tilted at just the right angle, contemplating me through the car's door with her hands on her hips.

A car farther back in line beeped at us. Easy to be brave when Mrs. Quarles' eyes weren't boring into you.

"Well, I don't have time to lecture you this morning with the rush. Move along and I'll just make a note to have a word with the girls' mother about more healthy eating choices." She jotted a note in her notebook and slammed the car door shut.

Chalk up another great start to my day. Not only would Laney hear about how Uncle Marty had locked Megan into the office creating a safety hazard, but Mrs. Quarles would tell her that I had fed the girls chocolate milkshakes for breakfast. Unless I figured out how to get their Excused Absence Forms signed, the girls would have to stay late on Monday for detention. And if we couldn't figure out who was after Laney, she could die. Uncle Marty would lose his hero status for sure.

Sigh.

Raj looked up when I dropped my stuff at my desk. "Oh, do you still work here?"

"Very funny." Before Raj returned his attention back to his work, I asked, "Do you know where I could borrow a red Land Rover today?"

"You know all our Rover cars are white, not red."

"No. I need a Land Rover, not a Rover. And it needs to be red."

Raj's face grew perplexed. "Why do you need a car? You work here. All our rides are free."

To keep my health, and receiving the free rides, I needed to bring a red Land Rover to Fernando Hernandez today. I knew what was good for me. I explained what had happened last night with Hernandez's drug gang at the restaurant.

Raj's leg started bouncing again. "I told you chasing Fernando Hernandez was not a good idea."

His leg had developed that tic this week. I wasn't sure if his caffeine overdose or sitting near me was to blame. "You were right, but I think he may be my best lead so far. His gang seemed like they wouldn't have a problem killing someone in the hospital."

Always the rational engineer, Raj said, "So, now you will call the police."

"Not quite yet. I have to bring this car to him first. I should be fine. They were interested in Rover so they wouldn't shoot the messenger." *Would they?*

"We don't have a red Land Rover."

"I'll have to find one."

While Raj returned to his work, I checked online for where I could rent the car today. Only two places in the whole Bay Area rented Land Rover cars. Our company, and our competitors, had almost eliminated the rental car business. The closest rental agency, located in Palo Alto, couldn't rent me a car until after lunch.

With nothing left to do but worry, I tried to focus on my own work for a few hours.

Shortly before lunch, Raj looked up when I slapped my forehead. "What?" he said.

I shook my head. "I forgot the business card with Fernando Hernandez's phone number written on it. I must have left it in my pants pocket from yesterday. I don't have time to run home to get the number, get the car, take it to Hernandez's, and get my work done." I groaned and put my head down on my desk for a rest.

Then I remembered I didn't need the business card. Fernando Hernandez's phone number was in Laney's calendar on her computer. I looked up in triumph. "Ha!"

"Now what?" asked Raj.

"I'm off to the races."

Raj shook his head. "Better race the Land Rover. I think they are faster than our cars."

I didn't respond. Instead, I pulled out my phone. With one, red Land Rover rented for the afternoon, I had no more excuses. My palms sweating and my heart racing, I called Hernandez.

24

Friday Noon

"Hóla?" answered a voice with a strong Latin American accent.

"Uh, hello. Is this Fernando Hernandez?" I wasn't sure whether I wanted a confirmation or not.

"It is. How are you today?" Hernandez replied with surprising hospitality.

"Um. Fine thanks. My name is Marty Golden —"

"Very pleased to meet you, Mr. Golden. I am Fernando Hernandez." Hernandez's politeness didn't match the typical rudeness of most Silicon Valley residents, all in a hurry to make it big. This proved to me that he must have grown up outside of the U.S. Perhaps drug lords teach their children good manners.

Swallowing hard, I said, "Mr. Hernandez, —"

He interrupted again, "No, you must call me Fernando."

I'd never met such a polite gang leader. Of course, I'd never met any gang leaders. "Ok. Fernando, could you give me your address? I'm supposed to take a red Land Rover to you today. It wasn't ready earlier, but I can bring it to you in an hour or two."

After a moment of silence, Fernando said, "I am very sorry. There must be some mistake. I did not buy a new car."

"I know. This is for a test drive. Your, uh, colleagues insisted that I bring you this car today."

"Sí, sí, sí. That is so very nice of them. It is not even my birthday. I have never heard of such a wonderful gift. Tell me, Mr. Golden, which dealer do you work for?"

"I don't work for a dealer. I work for the Rover car service."

"Ah. I have heard of them. Good for you. What a cool company."

That threw me off. Rover didn't feel cool to me. Our cafeteria didn't have "Pecan Month" and we didn't have dueling yoga rooms. It was work. Granted, I enjoyed my work, mostly. All my friends also worked in tech companies. After all, we lived in Silicon Valley. I hadn't expected a South American drug lord's son to have opinions on the coolness of my employer.

I decided to take a risk. After all, he couldn't hurt me over the phone. "Yeah, thanks. By the way, I'm Laney Tran's brother. Do you remember her?"

"Oh, Sí. She is from Human Resources, is she not?" Fernando's tone cooled.

"That's right. Did you talk to her on Monday?"

"I did. She called very early in the morning. She woke me up." Fernando's voice had turned indignant and then turned wistful, "You see, we had a magnificent party on Sunday evening. It was wonderful — great food, great wine, beautiful women. Ahhhh." He paused as if to close his eyes as he reminisced. Then he continued, "You should have come."

I was disoriented by his rapid personality changes and his retroactive invitation. "Wasn't her appointment with you at nine o'clock?"

Fernando snorted. "Sí, sí, sí. She insisted. That is much too early in the morning for work. I do not like to start work before eleven. Your sister, she started asking questions right away. I told her that was not the right way to have a polite conversation. There was not even cappuccino." Now he sounded perplexed at the very thought.

Despite myself, I chuckled, imagining the interaction between the two of them. "Yes. Laney can be a bit intense. She gets up and runs at five every morning, so nine is practically lunch-time for her."

"Aiyaiya! That is not civilized." Fernando sounded distressed and disbelieving. "She mentioned some kind of sexual complaint. Can you imagine? I don't know who is complaining about my sex. I have been with many women and there have never been any complaints. My wife, she has nothing to complain about. She does complain about many things. She would not call Human Resources. Did she call Human Resources?" Fernando's accent strengthened as his words sped up.

I couldn't keep up with his rapid-fire speech and I didn't know how to respond. "I can't believe your wife called Human Resources either."

Fernando raised his voice. "So, she did call Human Resources."

"No ... I didn't mean that. I mean, I don't know."

He kept going without pausing to interpret my stumbling response. "And to start talking about sex before we've had coffee in the morning is not appropriate. I told your sister that I would talk to her only if she came to my house so I could show her. She said she wasn't interested. How is that possible? It is very rude. I told her she was making me mad." Fernando was making even less sense now, but he seemed angry with Laney, me, and his wife.

An angry South American drug lord's son struck me as a dangerous person to upset.

Uncertain if I wanted to hear the answer, I asked, "What did you want to show her?"

"She was not interested. You should come." Fernando insisted, "Yes, come to my house. I will show you. And bring the red Rover over."

I heard yelling in the background. Fernando bellowed something back in rapid-fire Spanish. The loud, intense shouting match lasted a while.

The noise and fury worried me. Laney was investigating some kind of complaint against this drug lord, but I didn't understand why.

Fernando returned his attention to me. "Mr. Golden, you will come," he commanded.

I had only one acceptable answer. "Okay. I will come over. Where do you live?" I didn't think he would do anything to me in broad daylight in his own home. At least, I didn't think so. To be safe, I'd have my phone at the ready to call Mace. I wanted to get to the bottom of this. If Fernando had done something or knew something, I needed to find out. He gave me his address. He lived close to the car rental agency so at least I wouldn't waste a lot of time.

Less than an hour later, I stepped down from the Land Rover outside a small, well-kept house. The bright, red car matched several of the plants in his yard. Flowers and flowering succulents were scattered in a thick patch under the windows and around the edges of a small rock garden lawn. He might have attempted to murder my sister, but at least his yard looked nice.

I carried my phone with Mace's contact open on the screen. My finger hovered over the dial icon in case this went even worse than last night. As I approached the house, the front door flew open. A large man approached me and flung his arms open wide. Slowing, not sure what he'd try, I almost called Mace, but I hesitated. The man carried no gun, wooden spoon, or any other obvious weapons. None of the other gang members from the restaurant appeared. I checked behind me to be sure the two from yesterday evening hadn't snuck up on me again.

When the man stepped near, he reached out and pulled me into a hug. "Welcome, welcome!" He kissed first my left cheek, then my right. "You must be Marty, I can call you Marty, right? Now you are at my home, we are friends."

Looking behind me, he started bouncing on his toes. He gestured to the Land Rover that I'd parked in front of his house. "Bonito! What a beautiful car. We must drive it soon."

Again overwhelmed, I managed to keep my balance as he released me from his bear hug. "Nice to meet you. And you are Mr. Hernandez? Fernando?"

"Of course." Fernando beamed. "Do you want to see my meat?"

"No." *Definitely not!*

Fernando became indignant, his face reddening. "But you must. That's why you're here, no? My meat is excellent. Everyone talks about it. Come, come. I will show it to you in my backyard." Fernando grabbed my arm and started pulling me along.

"Wait, what are you talking about?" I said, growing concerned. I could see how Laney might have had a tough time with him.

Fernando slapped his forehead. "Of course, what am I saying. We must share mate first."

I couldn't understand his thick accent and worried about making him mad. "I'm sorry. I don't understand. Your, uh, associates told me I needed to bring you this car."

This stopped him in his tracks. He stared at me. "Yes, that is very nice. First, you must try my mate. It is a traditional Argentine tea drink. This is what we do with all our guests."

Embarrassed at my faux pas, I murmured, "Ok." I followed him into his house.

A small Latina woman, thin and fit, walked out of a back room dressed in form-fitting, workout clothes. Perhaps five feet tall, she walked straight up to Fernando and socked him in the arm. Hard. "You fix this. Stop talking about your meat all the time. You need to fix whatever is wrong at work. I am going to the gym now." She punched him again. "You fix it." And she left, giving me a single, small nod as she walked past.

Fernando turned and watched her leave with a smile on his face. "Ah, I love her. My wife, she is wonderful. Sí?"

I half shrugged, half nodded. *Just wonderful.*

"Come see my meat. It is still cooking on my barbeque."

Ahh. "Sure," I said, much relieved.

Outside his back door, a pressed concrete patio held a large table with ten chairs surrounding it. From the table, Fernando picked up a gourd-shaped mug packed to the brim with chopped green leaves. A metal straw stuck out of the chopped green leaves. He took a tea kettle and carefully poured some steaming water into the mug. He picked up the mug and, instead of handing it to me, he took a long slurp on the straw until he made a loud sucking noise. He sighed in contentment. "Perfecto."

I looked at the table for another mug, however, Fernando held the only one.

Refilling the mug with more hot water, he thrust it at me. "Welcome to my house, Marty."

I absently thanked him while I tried to figure out where he kept the extra straws. I didn't see them so I pulled out the straw and held it out to him. "Here's your straw. Where are the extras?"

Fernando gasped. "No, it is not polite to move the bombilla." He took the straw and mug from me, put the straw back in and handed it to me again with two hands.

I pulled back. Germ-phobic in the best of times, I did not want to share the straw of this stranger, a drug lord's son who may have hurt Laney. "No, thank you."

Fernando scowled at my polite words. "You insult me in my own home?"

Great. I insulted the drug lord. I winced. "No. I don't mean to. It's just … I don't want any."

"In my culture, refusing mate means you don't want to be friends. Do you not want to be friends, Marty?" The bigger man leaned in closer as his frown deepened.

I don't think so. Swallowing my disgust, I reached for the mug and took a big sip. The mate had a bitter, pungent flavor that I didn't like. I kept it down and made sure to make a big sucking noise. I handed him back the mug and pretended to smile.

In another rapid mood swing, Fernando grinned and clapped me on the back. "Come, take a look at my grill. I built it myself." Placing his hand on the center of my back, he propelled me to the side of the patio next to his house where we could overlook his grill. A large grilling station dominated the area. Built with red bricks, the large, rectangular barbeque featured a movable, metal grill with V-shaped grates and attached by a chain through a flywheel on the side with a hand-operated winch. The red bricks extended around and above the grill to form sides and a roof that reflected the heat back to the grill while allowing the smoke to flow out the top. The grill rested a few inches above a fire of charcoal and hardwood chips.

He had quite a setup. "Wow," I said.

Complimenting his grill made Fernando preen. "It's Argentine-style. That is the best for meat. Even the bricks come from Argentina. Americans do not understand meat. You use grills with gas. Gas! Unbelievable. Gas is for cars. And from beans." Fernando guffawed at his own joke, then continued, "Meat takes time. Americans want everything now, now, now. No patience. Argentines know that meat takes time. Treat it like a woman. You need to be gentle, caress it, warm it up just right to get it ready."

He paused for effect. "Then it explodes!" Fernando punctuated his own explosion with his arms as a little spit came flying out of his mouth.

Fernando didn't need anyone to interact with him to stay

engaged in a conversation. His passion alone could sustain a conversation by himself. After all, this was important. This was grilling. He could easily be misunderstood by others.

Fernando repeated, "It explodes with flavor. But you have to give it enough time. Exactly the right amount of time. Here." He pushed a spoonful of an oily green sauce in my direction, "Try my chimichurri."

"Uh. Not right now. I'm sure it's delicious."

He reddened and waved a large carving knife in my direction. I feared I had offended him again. I did not want to offend him.

He furrowed his brow in confusion at my response. After a moment, he nodded, "Of course. I apologize. You shouldn't try chimichurri by itself. You must eat it on steak. That is the only proper way. I apologize." Fernando gave me a small bow before he commanded, "Come here."

I obeyed.

An amazing smell wafted past my nose as we approached the grill. Beaming with pride, he turned back to me. Bringing the fingers and thumb of his right hand together, he raised it to his lips, kissed them and joyfully tossed fingers and thumb into the air. "Incredible, right? Five hours it cooks. Wait until you taste it. I will cut off a small piece for you."

He carved off a chunk about the size of my head. He handed it to me on a platter with a fork and mini version of his own carving knife. With great anticipation, he took the spoon from the container of his green, oily sauce and spread some on my plate. He looked at me with eyebrows raised. "Now, eat. Eat my meat with the chimichurri sauce. It is the only way."

I cut a small piece, dipped it into the green sauce and hesitantly put it in my mouth. *Heavenly.*

Fernando saw my reaction. "Sí? It is incredible, is it not? How can someone not like my meat?"

Mouth full, I nodded. Maybe Fernando would adopt me. Why hadn't I come to his party on Sunday? Had Laney tried some?

Fernando waved his arms exuberantly and kept the conversation going without needing my involvement. "I do not understand. Why would someone complain about me at work? I work very hard. I do not waste time with silly talk about TV shows or American baseball. I am very good engineer. I work on my software and I tell people about my grilling. That is all."

"Wait. You're an engineer?"

"Yes. Didn't my colleagues tell you?"

I shook my head. "Do you, uh, hang out at the Restaurante El Salvador often?" I didn't know how else to ask about his gang without provoking him again.

"El Salvador? No, I know no one from El Salvador. We beat them at fútbol in the World Cup this year, but that is all I know of El Salvador."

This didn't make sense. He didn't act like a drug lord. At least not like the ones I'd seen on television or at the restaurant. While we stood there looking at each other, with the wonderful smell from his grill still drifting across the yard, my phone rang. I excused myself as I answered.

"Hi, Marty?" Meghan Emerson's voice came out of my phone. She sounded breathless, but not from her excitement to talk to me.

I hadn't expected to hear from her. I hadn't even added her as a contact into my phone. "Yes. How are you?"

"I just got home." Meghan's voice wavered. "My house ... my house has been broken into."

25

Friday Late Afternoon

Both Meghan's and Laney's homes getting burglarized on two consecutive days couldn't be a coincidence.

"Yours, too? Are you ok?" I asked.

Meghan's voice steadied. "Yeah, I'm fine. What do you mean by 'yours, too'?"

"Someone broke into Laney's house yesterday."

"That's too weird. Now I'm scared."

"Did you call the police?" I asked.

"Yes. As soon as I saw my front door was ajar, I ran over to a neighbor's house. I called you because, I thought, maybe, you were right about some strange connection between me and Laney. This could have been them harassing me, but it feels different. They ignored me all day at work. Why would they break into my house?"

"I don't know."

"This is too much, though. Why would someone break into my home and hers?" Without waiting for a response, Meghan added, "Hey, the Campbell police are just pulling up. Can we talk later?"

"Yes. Definitely." My father didn't raise an idiot. A woman asks if she can call, there's only one answer. I also wanted to figure out why someone broke into her home and Laney's.

I almost called Mace. He should know about this. Yet, yesterday, I'd promised Meghan that I wouldn't tell anyone else about her situation. Besides, after my calls to Mace this week, he'd think I sounded like the boy who cried wolf once too often. I'd need to talk to Meghan first and convince her to tell Mace what had happened. Mace would believe her. Tag team was my new strategy.

My mind whirling, I turned back to Fernando. "I'm so sorry, but my, um, daughter, doesn't have her key. I need to go home to let her in." Did it count as a lie if it actually happened yesterday?

"Of course, of course. Family is the most important thing. You must go to her now. We can do the test drive some other time." Fernando looked down and his face again turned red. "Perhaps you could do a small favor for me?"

"Sure," I answered before I'd fully thought through my words. After all, we had drunk mate together. Now, we were friends. I held my breath, hoping he wasn't an engineer, who moonlighted as a South American drug lord, rampaging through the neighborhoods of Silicon Valley and about to pull me into some nefarious plot.

He turned bashful before almost whispering his request. "Would you mind submitting my resume for a job at Rover?" Fernando handed me a piece of paper that he grabbed off the table. "When you told me you worked at Rover, I printed a copy to give you."

He grinned when I took it. "Do you want to take some steak with you?"

I did. "Wow. Thank you. That's very nice. Maybe just a little bit."

I left his house with my arms full. I nibbled the whole way back to the rental agency and as I waited for the Rover car to take me home. Sí, his meat was truly delicious.

* * * * * * *

When I returned to my building, I picked up Skye and Megan from Mrs. Kim's apartment and brought them back to my place. They sat down on the couch and flipped on the television. After I put Fernando's meat in the refrigerator, I checked the pockets from last night's pants for the business card. Pulling it out, I compared the number to the one I'd called today from Laney's calendar.

My breath caught in my throat. It was a different number. As I'd started to suspect once I'd met him, I had visited the wrong Fernando Hernandez. Somewhere in Silicon Valley, Fernando Hernandez, the gang leader and maybe drug lord, didn't get his test drive in a red, Land Rover today. I had left him hanging while I enjoyed my Fernando's grilling prowess. Now the men from El Salvador Restaurante would come find me and Laney. They promised that I wouldn't like that.

Heart beating in my ears again, I pulled out my phone to call Sergeant Jackson for help. For once, I paused before I dialed him. What would I tell him? Mace wouldn't appreciate that I had gone to check out a suspect, nor that I had rented a red Land Rover to go visit the suspect's house alone. Laney wouldn't like learning that I had taken her girls into a drug gang's hangout, regardless of how delicious their food was. At least the gang didn't know where Laney or I lived. I'd have to go in the back door at the Rover offices for a while until they forgot about me.

I put my phone back in my pocket, proud of my careful reasoning. I wouldn't return to the restaurant. Gangs must have more important issues to handle than tracking down rogue software engineers. I'd never see the gang again. *I hope.*

I sat down at the desk in my home office. Laney might have her

work cut out for her, from an HR perspective, with the engineer
Fernando. But at least, she didn't have anything to fear from this
Fernando except high cholesterol. I put his resume into my bag
to bring to the office. I wouldn't mind having my new friend,
the meat grilling genius, Fernando Hernandez join Rover. He'd
certainly make our potluck lunches much tastier. Perhaps I could
talk him into bringing something from his grill on birthday cake
days.

Leaning back in my chair at my desk, I finally had a few minutes
to think. I realized I hadn't followed up with Jean Rollag since I'd
decided not to leave him a voicemail on Wednesday. Although I
couldn't be certain that the meat-loving Fernando was merely a
random client of Laney's, he didn't seem like the type to attack her.

Rollag still felt like the most likely suspect. He'd want to quiet
Laney and his old friend, Sierra, so his long-ago Stanford bribery
wouldn't cost him billions in the upcoming IPO. He might have
dropped the drone on her car from a floating hammock in a secret
lab inside DroneTech. If I told him that I also knew about his bribe
to Sierra and was going to tell the world, perhaps that would stop
him from trying to kill Laney. His secret would be out so there'd
be no point in going after her again. That was all I cared about
anyway.

I half-smiled at my own brilliant deductive reasoning. Mace
would be impressed at how I solved the case. Not wanting the
girls watching television to overhear me confronting their mother's
attacker, I closed the office doors before I called Rollag. Sitting
down in my office chair again, I focused to collect my thoughts,
then picked up my phone.

"'Lo, who's this?" answered Rollag in a brusque voice.

"Hi, this is Marty Golden. I talked to you on Wednesday
morning in the Starbucks about my sister, Laney, your HR
consultant."

"Oh yeah. Hang on while I step out of this meeting." Rollag's voice perked up after he was alone. "Is she interested?"

Ass. Did he think I'd interrupted his business meeting to pimp out my sister? "No, definitely not. I wanted you to know that your secret's out. I know how you messed things up in college and I'm going to tell your VCs."

This made Rollag angry. "Screw you. You think you're going to blackmail me? The VCs already know about my arrest. Tell your sister to forget it, too. I'm no longer interested."

"She's never been interested in you!" *What a complete jerk!*

"Fine. I'm leaving tonight for a vacation in Australia anyway. Plenty of babes there. Don't call me again." Rollag hung up on me.

I was pissed all over again. Did all companies worth ten billion dollars have rude, arrogant founders? Did those go hand-in-hand?

Wait. What did he mean by his 'arrest'? I'd only called to tell him that I knew of his bribe to Sierra.

I turned to my computer and started to search for anything online about Jean Rollag getting arrested. Nothing came up in the first few pages of the search. Although he was getting a lot of press recently, I found nothing about an arrest. But everything gets stored online these days. It would take a bit more effort. I tried some advanced search engines, the kind that engineers built because they thought they could outsmart the incumbents, but only other engineers used, and then they went bankrupt. Finally, I came across something. Something big. I checked one more website before leaning back in my chair.

Whoa. I needed to bounce this off someone. I called Raj. "Hi, it's Marty. Any red alerts at work?"

"Ha! No, Captain Kirk. The boss beamed up to Palo Alto for some very important meetings this afternoon. We all live long and prosper today." Raj sounded triumphant at managing to use Star Trek jargon on me for once.

"Good one." I paused to appreciate his ability to incorporate lines from a 1960's sci-fi series into his third spoken language. Before he could try Klingon, I said, "Hey, I found something weird about Rollag and I don't know what to do next."

"Did you find any Tribbles?"

Surprised to find I was too excited to banter further about Star Trek trivia, I told him, "I found an old article from a small tabloid in Australia called the Melbourne Observer. The headline read "UM Student Nabbed for Soliciting Prostitution." You'll never guess who the story was about?"

"Rollag," answered Raj with uncomfortable directness. "You said you found something weird about Rollag, correct?"

I hadn't expected him to answer my rhetorical question. "Yes, it was about him. Rich American college kid on a semester abroad program to Australia gets arrested during a vacation to Italy with a prostitute. As if going to Australia for college wasn't enough of a vacation."

I snorted in disgust at the thought. I never had that kind of luck. I worked hard in college and my parents didn't have much money. No trips to Europe or Australia ever came my way. My biggest travel highlights during college were a few road trips in beat-up cars stuffed with enough guys to cover gas costs and share hotel rooms during Spring Breaks, all entirely self-funded. No indulgent, wealthy parents offered to fund my startup while I didn't worry about finding a job. I wasn't being entirely fair to Rollag, who had started his company while still in school and got venture funding lined up before graduating. I still didn't like him.

Continuing, I said, "I'll bet Rollag's parents hired a lawyer to use Europe's "right-to-be-forgotten" laws and remove mentions of his French arrest from search engines."

"That must have been expensive," said Raj.

"It does explain why we didn't see the story when we looked Rollag up in the office earlier. But that's not even the best part.

You'll never guess." Unable to stay seated, I started pacing circles around my small home office.

"What?" Raj didn't match my level of enthusiasm. After imitating the IRS badge and meeting the drug gang, he advocated a more cautious approach.

"Rollag's bio on the DroneTech site says that he graduated from Stanford with honors."

Raj switched into his didactic mode. "Graduating is very important. My parents worked extra jobs so my brother and I could both go to the Indian Institute of Technology. It is most prestigious college for engineering in all of India."

"Yeah, I know. That's impressive, like M.I.T. here." I moved on. "But, Rollag bribed someone at Stanford to change his grades from his semester abroad in Australia. Otherwise, he wouldn't have been able to graduate from Stanford on time, or with honors."

"That is most improper." Raj sounded offended that someone would diminish the value of a degree from such a respected university by cheating.

"Exactly. He's a liar and an arrogant ass. Now I know Rollag did two bad things. But his venture capitalists only know about one of them, I think. Remember the DroneTech story that their VCs had a reputational clause that gave them a much bigger share of the company if either of the founders had done anything that could damage the company's reputation?"

"Ah. Now I understand. What is it that you will do now?"

Losing my adrenaline rush and worn out from the busy week, I sat down again at my desk. "I'm not sure. That's why I called."

"Do you really believe Rollag hurt your sister?" Raj sounded doubtful.

Now that he said it aloud, it did seem unlikely that a founder of a huge company could possibly be involved. "Maybe. I don't know," I said, frustrated with the whole situation. "Well, either way he doesn't seem all that interested in doing anything else to hurt her.

He told me he's leaving the country for a vacation. At least he won't be here to hurt her for a while."

"Perhaps she is safe then? Or perhaps he hired someone? Or perhaps there is another reason she got hurt?" Raj neatly summarized the three options. I'd have preferred he simply solved the case.

"I don't know. Maybe there is something else going on. I think I need to do a deep dive into Laney's computer for —"

Raj cut me off. "Yes, yes. Search her computer, but no more visits to Fernando Hernandez."

I must have had the right plan. Raj rarely interrupted others. Channeling my own Star Trek Captain Picard persona, I said, "I will make it so!"

We hung up so I could get to it. I considered telling Mace about Rollag's secrets now. Rollag certainly had the motivation to keep his secret from getting released. Perhaps he'd hurt Laney in fear that she'd make them public. Mace might talk to him, but I still had no proof he had done anything to her.

Even if he hadn't hurt her, Rollag was still offensive. Cosmic karma would get him. With a little help from me. I felt confident that the DroneTech venture capitalists would appreciate hearing my information about Rollag bribing Sierra so he could graduate. In fact, I envisioned billions of reasons why they'd find this news fascinating. I couldn't stop an evil grin from spreading across my face. Most unattractive I'm sure, but at least I didn't cackle.

Taking out Laney's computer, I checked to see if she'd done more research on DroneTech. I hadn't searched for Sierra Smith earlier. Laney had some brief notes from their conversation, but these only disclosed that they had discussed Rollag's and Sanders' escapades while at Stanford. Laney's notes made no mention of bribery.

I'm a better fake IRS agent than Laney. I did a Megan–like chant in my head.

Reading further, I found that Laney had briefly listed Rollag's earlier arrest as a detail from her initial meeting with the venture capitalists. Rollag hadn't lied to me that the VCs knew about his arrest. But, they didn't appear to know that he'd used bribery to graduate.

The evil smile crept back onto my face and then dissolved. Since Rollag had told me the truth about his arrest and Laney didn't know of the bribe, then why would he want to hurt her? Without that tidbit, Laney had nothing that would damage him. I groaned in frustration. The whole week had gone by and I'd made no progress in protecting Laney. If Rollag didn't do it, then who else wanted to hurt Laney?

26

Friday Dinner

My phone rang. Meghan's name popped up on the display. After her previous call, I'd added her as a contact. I answered quickly, "Hi. How are you doing?"

"I'm fine. A little scared, but okay. Whoever broke into my house didn't take anything. They just made a weird circular mess in the rooms."

The hairs rose on the back of my neck. "That's exactly what happened at Laney's house. It looked like they were searching for something but didn't find it."

Megan didn't wait for me to finish speaking. "I'm almost finished straightening up and I need to get out of here. Now." I heard drawers closing in the background. She sounded a bit out of breath as if she'd been rushing around cleaning up. "Did you eat dinner yet?" Her voice remained a bit shaky.

"No, not yet." I could always eat.

I heard a car door slam. "Perhaps we could grab a bite and talk some more? What do you feel like?" Her voice calmed and also changed to that almost studio-like sound that meant she must be sitting in a closed car.

A date? Unsure of our status, I replied, "Anything except Mexican, Korean, or spaghetti."

Meghan laughed as my answer distracted her. "Unusual response. There must be a good story there. How about meeting in thirty minutes for Chinese? I know a good place."

Of course, I agreed. After we finished talking, I walked down the hallway to Mrs. Kim's apartment. She gave an eager smile of agreement when I asked if she'd come over to have dinner and watch the girls tonight. I had enough meat leftover from Fernando to feed her and the two girls, and likely the rest of the neighborhood. Maybe she only agreed in order to get her teacups returned? Or maybe not. I didn't understand it, but she and the girls had formed a tight bond in only a few days.

⸙ ⸙ ⸙ ⸙ ⸙ ⸙ ⸙

Soon after, the Rover car dropped me at the small, Chinese restaurant that Meghan had suggested. Located in the small, downtown Campbell district, I figured it must be one of her neighborhood favorites. Meghan stood outside in a nice blouse, skirt and low heels. Thankful that I'd changed out of my work clothes into chinos, a button-down shirt and loafers just in case this was a date, I approached her. *Glad these shoes didn't smell.*

I reached out to give her a handshake right as she leaned over to give me a hug. *Awkward.* Not quite friends, yet unsure if it was a date, the proper etiquette for the situation escaped me. I'd greet someone in a work setting with a handshake, a male friend with a pat on the shoulder or arm, or a close female friend with a hug or a kiss on the cheek. I couldn't quite classify the woman who might be ensnarled in a plot that had triggered a near-lethal attack on my sister and left me with my two nieces.

Meghan extracted herself from our uncomfortable, failed greeting shake-hug and walked ahead of me into the restaurant.

Her head scanning from side to side, she seemed to be checking out the place. I saw no gang members. Everything looked fine, even nice, to me. A large fish tank, stocked with colorful koi whose metallic scales glittered under bright lights, greeted us. Flanked on one side by a golden dragon statue and an intricately carved jade statue on the other, a host stand stood unguarded a few steps inside the door. Several elaborate fans attached across the white, painted walls rested between lantern-shaped, red and golden lamp sconces. A few couples occupied scattered tables, but otherwise, the place was quiet for a Friday evening. Meghan's thorough assessment of the room complete, she relaxed. With nothing outwardly amiss, the place passed her review. I'm glad it met her standards because, after a week full of dinner mishaps and mayhem, a nice evening out for good Chinese food seemed appealing.

A young waitress, perhaps still in high school, nodded hello to us as she set a plate down on the table by an older couple. She came over to greet us and took us to a table near the back of the restaurant. Forks and paper napkins lay on top of paper placemats decorated with Chinese zodiac symbols. She handed us plastic menus. "Welcome. Can I get you something to drink?"

I ordered a Tsingtao beer while Meghan requested green tea.

Finally situated as the waitress left, I asked Meghan, "So what did the police say?"

"Not much. They asked me and my neighbors a few questions and looked around. I didn't see anything missing. Only a big mess. The oddest part was it almost seemed organized. Like the people who make crop circles invaded my house." Meghan grunted in exasperation.

"That's exactly what happened at Laney's house yesterday. I didn't notice anything missing either."

We picked up our menus. Meghan took a quick glance before setting it down.

I'd barely had a chance to look at it and couldn't decide quite so quickly. Stalling for time while I scanned the menu, I asked, "Do you have any favorites?"

"Oh, I like everything here." Meghan swiveled her head from side to side as she checked out the other tables.

Her rapid decision making had me pulling out all the delay tactics. "Do you want to eat family-style?" *Like who doesn't in a Chinese restaurant?*

"Sure. Why don't you order whatever you like? I really do like everything here."

Sure, no pressure. I studied the menu, trying to discern the right choices to order.

The waitress brought a ceramic tea kettle, stained yellow around the spout and showing cracks with age, along with two small teacups. She smiled and left.

Meghan's mouth turned down into a slight frown. "Didn't you order a beer?"

"It's no big deal. I'll get it when she comes back. I like tea too." I buried myself back in the menu options.

"But still." She didn't sound pleased.

I changed the subject. "I wonder if whoever broke into Laney's house might have been looking for her briefcase. I have no idea why they'd want it. But it's at my apartment, not her house or hospital room."

"Did you look in it? What did she have — the nuclear launch codes?"

At her small jest, I glanced up from the menu. She must be feeling calmer now if she was cracking jokes. "There's not much in there. A mostly empty notebook and some old newspaper clippings from Spokane. I didn't see anything incriminating or, really, anything anyone would want. She didn't even have detailed notes on her clients in her notebook."

"It's so strange. I can't think of a connection between her and me besides my harassment complaint." Meghan shrugged her shoulders. "I'd only met her last Friday for the first time. It has to be something more than that. Why would they break into my house the day after breaking into hers?"

"I don't know. This whole situation has me confused."

"Me too. When we talked last Friday, she mentioned she was going to the agency later that afternoon for some event. Do you think something happened there?" Meghan's forehead and nose wrinkled as she tilted her head in thought.

I shrugged. "I don't know. All she mentioned in her notes was something about an exec meet-and-greet."

"She probably met the CEO." Meghan had an unusual expression on her face that I couldn't interpret.

"Why? Is he an interesting guy?" Her expression puzzled me.

"He's a bit odd, but he could be our governor one day."

"Aren't all politicians odd?" I tried to avoid reading or talking about politicians. This wasn't all that hard to do as an engineer in Silicon Valley.

Meghan gave me a wry smile with a small chortle of amusement. "You remember that our current governor used to run the State Water Resources Control Board, right?"

"Oh yeah, of course. With the whole state focused on water, that's such a visible position. There's certainly a ton of press coverage for all their decisions." Although politics don't interest me, I knew that much.

This got Meghan started. "When he became governor, he appointed the new head of the Control Board. And now that guy is ready to retire at the end of this year. The governor gets to appoint someone else to run the Control Board. The NorCal Water Agency CEO has to be a leading contender. He beat out the other local district leaders to run the merged agency when the state forced all the smaller water districts to merge into the three big regional agencies."

"Boy, talk about moving up fast. From running a county water district to regional water agency CEO to Control Board to governor in a few short years." How hard could it be to run a water agency? *I drink water.* I'd bounced from startup to startup without this guy's luck.

Meghan didn't notice, or ignored, the frustration in my comment. "Maybe not guaranteed, but he'd have a good shot at becoming governor and he's not yet forty."

The waitress' return interrupted us. "Have you decided yet? What can I get you?"

I forgot all about the beer as the pressure to decide hit me. I took one last look at the menu in case a new special had spontaneously appeared. Unsure what Meghan might like best, I decided to play it safe. "We're going to share. Could we get the beef with broccoli, kung pao chicken, white rice and wonton soup to start?"

Meghan said nothing, but she looked satisfied. *Phew. Survived the food ordering test.* Thank goodness Meghan wasn't as picky an eater as my nieces.

After the waitress left, Meghan asked, "By the way, what was with your comment about no Mexican, Korean or spaghetti for dinner? Did you have some weird combo platter last night?"

I started describing this week's dinner experiences with Skye and Megan.

Meghan almost spat out her sip of tea when I told her about the confusion of kimchee for salsa. "How did you let them talk you into putting spaghetti into taco shells?"

My face screwed up into a grimace. "Either their mother lets them eat that or they're conning me. I'm not sure which, but the more time I spend with them, the more I'm leaning toward the con job."

Meghan raised an eyebrow. "Why did you eat it too?"

I chuckled at my own stupidity and shrugged. "I don't know. It didn't look so bad at first." I paused for effect. "I was wrong."

The restaurant had started to fill up, but the tables were spaced out across the room. I liked that we could talk without other diners practically sitting in our lap like too many of the wannabe trendy restaurants in the area. When did being able to hear your date stop being hip?

Growing up, my father had always told me to get your date to talk more than you did. I switched gears. "What's the big project that you're working on at the water agency?"

"They hired me to finish an environmental impact analysis for a project with a cool new technology to turn Central Valley farming runoff water, contaminated by fertilizers and other agricultural byproducts, into clean drinking water."

"Isn't ocean water used for desalination? Can they really remove all the, um, pollutants?"

She smirked. "You do know that all our groundwater contains the, um, pollutants that get extracted by a treatment plant before it goes into our water lines?"

"Delightful." Flirting a little, I made sure she saw me take a large sip of water.

Meghan smiled. She had a nice smile. She continued, "This new plant in the Central Valley farming region could distill out the dangerous chemicals. They'd sell the recovered chemicals back to the farmers to use again while providing clean water to the community. With so much sun in the middle of the state, solar power is cheaper there than powering reverse osmosis like they do at the ocean desalination plants. Best of all for the environment, there's no wastewater to put back into the ocean and damage sea life."

"Wow. Sounds like the holy grail. Cheap, clean water where it's needed, and no environmental impact. What's the catch?" I appreciated her passion for her work. Designing a new product, or cool feature, felt the same way to me.

Returning to the table, the waitress set down a soup tureen. She served us each a bowl of egg drop soup, smiled and turned to leave again. The wonton soup that I'd ordered must have run off with my beer.

Meghan's frown returned as a scowl. I started to tell her that I like egg drop soup too, but she surprised me and the waitress. In a loud, commanding voice, she started speaking in rapid Mandarin. I only recognized her first phrase, "Nǐ hǎo," or Hello. The rest was a blur of sound and it didn't sound pleased.

The waitress bowed and started to reply when a Chinese woman wearing a chef's white apron burst out from the kitchen. I gasped. How could this happen again? Sitting up straighter in my chair, I braced for the conflict. I didn't glance at Meghan as I focused on the chef, on the lookout for a wooden spoon. Angry chefs approaching me had become all too common.

The chef, who looked about our age, reached the table in three strides. "Hey!" She spoke in a loud voice that drew the attention of the tables around us.

Really, egg drop soup was fine.

Meghan stood and faced the chef. "Li Na!" It sounded like a call to arms.

"Meghan!"

The women hugged.

And with that, the confrontation came to an abrupt, yet peaceful resolution.

Relieved that I wouldn't experience a repeat of last night, I unclenched my jaw.

Meghan stepped back from her hug. "I thought you worked at your new restaurant on Fridays?"

The chef, Li Na, shook her head. "Usually. But I have a new chef here and I wanted to train him. Why didn't you tell me you were here?"

"I didn't see you and I didn't recognize her." Meghan gestured toward the shocked waitress still half-bowing near the table. The waitress didn't encounter many customers with green eyes and pale complexions who spoke better Mandarin than she did.

"This is my cousin, Sue. She started here as a waitress this week." Li Na faced her niece. "This is Auntie Meghan," she said as if that explained everything.

Li Na then looked at me, looked at the table, and raised her eyebrows at Meghan. She clapped her hands three times loudly and shouted something in Mandarin toward the kitchen.

Her clapping had a magical effect. As if she were Dorothy clicking her heels and we were getting whisked away, our table was transformed. In rapid succession, three men came out from the kitchen. They removed the tureen, placemats, forks and tea. They cleared the table in a flash. The next moment, a nice, white linen cloth covered the table, along with napkins folded into swans and beautiful ebony chopsticks. A beautiful china kettle with an intricate, stylized design replaced the stained and chipped tea kettle.

Li Na gave me a firm handshake and dipped into a small bow. "Welcome to my restaurant. I am Li Na. And you are?"

I may have stammered something resembling my name.

"Welcome, Marty. I am very glad you are here with my sister Meghan. Never mind what you ordered, I will make you something very special for you both."

"Uh, thanks."

"What do you like? Chicken, vegetables, noodles, seafood?"

"Uh, sure."

"Spicy or mild?"

"Medium?" I wasn't sure what was happening, but I didn't expect to see the egg drop soup again. One day I'd have a normal dinner. Just not this week.

"Great. I've got it. I'll bring you something wonderful. Sit down and enjoy." Li Na winked at Meghan, turned, and disappeared. No flash of light accompanied this feat. The three men followed her into the kitchen like an honor guard and our waitress, Sue, slowly backed away, never quite straightening from her half-bow.

Meghan's face reddened as she noticed the whole room staring at us. She sank back into her chair without speaking. I understood. Surely sitting down would make everyone stop staring and they'd fail to notice that our table now looked like we'd been transported from the middle of a normal Chinese restaurant in suburban California into a five-star restaurant.

My turn to smirk. "Eat here often?"

She burst out laughing. The other tables stared again. Or possibly they hadn't stopped. I hadn't checked.

Meghan waved her hands in apology. "I'm sorry. I didn't mean for a whole scene. I got annoyed that the waitress kept bringing us the wrong things."

"It's completely understandable. Whenever I complain to a waitress, I also get upgraded to a special dining experience."

She giggled. "I honestly didn't think Li Na was working here today. After what happened earlier, I just wanted some comfort food in my favorite restaurant."

I felt the same way. "How do you know Li Na? Is she really your sister?"

"Not my real sister. I met her when I lived in her parents' house for a year abroad in China during college. Li Na had recently graduated from college. We spent most evenings and weekends together. We became like sisters. About ten years ago, she immigrated to the U.S. as a chef. Now she owns two restaurants."

"Impressive. Okay, so I guess ordering standard American Chinese dishes didn't amaze you."

"It was sort of cute. I could tell how hard you were trying. And I really do like everything here. But, yeah, I do tend to eat a bit more exotically in Chinese restaurants than the average American."

I sat back and took a sip of the green tea from the fancy, unstained, china tureen. It was excellent. While we waited for our surprise dinner to arrive, I said, "I think you were telling me about your project before all this." I waved my arms to encompass the transformed table.

"Yes, well." She caught her breath. "They're bullying me to approve the impact assessment so the project can stay on schedule. I think that's why my predecessor quit or was fired."

"Is there a problem with approving the project?"

She gave a small shrug. "It's no big deal. They need to move the project to a different part of their land before any decent analyst would approve it."

"Why?"

"By chance, they picked a site directly on top of a habitat for an endangered species. They didn't do enough testing before they started the infrastructure preparation. They thought the environmental impact analysis would be routine and then they discovered they had a problem."

"Will the assessment kill the project? That would get someone mad," I said.

"What's nutty is they only need to move the project about a quarter mile away. They own that land too and the preparation that's already finished would mostly still work. It would be a pretty minor hit to their budget."

"Then, what's the big deal?"

"I think it's because moving would delay the project by a few months," said Meghan.

"Ok ... I mean we need the water, but this isn't the first time a project got delayed."

"For our CEO, this is a terrible time for a delay in a major project. Even for a few months. It would make him look bad and the governor might pick one of the other regional water agency leaders to run the state board. And that would interfere with the CEO's political plans."

Our waitress, delivered our dinners, placing the plates on the table with special care. I have no idea what I ate. It was delicious, whatever it was. We enjoyed the food for a while without speaking. Neither of us looked around to check out our neighbors' reactions to our special meal. I only hoped I could get it again when I came back. I'd have to learn the secret Mandarin password to access the special menu.

I finally came up for air. "What's the endangered species?"

"It's a specific type of ants often called Texas Crazy Ants."

This time, I burst out laughing. People around us stared again.

Meghan looked puzzled. "Ants usually aren't funny."

"More damn ants." Still chuckling, I told her about Skye's science fair project and her escapades yesterday.

By the time I finished, Meghan was laughing too. "Hard to believe she's just in seventh grade. I'll have to meet her one day."

I liked that idea. Another one came to me. "What's your degree in?"

"I got a Ph.D. in Environmental Science from UC Santa Cruz."

"Go Slugs," I said, referring to UCSC's bizarre banana slug mascot. *Only in California.* "So, you're Dr. Emerson, right?"

"Yes, but I only use my title for work or see it on a formal invitation. Why?"

"Well, I hate to ask. Would you mind signing an excused absence form for the girls? I need to get a doctor to sign them or they'd be considered unexcused."

Meghan snorted. "Seriously?"

I shook my head. "Yeah, the school secretary was pretty adamant and rather intimidating. I don't want to get the girls into trouble in a new school. Or me."

Meghan's eyes twinkled. "You look worried. You know I'm not that kind of doctor?"

I set down my chopsticks. Just the thought of Mrs. Quarles made me lose my appetite. "I am worried. You haven't met Mrs. Quarles, the school secretary. She almost wouldn't let me take the girls out of school early today."

"That's silly. You're an adult and their guardian." She sounded incredulous.

"She was scary."

Shaking her head in humorous disbelief, Meghan signed the small slips that I produced from my wallet.

I resisted the urge to high five someone. *No detention for me!* After all, Mrs. Quarles hadn't required that the doctor must practice medicine. My brief sense of triumph faded as I realized how silly I must sound that I struggled with a school secretary. Quick thinking kept me from digging myself into a bigger hole as I avoided telling Meghan about Mrs. Quarles' displeasure with the girls' breakfast this morning.

A fancy sweet dish appeared on our table. It had a name that I couldn't pronounce again after Sue told it to us. We shared it for dessert, along with more tea.

Meghan took a bite of the dessert. "It's hard to imagine that we'd have a governor who goes by Billy Bob."

"Billy Bob? Who's that?"

Meghan looked at me in surprise. "He's the CEO I've been talking about. He's the head of the NorCal Water Agency. William Robert Allen. They call him Billy Bob at work. Well, I guess you have to know him to call him that to his face, but that's his nickname."

"It's not enough that he has three first names? Does he need a nickname with two more first names? Seems as if he should pick a name and stick with it like everyone else. Did he get the job because he had more first names than anyone else?" I may have tried too hard to make her laugh again.

Meghan gave me a faint smile before answering, "He doesn't act like it, but I suppose he must be smart. He got a degree in mechanical or civil engineering from Gonzaga. Now that he's running the agency, he can go to meetings and sign off on work that his staff does."

The name and school clicked into place for me. My ability to remember what I read and other useless bits of trivia came in handy again. William Robert Allen, or Billy Bob, was the editor in the old Gonzaga Bulletin photo of that fire in their offices. I told Meghan about Laney's clippings.

"That's weird. Why would she have those old papers?"

"I don't know. She recently did a quick day trip to Spokane. Maybe she got them while she was there." The light bulb went off in my head. "Do you think Billy Bob had something to do with Laney getting hurt?"

Meghan didn't answer as she twisted her napkin into knots. She shrugged with a helpless gesture and looked down at her tea. After a few seconds of tension at the table, she picked up her cup and took a final sip of tea. With a solid clink, she set her cup back on the saucer and looked up at me with her jaw jutting out. "I've had it. Come on, let's go."

"What? Where?" I stammered. *Now what have I done?*

"They piss me off and I can't trust them. No job is worth this crap. I want to go to the office and get my files. I'll take them to the newspaper or the police."

Relieved I hadn't upset her, I said, "Ok. But I thought you couldn't take your computer out of the office and they'd already gone through your files."

"I don't need my computer. I have a paper copy of the original data from the analyst who left. When I started getting harassed, I stored the important files in a co-worker's drawer. She didn't like what they were doing to me either."

"How do we get in?"

Meghan waved to catch Sue's attention so she'd bring us the check. "I've still got my badge and Ernie likes me."

I felt a small stab of jealousy. "Who's Ernie?"

"He's the night security guard at the agency. I think he's related to one of the bigwigs. He's an old sweetie. I work late a lot and we often chat for a while when I leave. I even talked him into volunteering to work the front gate for this weekend's Renaissance Faire. He complained he didn't see many people working on the night shift. Working the front gate will solve that."

"Once we get the files, I know a cop that you should meet." This time Mace would be pleased to see me again.

Meghan excused herself to the restroom. While she was away, I shared my new experience with my kids.

GROUP TEXT TO AMANDA, ELI

MARTY: I just got the secret menu at a Chinese restaurant. It's magical

ELI: Did you find it online like we did for In-N-Out Burger?

MARTY: No, the woman I'm having dinner with speaks Mandarin

AMANDA: You went out with a Chinese woman?

MARTY: No, she is Irish-American

AMANDA: You're on a date right now?

MARTY: Yes, well I don't know if it is a date

ELI: Smooth Dad

AMANDA: Get off your phone Dad and pay attention to your date. Geez!

Meghan returned before I could explain further. Just as well because it was now time to dive into the Water Agency.

27

Friday After Dinner

The NorCal Water Agency building stood north of downtown San Jose. They'd taken over a modern office building from a defunct startup which had grown large enough to build a beautiful building but didn't keep growing fast enough to actually pay for it.

Meghan parked on a side street to prevent coworkers from seeing her car in the parking lot. We shouldn't have worried. When we walked along the sidewalk leading to the building's entrance, it was clear that everyone had left work for the weekend, with only a few pieces of trash blowing around the empty parking lot in front of the building. All the lights remained on even though no one was there.

As we neared the entrance, Meghan slowed and took my arm. "I have an idea. Follow my lead."

I had no ideas so that worked for me.

The front doors slid open as we strolled into the lobby. An older, heavyset man with thinning hair and a large nose sat behind the counter just inside the lobby. We continued forward to the counter. I put on my nonchalant face, slowing to a stroll and swinging my arms in a jaunty fashion from front to back. Just another, perfectly normal, evening stroll to the Water Agency. *Don't mind us, we're not here to steal anything.*

Proud of my acting skills, I forced a smile on my face. Indicating a lack of appreciation for my efforts, Meghan shot me a piercing, sideways glance and pinched my arm. I tried to maintain a demeanor of casual calmness, aiming to remain unruffled despite the critical review.

On the other hand, Meghan's cool manner came across as natural, not playacting. "Hi Ernie. How's it going tonight? I'll see you at the Renaissance Faire tomorrow night, right?"

"Hi'ya Meghan. Haven't seen you all week. Absolutely, I'll be there tomorrow. What brings ya back to work on this beautiful Friday evening?" Ernie had a slight drawl to go along with a smile that appeared sincere. More than merely relieved to have a break during his monotonous evening, he leaned forward, face softening into a warm welcome for his friend.

"I wanted to show my friend the museum." Meghan smiled at Ernie and leaned in to my shoulder. "Can I take him upstairs for a short bit and then we'll be out of your hair?"

Ernie theatrically ran a hand through what little hair remained on his head. "Not much there to worry about." With a more skeptical expression on his weathered face, he sized me up. After a short assessment, he reached a hand over the counter. "Good to meet you. I'm Ernie."

I shook his hand. "You too. I'm Marty."

"Y'all been together for long?" asked Ernie.

I wished I could talk like that. Saying y'all made me feel friendlier, like I was friendly with an entire auditorium full of people. I couldn't pull off a y'all without getting mocked. If I wanted to use it myself, I'd either need some acting lessons or new friends. *Wait, did he ask me a question?*

"Not really." Meghan didn't elaborate on our barely two-day-old relationship. Ernie didn't ask for any details. After all, gentlemen, especially Southern gentlemen, don't pry.

"Well …," said Ernie, pondering the situation. "I'm not supposed to let strangers into the building during the evening time, but now that we've all met, I reckon it's fine for y'all to go on upstairs to have a look-see." After this display of impeccable logic, he added, "As long as y'all don't stay too long."

"Thanks a bunch, Ernie. Aren't you just the sweetest. We'll be back down in a jiffy." Meghan's voice picked up a little of Ernie's drawl.

Perhaps sensing that I might attempt a drawl, Meghan yanked me away from the desk, along to the glass door leading out of the lobby. She swiped her badge and the door opened. We walked through to wait by a small bank of elevators.

"Y'all sounded cute," I drawled to Meghan, making her wince. Taking the hint, I jettisoned the attempt. "What's the museum? I thought we were going to your office?"

"That's what we call the executive lobby on our floor. There are two Jackson Pollock paintings there."

"The Water Agency has Jackson Pollock paintings? I knew my water bill was too high."

"People say Billy Bob bought them with his own money and registered his office as a public museum. He displayed them here so he didn't have to pay sales tax." Meghan punched the up button again and one of the elevator doors slid open.

"A museum. Do I get a map?"

"Just a free audio guide," said Meghan, her eyes sparkling.

"Wasn't Pollack the artist who did the drip paintings where he sat on a chair on his huge canvases and splattered paint all over them?" I'd seen a special on him one day when I was sick.

"Yes. He was known as an abstract expressionist." Meghan sounded like she led tours.

"He basically invented the toy market for spin art machines."

Meghan half-heartedly acknowledged my attempt at humor. Turning serious, I asked, "Think anyone's working tonight?"

"Doesn't look like it."

We rode the rest of the way to the fourth floor in quiet anticipation. When we got off the elevator, we didn't hear any noises. The elevator bank was located near one end of the rectangular building. To the left down the main hallway, I saw several meeting rooms, an emergency exit staircase, and a bank of wide file cabinets. Another conference room lay directly in front of us across from the elevator lobby. To the right, the hallway ran the full length of the building.

Meghan turned to the right out of the elevator lobby. On the right sat a luxurious waiting room with several offices visible behind the fancy secretary's desk that stood guard.

Meghan pointed to the waiting room. "The paintings are in there."

"Why are you whispering?"

"Just a habit I guess. Voices really carry in this hallway and heels are crazy loud. For some reason, they didn't put down any carpeting." She headed toward the waiting room. "Here, let me show them to you in case Ernie asks you about them. Then, let's get my file and get out of here. I don't want to hang around."

I followed her into the waiting area of a small executive suite. Behind the protective desk, a heavy-looking, wood door sat open, revealing a large office with a glass conference table surrounded by black leather chairs. Beyond that sat a mahogany desk with a top-notch, leather executive chair. *Primo.* It could have been one of those ultra-high-end, majestic chairs that billionaire villains in the movies sat in while they plotted world domination.

A conference room next door to the large office held an expensive-looking wood table, six chairs and a large display screen on the opposite wall. The door to a final, smaller room in the suite was closed.

Megan stopped inside the waiting room and waved to the large office. "Billy Bob's office." Turning around, she pointed at the wall to the right of the entrance doors to the waiting room. "Those are the Pollock paintings. They hung them so only the execs see them every day. Ironic for a so-called, public museum, don't you think?"

I turned to scrutinize the paintings mounted in swanky frames. The smaller one held a tiny three by five-inch paper drawing made with crayon and black ink. It looked like a stick figure of a man, with red and yellow flames coming off his body, who was diving down into a wormhole chasing after a yellow star-shaped umbrella.

It didn't resemble any Pollock paintings I'd ever seen so I moved to the larger painting, almost two feet by three feet. The title underneath read "Jackson Pollock, Untitled (1951)".

"Did Pollock run out of ideas to name his works?"

"Come on." Meghan turned to walk through an open door at the end of the suite.

I assumed the pose of a serious art patron, one hand on my hip and one to my chin as I tilted my head. "Hmmm. It looks like a snowman got dropped from a balcony and exploded—"

Meghan dismissed the paintings. "I'm not a big fan of these."

I was on a roll. "Or it looks like the Jack in the Box guy got hit by a truck and his guts got splattered. Like that Christmas song about Grandma getting run over by a reindeer. Except this is Jack in the Box and Pollock stood nearby and captured the moment."

Meghan stopped, staring at me with her mouth slightly agape. After a few beats, she closed her mouth and shook her head as if to clear her head. "Let's go get my papers."

I should stick to programming.

Meghan walked out through the executive suite into another

room. Unwinding myself from my art patron's pose, I stumbled after her as I tried to extract my foot from my mouth.

I stopped dead in my tracks when I walked through the open door after Meghan. This was the nicest break room I'd ever seen. Separated from the hallway by full-length, glass walls, the room held a fancy coffee bar surrounded by a marble top and padded stools. With the fancy machines behind the counter, my Starbucks buddy, Brody, would appreciate this setup. A few high tables, with more high stools near them, dotted the room. Several refrigerators, microwaves, vending machines and a long closet lined the wall back to the executive suite. The other end of the room, also glass-walled, had a wide opening leading to a game room containing a ping-pong table, foosball game, pinball machine and wall-mounted Velcro dart board.

"Wow. You have both a game room and a break room on your floor?" Breathless, I managed to get the words out. Whispering felt like the appropriate level of reverence this deserved.

She gave me an "are you serious?" look that I'd seen several times already. "And a barista who staffs the coffee bar in the mornings too. Crazy, huh?" Meghan kept walking. After all, she saw this every day.

I trailed her, taking it all in. As I passed the pinball machine, an unseen tractor beam seemed to pull me in. Again, I had to check for drool. "You have an antique, *Star Trek: The Next Generation* pinball machine. That's my favorite one of all-time." I ran my hands lovingly over the controls and looked at the backdrop picture with Captain Picard and the rest of the characters from that long-ago show. "Space, the final frontier." My reverential tone returned. I hoped Meghan wouldn't hear me.

Meghan had nothing wrong with her hearing. She stopped before leaving the game room and scoffed. "The game's noise got so annoying that facilities turned the volume off."

Sacrilege. My mouth gawked openly this time. I recognized my Trekkie zeal could get out of hand, especially for the uninformed. So, discretion won out and I decided not to say anything to Meghan. Anything else I said at this point would not improve my standing.

With a tinge of exasperation in her voice, Meghan said, "I'll go get my papers and meet you here."

The noise of her footsteps echoing like staccato gun blasts as she walked out into the hallway broke my trance. She wasn't kidding about the echo chamber effect of this hallway. Glancing out the glass walls, it was clear that no one remained working on this floor tonight. *Free time.* I scurried back to the executive suite. I wanted to try out Billy Bob's throne.

I eased into the luxurious chair. *Posh.* Wonder if my boss would buy one for my cubicle? Billy Bob's desk, clear except for a computer and keyboard, also felt expensive under my hands. Then, remembering the stories Meghan had told me at dinner, I jerked my hands back. Billy Bob, or his people, were scum. I didn't want to touch something contaminated.

But, was he a stupid enough scum to keep a file on Meghan in his desk? I pulled on the drawers, but they were all locked.

With nothing else to do except act imperial, I leaned back and spun to look out the window at the view of the foothills of the Santa Cruz Mountains. In a chair this comfortable, I could get lost for hours daydreaming. No wonder real thrones looked so uncomfortable. Kings and queens would never have lasted if they'd lolled around all day, sprawled out on their comfy cozy thrones. Evildoers galore would have done mischief to the good people of the land.

Like making drones fall and murdering old ladies in the hospital. Reality intruded.

I sighed. Who was I kidding? This was as close as I'd get to occupying a CEO's office. I shoved off to return the chair from fantasy land. When my spin brought me back to the desk, my chair bumped into Billy Bob's keyboard tray and his screen flashed on.

No password. Of course, he locked his desk drawers and not his computer. The technically inept were taking over the world.

Leaning forward, I did a quick search on his computer for anything about Meghan. If I could find proof that Billy Bob had known about the harassment, then she could use that. When nothing came up, I tried a search for Laney.

Nothing.

I had one more idea to try. Opening his browser, I checked the history, looking for anything unusual. Realistically, I didn't expect to find evidence of another leader giving bribes while in college. But, I hadn't anticipated learning that Rollag had bribed Sierra Smith either. Billy Bob was a political junkie, visiting multiple news and political blogs every day. Wondering if any extremists had celebrated drone strikes on part-time HR consultants, I looked back to Monday.

I froze, stunned to find a link to a Mercury News report about a drone accident in San Jose. Why had Billy Bob opened this story? Was he checking on the outcome of his drone crash?

28

Friday Evening

I quickly clicked on the link. Up popped a story about an accident involving a falling drone. A photo showed the side of an ice cream truck smashed almost in half, with a large, brightly painted ice cream cone tilting over, appearing almost to drip onto a neon yellow, retro style VW Bug.

The car was too unusual. It had to be Sunshine, Laney's car. How many neon yellow, retro style VW Bugs could have crashed into an ice cream truck in San Jose on Monday?

I felt bad that Laney's car was totaled. She talked about it all the time, to everyone. I'm sure she'd bragged about it when she met Meghan. She'd probably even told Billy Bob about it when they met. Heck, she loved that car almost like a third child. A few years ago, Laney had spent hours agonizing over the custom paint options. She claimed the bright color cheered her up.

Although Billy Bob was a scum for threatening Meghan, he couldn't have caused the drone crash. He was a politician who ran a water agency. They had an awesome break room, but no drone control room, or secret lab with floating hammock.

I heard Meghan's footsteps approaching and shut down the

computer. I popped out of the chair and hustled into the break room to meet her. She carried a Victoria's Secret shopping bag that looked heavy.

I gestured to the bag with a puzzled expression on my face and Meghan responded, "They're the results from the initial environmental survey, which found the Dorymyrmex insanus ants under the planned construction site. I want to take these to the state board or the newspaper. Maybe both."

"How will we get it out past Ernie?"

Meghan gave me a devious grin. "Ernie will be too embarrassed to look inside."

I had to admire the trick even if I couldn't use it myself. "Not the first time you've done this, is it?"

"No. Not exactly." Meghan didn't elaborate.

As we turned to leave the break room, a ding echoed from the elevator bank. Someone else had returned to the office.

Meghan seized my arm. "In here." She opened the louvered door to a large supply closet and tugged me inside with her. As she pulled the door closed, I heard people getting off the elevator. Meghan looked at me and raised her finger to her lips.

Sure. Even I was smart enough to realize we didn't want to explain why we were taking a Victoria's Secret bag full of forbidden papers off the floor without permission and after hours.

I briefly glanced around me in the closet. The louvers let in enough light that we could see each other and the shelves in the dim light. The shelves around us contained typical office break room supplies, including coffee cups, paper plates, napkins, plastic silverware, aluminum foil and plastic wrap, a few boxes of pens, birthday candles, and a small lighter, spare ping-pong paddles and balls, and a case of twelve extra boxes of foosballs. That made me pause. I understand having a spare foosball or two around in case one gets lost, but who plays such an aggressive match of foosball in an office game room that they need twelve boxes of spares?

I thought perhaps two men had gotten off the elevator. The steps sounded heavy and without the clip-clack of women's heels. They stopped after a few steps, probably outside the executive suite.

I heard a man's voice with a slight Southern twang from the hallway. "I've got some work to finish."

Meghan let out a small gasp. "That's Billy Bob. He can't find me here with this," she whispered as she pointed to the Victoria's Secret bag.

Billy Bob continued in a condescending tone. "You sit in there and figure out how you're going to go back and fix your screw-up. I'm going to see if there's any new gossip coming out of Sacramento."

"What's he doing here now?" I whispered back, worried that they'd hear us.

A second man in the hall with a gravelly voice answered Billy Bob. "Boss, I don't think I can get in."

"Who's that?" I asked her.

"It sounds like Spike. He's the security goon who bothered me on the elevator."

"He can't get in where?" I asked her.

Meghan again raised her finger to her lips to shush me.

More steps echoed down the hallway as they must have walked into the executive suite.

"Hey. I think someone used my computer." Billy Bob's voice sounded upset. It echoed through the quiet of the floor.

"Probably the cleaners again," answered Spike.

"Don't be stupid. They wouldn't do that again, not after the last time." Billy Bob didn't seem likely to win any boss of the year awards.

I could practically see the sneer on his face from around the corner and behind the closet door.

Then it hit me.

A bolt of fear ran through me. "I think he was talking about Laney."

Meghan gestured more vigorously for me to be quiet.

"Want me to check the video recording?" Spike yelled back to his boss.

Billy Bob hadn't crashed the drone on Laney. He couldn't have. But Laney would have told him about her car. She told everyone she met about Sunshine. In his obsession with the news, he must have seen the report about the crash and her hospitalization and then sent Spike to murder her.

But, why?

Billy Bob answered Spike, "Yeah. Go see who's been in here tonight."

Panicked, Meghan whipped her head around to stare at me. "We've got to get out of here."

"I think he did it," I said. Why would the CEO of the NorCal Water Agency want to kill Laney?

I had to stop him.

Them.

I reached for the doorknob.

Meghan yanked back on my arm and whispered in my ear, "No. You can't go out there. It's too dangerous."

Today is a good day to die. Yet, she was right. Following Star Trek quotes probably wasn't the smartest way to make decisions. I whispered back, "We need to call the police."

The hallway went silent. Spike might have gone into the conference room. Maybe he'd even closed the door and had his back to the hallway. But, we couldn't risk going back to the elevators and Spike seeing us.

I fretted. "We can't just wait here. We need to get out of here before Spike checks the recording." I pulled out my phone. "I know a cop. I'll call him and talk quietly."

Meghan put her hand over my phone. "No. They might hear you talking. I've got another idea." She grabbed a pen and the lighter from the shelf. Pointing behind me, she said, "Hand me the ping-pong balls."

"Are we going to challenge them to a game?" I handed her the balls. Even I didn't think my comment was funny.

Meghan poked the pen into a ping-pong ball. She pulled a long piece of aluminum foil from a package and wrapped it carefully, and quietly, around the ball and formed a tube of aluminum foil around the pen. Then she pulled the pen out of the ball leaving just the aluminum foil tube extending out from the foil-wrapped ball.

I watched with fascination. I'd seen all the old episodes of MacGyver and then MythBusters when I was growing up, but I'd never seen any of them use aluminum foil and a ping-pong ball to beat up the bad guys. We weren't trapped in a locked room and her contraption didn't seem all that useful as a makeshift lock-pick anyway. I was mystified and kept watching.

Next, Meghan knelt and held the lighter to the outside of the ping-pong ball wrapped in aluminum foil. After a few seconds, it burst into flame and she backed away. A few seconds later, acrid white smoke gushed out the tube formed by the aluminum foil.

Tendrils of smoke rose up, enough to trip the smoke detector set in the ceiling of the small supply closet. The red light on the detector started flashing faster. The flames disappeared, but, improbably, more smoke poured out the tube. It stunk. I pinched my nose to keep myself from gagging on the burnt plastic smell. Who knew smoke from a burning ping-pong ball would be this noxious?

There was more than enough smoke to activate the building's fire alarm system. This wasn't a timid home alarm with low battery strength that might not get heard through closed bedroom doors.

No, the NorCal Water Agency had an industrial-strength alarm, maintained in the prime of its life, sounding a full-bodied warning that everyone needed to escape now or risk death by ping-pong ball.

"Hey! What's that?" Billy Bob's voice sounded frightened. Panic must have confused him because fire alarms have a distinctive sound. "Do you see a fire?" he shouted to Spike.

Spike didn't answer. Running footsteps pounded down the hallway. Billy Bob's voice again sounded over the blaring alarms. "Spike! Get back here. These paintings are worth more than you are. Grab the other Pollock! I don't want these damaged."

The smoke and the smell from the burning ping-pong ball had nearly overpowered Meghan and me. I nudged open the closet door and tried not to cough or draw attention to us as I stepped out into break room. I shouldn't have worried. Billy Bob and Spike weren't in sight.

I took a quick peek out the opening into the hallway. Billy Bob had flung open the fire door to the staircase, past the executive offices and the elevators. His left hand grasped the tiny Pollock drawing as his body disappeared through the door. The courageous CEO had left the big painting for Spike to carry down four flights of stairs. Billy Bob didn't even stick around to hold the heavy fire door for Spike. Spike, a heavyset, wide man, had close-cropped hair on the side of his head and spikes of thinning, light brown hair jutting out in all directions from the top of his head. He trotted with his arms spread wide as he hurried after Billy Bob, holding the heavy, two by three foot frame. I ducked back into the break room so he wouldn't see me.

The fire alarm's volume ramped up to eleven as if it worried that we might not have noticed its earlier efforts. It was hard to hear myself think. Between the klaxons in the DroneTech control room and tonight's fire alarm, I'd probably caused permanent hearing damage.

"They're going down the staircase past the elevators," I shouted to Meghan from just a few feet away.

"Let's go to the other staircase. We need to get out of here before the fire trucks come." Meghan grabbed her Victoria's Secret bag. Then she turned back, leaned over and picked up the burnt-out ping-pong ball by a corner of the aluminum foil. She closed the closet door behind her and put the aluminum foil in her bag. Unlike the fictional MacGyver, environmental analysts don't leave messes behind. Plus, she avoided leaving evidence of attempted arson.

At that moment, the sprinklers in the break room erupted with a surge of water spray all over us and the break room. We leaped out of the room right as the sprinklers in the hallway turned on. Unable to avoid a drenching, we hustled, squishing and splattering wet footsteps past the cubicle farm to the other end of the building and into the staircase.

In the stairway, we shook off what water we could and checked the plastic bag to make sure Meghan's papers were dry. Four floors down, I paused before opening the emergency exit to the outside. "Was your car on this street or the other side of the building?"

Meghan swept past me without hesitation. "It's here." She pushed open the door and we were outside. The alarms sounded quieter outside the building, but still loud enough to disturb the otherwise calm evening. In the distance, I could hear a fire truck siren approaching. Meghan had parked her car only a few steps away. We jumped in and she pulled away before even putting on her seatbelt.

We were drenched and smelled like burnt plastic. A few blocks away, she pulled over and stopped the car. In a shaky voice, Meghan asked, "Now what?"

I caught my breath too. "I think you should meet Sergeant Jackson. He's from the San Jose Police and is looking into Laney's case."

Emotions roiled across her face as she considered her options. Then, she shrugged. "Well, I don't know what else to do. And the police will see us leaving the floor on the security cameras anyway."

Security cameras! "Oh crap. I forgot."

Ever the logical scientist, Meghan said, "Well, we're caught either way. Ernie also knew we were on the floor."

I took out my phone and called Mace. Might need to add him to my phone's favorites list if this kept up.

Mace answered with a grumble. "What do you want now?"

At least he still answered my calls. I dispensed with the pleasantries as well. "Something happened that you need to know about."

"This better not be another Amber Alert."

"No. It's about my sister. I think we know who's trying to kill her."

Mace focused on the wrong word. "We?"

"A friend of mine who works at the NorCal Water Agency."

"Didn't I just hear a call from dispatch for a fire at the Water Agency?" Mace's voice took on a suspicious edge, a tone I knew well.

"Yeah, but don't worry. There's no fire."

"How would you know? Don't tell you're involved in that too?" Mace's voice rose as his questions started evolving into an angry interrogation.

"Look. I'll explain everything but you need to meet Meghan."

"Your niece? I told you no more missing kid reports."

"No, this is an adult Meghan. Can we just meet you wherever you are now?" I was tired and scared and needed his help to protect Laney.

Mace heard it all in my voice. "Ok. This better be worth it. I'm almost done with my shift. I'm finishing up some paperwork at a Starbucks."

Naturally, it was my new home away from home. I told Mace that I knew how to find him and that we'd be there soon.

After I hung up, I turned to Megan. "He's in that Starbucks where we first met. I've been in that place three times this week already. Boy, I miss the days when cops went to donut shops."

"Lots of people go to Starbucks every day. It's healthier than a donut place."

"Not all their stuff." I didn't explain further.

Meghan started the car and headed to the Starbucks for our meeting with Mace.

I glanced over as she drove. "That was pretty quick thinking in there. Where did you learn that trick with the ping-pong ball?"

Meghan relaxed a little as a small smile broke out on her lips. "I've always been interested in science. Not just what we learned in class. Besides, I had three older brothers growing up. With all the crap they pulled on me, I had to find ways to get back at them."

"I think Skye would like you. You know about two of her favorite things — ants and science tricks."

29

Friday Late Night

We squished our way into my now-favorite Starbucks. This time I smelled of burnt plastic rather than fish. I was starting to understand the Starbucks founder's idea that his shops could become the 'third place between work and home'. They certainly kept coming between my home and work, although he probably didn't intend it that way.

Some fascinating customers must walk through Starbucks on a regular basis because no one noticed, or at least they pretended not to notice, when Meghan and I made our entrance to the coffee shop dripping wet, stinky and bedraggled.

Brody had his back to us, but his distinctive spiked blonde hair with orange tips made his presence obvious. Mace looked different from how I'd ever seen him. His face looked relaxed as he sat at a table, laughing at something that Brody had said. Brody turned to check who'd entered the coffee shop. He took a few steps toward us and greeted us with his usual upbeat manner, without any hint of surprise of our condition or time of day. "Aloha, John! Hanging ten? Your order will be right up. And a green tea for the lady, right?"

Meghan smiled and nodded appreciatively to him.

"Right on, dude. Coming up." Brody walked past us to the coffee machines.

Meghan asked me, "When are you going to tell him your name isn't John?"

"I don't know. I hate to make him feel bad. He's so friendly all the time."

We squished over to the table where Mace sat. He straightened and reverted back to the stern cop who I'd imagined as a movie action hero in my daydreams.

"Did he just call you John?" Sergeant Jackson's voice growled low, all signs of his good humor evaporated.

"It's an odd story," I said.

"I'm starting to think that everything about you is more than a little odd." His eyes taking on that familiar glare as he shook his head in annoyance.

I overlooked this and introduced Meghan. Mace stuck out his hand, but she didn't take it. Without speaking, she cocked her head to the side and considered Mace with a long, searching look.

After an awkward silence that lasted too long, I started my introduction again, hoping that Meghan merely needed a redo.

As I said his name again, she burst into laughter. "Wait, you aren't … Are you?" She paused as if that were an actual question that could be answered.

Mace lowered his hand and looked down at his papers without commenting on Meghan's reaction. His neck flushed.

Meghan giggled. "No, really. Are you … that Mace Jackson?"

I looked back at Mace. He busied himself with organizing his papers on the table, fumbling through them as he pretended to ignore us, and mumbled to himself again. I could feel the heat of his embarrassment radiating off him.

I didn't know which Mace worried me more — the normally cool, tough cop who thought I couldn't get my act together, or this fumbling fool who couldn't face a giggly Meghan. I tried to add my own value to the conversation, "Huh? What?"

Meghan tittered as she tried to suppress her laughter. She fumbled in her purse, all school-girl jittery, and pulled out her phone. She thrust it toward Mace. "Would you? I mean —"

Mace's low rumble interrupted her. "I don't … I mean, I no longer." He slumped in his chair, his posture all wrong for a movie star.

"Really? Please?" Meghan wheedled, outstretched arms holding her phone ready to take a selfie in an appeal to Mace.

As they froze, silently staring each other down, I broke in. "Could someone tell me what on earth is going on?"

"You didn't know?" Meghan turned her attention back to me after spending the last few moments staring at Mace.

"Please." Mace pleaded.

I'd seen Mace as the action hero cop in control of the situation and as the annoyed cop at his fumbling, amateur assistant, but never as the supplicant begging Meghan not to spill the beans.

"Know what?" I looked to Meghan in confusion.

Gesturing to Mace, Meghan replied, "You didn't know this was Mace Jackson, the model?"

"Which model?" I asked. Robots, like R2-D2, had model designations. I didn't realize cops had them as well.

"The famous underwear model." Meghan waggled her eyebrows at me.

My mouth dropped open as her explanation sunk in. I turned and gawked at Mace, reassessing him for the first time since I met him on Monday.

"That was a long time ago," Mace said in a soft voice.

"No more than ten years," responded Meghan.

I couldn't remember people's names who I saw every day at work. Meghan's ability to recall a model's face and name from ten years ago stunned me.

Mace squeaked as he started speaking. He halted and cleared his throat. "That's a past life. I'd appreciate it if you would let it stay in the past." He shuffled the papers some more as he sought to regain his composure. Clearing his voice again, he asked, "Now, did someone threaten to kill your sister?" Self-control reasserted, he straightened his shoulders and set his papers aside.

His words brought Meghan and me back to reality. We needed to focus on the reason we called him in the first place. We eased down to our seats without speaking. Meghan kept sneaking glances at Mace and then tittering quietly to me. His past might be past but we hadn't put it behind us. Meghan and I would need to laugh about Mace's history again later. I liked the idea of seeing Meghan again.

Mace spoke again. "What's going on?" The return of his police officer's demeanor and command voice had the desired effect. We both snapped to attention. Meghan gave a quick summary of her harassment at work, the break-in at her house, Billy Bob and Spike's conversation at the water agency and our daring escape.

Jackson leaned back in his chair to study us. His forehead wrinkled. He asked Meghan, "They admitted to murdering the old lady in the hospital and breaking into your house?"

"Well, no, not exactly, —"

I interrupted her. "It's what he meant. He'd seen the story of her accident on Monday afternoon."

Jackson ignored my explanation. He squinted at me, voice harsh. "And you deliberately set a fire in a public building that caused the fire department to respond?"

I flushed and babbled. "No, I didn't ... I mean yes, we did. Well, it wasn't a real fire —"

Meghan interrupted, "I set off a small smoke bomb. We needed to escape so we could contact the police."

"Hmmm." Jackson still gave me the stink eye.

Why me? It was Meghan's idea.

"Hold on a minute. Let me call dispatch and make sure the officer is still on your sister's floor while we straighten this out." He turned in his chair and made a quick, quiet call.

I was relieved that Laney was still protected. Did this mean I wouldn't get arrested tonight? Well, at least, not yet. While he spoke, Meghan caught my attention with widened eyes that she shifted to indicate Mace and then back at me. She did this several times as if to make sure I remembered who sat next to us. Despite a mere shrug from me, she nearly burst into laughter on her own. She suppressed her giggles, nonetheless, a small snort escaped. She swallowed her laughter and took a deep breath to restrain herself.

Mace finished his call and turned back to Meghan before her giggles returned. "Tell me more about the CEO."

Pulling herself together, Meghan said, "Billy Bob's our CEO…"

"The CEO's name is Billy Bob?" Jackson puffed out his lips in disbelief.

"His full name is William Robert Allen. Everyone calls him Billy Bob."

"You've got to be kidding me," said Jackson, still incredulous.

Why an underwear model turned cop, named Mace Jackson, would think anyone else had a ridiculous name struck me as entertaining. I swallowed my own laugh. Meghan might get away with it, but I didn't want to consider the consequences that laughing outright at Sergeant Mace Jackson could mean to me. His glare and harsh voice were scary enough.

Meghan pulled up a picture of Billy Bob on her phone from a quick internet search and showed Mace. "He's had like five different government or related industry jobs in the last ten years. Each time he stays for a year or two and then jumps to a new place with a promotion or bigger role."

"He looks pretty young to run such a large agency," said Jackson, peering at Meghan's phone.

"Yeah, he must be good at sucking up to his bosses. Our board sure seems to like him and the governor does too. The office rumor mill says Billy Bob will get appointed to run the State Water Board."

"Impressive. So why would a guy like that harass you?" asked Jackson.

Meghan opened up the folder from her office and took out the report we had just snuck out of the office. "Because of this." She handed it over.

Jackson scanned it briefly before looking back at her. "Why is this important?"

"It's the initial environmental analysis done on the site where Billy Bob plans to build NorCal's big, new water desalination plant."

"It looks like a map with a bunch of numbers and symbols on it. What does it mean?"

Meghan looked smug. "That he can't build the plant at their planned location. They'll need to move it to another part of the parcel. Not a disaster, but it will delay the project by at least six months."

"So?" Jackson looked puzzled.

That had been my reaction too. Now, proud that I knew the answer, I chimed in. "This means a publicity black eye right as the governor is making his final decision about who will get the vacant position to run the State Water Resources Control Board. If Billy Bob's first big project is delayed, the governor is likely to pick someone else."

"That's why he has his goons pressuring me to sign off on the project as it is. But I won't let them use my license like that. I won't do it," said Meghan, her voice grown louder with each statement, ended with her thumping the table with a righteous fist.

Mace paused to give her passion its due, before asking a follow-up question. "Ok. I can see, maybe, that he might want to lean on you to go along. But, what does that have to do with Laney Tran?"

The question seemed to deflate both of us. We had no answer for that. Our shoulders sagged as we sat in silence. Meghan excused herself to the restroom.

Mace glanced down at my hands. He noticed the pink Band-Aid on my finger and scoffed, "Princess?"

I shrugged. I couldn't see telling him I'd had an owie and found the first Band-Aid available in Laney's house to cover my paper cut.

Now we sat in uncomfortable silence. I considered telling him about Fernando's gang threatening me and Laney. I couldn't come up with a good way to bring it up without him yelling at me again. I almost asked him to tell me more about his modeling career. However, in a rare moment of discretion, I looked around the Starbucks instead. The place had emptied except for us and the two baristas. One mopped while Brody manipulated the beeping, hissing machines. My phone buzzed with a text and I gratefully took it out to engage with someone who did want to talk to me.

GROUP TEXT TO AMANDA, ELI
AMANDA: How'd rest of your date go?
MARTY: Interesting. Isn't it late for you?
AMANDA: It's Saturday night. What does that mean?
MARTY: Can't talk now
AMANDA: You're still with her???
MARTY: Yes
ELI: Whoa!
MARTY: It's not like that. Gotta go. Talk tomorrow
AMANDA: Wait! Tell us more

I put away the phone as Brody walked up with our drinks. He

nodded at Mace while he set down a steaming cup of green tea at Meghan's spot. With a flourish, he set mine down in front of me. "Here is your super-duper drink. Have a wonderful night!"

Mace looked up at his enthusiastic energy. Caffeine fumes must power Brody through his workday. I nodded my appreciation for his service and passion. "Thanks, Brody. Are you almost off work?"

Brody's eyes sparkled with delight. "Totally. Tonight's an extra shift so I can go surfing tomorrow. I'm pooped now, but the waves will be totally radical tomorrow."

His throwback language made me chuckle. "Well, then, you have a wonderful day tomorrow."

"Most definitely, dude." Brody exchanged smiles with Meghan as she returned to her seat.

Before Brody left our table, Mace waved one hand in the general direction of my drink. "What on earth is that?" Mace used a much more pleasant tone than he ever used to me.

Brody responded with a wink to Mace and a sing-song voice, "It's a Triple, Venti, Half Sweet, Non-Fat, Extra-Hot, Caramel Macchiato."

"You're kidding." Mace first looked at Brody to figure out if I'd truly placed such a ridiculous order. He shifted his eyes to Meghan. "He's kidding, right?"

Brody caught his eye. "No. It's totally righteous, dude. Do you want one too?" A smile flashed across Brody's face as he leaned forward for Mace's decision.

I waited for Mace to make a snide comment. He surprised me again. Looking at Brody, Mace gave a half-smile and shook his head. "No. Thanks though."

"Cool, dude. Well, you all have a wonderful night! Don't forget, we close in fifteen minutes." Brody left us to finish cleaning.

Mace turned his full attention back to Meghan.

"I can stop by the water agency to talk to Spike on Monday and try to scare him away from bothering you. But, I'd need more to go after Mr. Allen. It doesn't even make sense that a successful CEO would be involved in break-ins and attempted murder."

Meghan gritted her teeth. "Monday!?"

I jumped in before they started arguing. "It is weird to think of Billy Bob as a bad guy."

Jackson switched his focus to me. "Why?"

"In college, he was some kind of big man on campus. Laney has some old newspaper articles in her bag that she got from Gonzaga. He was the editor of the school paper. He even saved a girl from a fire in the newspaper building."

"They didn't start the fire, did they?" said Jackson, evidently still peeved at us.

"No. Some printing equipment caught fire. There was a big picture of him on the cover and a long article that made him out to be the hero."

Jackson snorted. "He was the editor, so of course the paper made him sound good."

I agreed. "They did go overboard. They interviewed his roommate, his brother — even called a next-door neighbor from his hometown. I'm not sure how it was newsworthy that Billy Bob walked the neighbor's dog during high school while the neighbors were on vacation, but even that tidbit made the article."

"They didn't interview his parents to find out how he slept as a baby?"

I answered despite Mace's sarcasm. "No, his parents died when he was in high school. His grandparents raised him but they passed away during his junior year in college."

"Geez, what a sob story." Jackson didn't have a soft heart.

Meghan shot the detective a hard look. The real-world version of her cover model didn't match up to her expectations.

I jumped in. "I think he told Spike to murder Laney in the hospital. A story about her crash was on his computer. You know how the saying goes, where there's smoke, there's fire."

Meghan groaned, but Jackson responded, "Unless it's a ping-pong ball."

"Or popcorn," I said.

"What?"

"Never mind, work joke."

Mace moved to stand up, "My shift ends soon and I'm heading home. Maybe I could get Spike to talk. But, I'll have to talk to my captain before going after Mr. Allen. Picking up the CEO of a major public agency isn't something to do lightly. Basically, we just have you overhearing some vague statements and breaking into his computer. I should probably arrest you both."

Discounting Mace's halfhearted threat, Meghan clenched her fist. "How can you not believe me? What about this file? They're trying to coerce me."

Responding to Meghan's anger, Jackson sat back down. "Look, I believe you. We'll do what we can to protect you and Laney. I understand it's frustrating. But I can't rush in to arrest someone without more solid proof, let alone the CEO of a major public agency. There's nothing to link the burglaries of yours and Laney's houses."

"What if Billy Bob admits to doing something illegal?" I asked.

Jackson gave me a dismissive blink that made me feel like an insect. "Sure. I'll call him up and ask him if he's done anything illegal recently." With a derisive sneer, he turned back to Meghan.

Before he could speak, I said, "No. I mean what if we get him to say something to us and you record it?"

"You want to do a sting on Billy Bob?" Meghan asked me, with both excitement and nervousness competing for attention in her voice.

Jackson interjected, "Not Marty." His eyes flicked to Meghan. "It would have to be you. Billy Bob's never met Marty."

Meghan's voice caught in her throat. "You want me to do a sting on Billy Bob?"

"It actually isn't a terrible idea," admitted Mace, reluctant to credit something I'd proposed. "We can be in the next room. If you could get him to confess to directing Spike to kill Laney or telling his people to hurt you, then we'd have it in his own voice and could charge him with conspiracy to commit murder."

"I don't know." Meghan hesitated. "This seems dangerous."

"We can keep you safe. We'd have a few cops nearby in case he tries anything. It's not like you'd be talking to a gang leader."

I reddened, but my luck held as no one noticed. This wasn't the time to discuss my experiences last night.

Jackson continued, "You said yourself that he could be on his way to becoming governor. Maybe he only wants your file back. Top executives typically don't get violent."

Meghan still didn't appear enthusiastic about the idea, but she agreed. If nothing else, it might stop the harassment.

I leaned forward, eager now to turn my idea into reality. "What do we do next?"

"You. Don't. Do. Anything." Jackson almost jabbed me with his words. "Meghan should contact Billy Bob and get him to meet her."

"What should I say to him?" Meghan's voice turned timorous as the idea of confronting Billy Bob sunk in.

"Make it as short as possible. You want to sound scared and desperate," advised Jackson.

"I am scared and desperate."

In command mode, Jackson didn't stop to console her. He continued with his instructions, "Since we don't know exactly what he wants, don't make any guesses. If you get it wrong, he'll know you're lying."

"Do you think he'll be suspicious if I don't ask him for something, like money?"

Mace shrugged. "I don't know. You don't want to scare him

off, but we should have a believable reason why you're suddenly willing to help him."

They paused and Meghan took another sip of her tea while we all pondered.

I broke the tense silence, blurting out, "How about 'I have what you're looking for. I'll give it to you if you'll just leave me alone.' "

Both Meghan and Mace looked up, startled. With eyes widening, they stared at me for a moment, absorbing my suggestion.

After a long enough pause that made me wonder if they'd forgotten, Meghan said, "That's pretty good."

With a quiet grunt, Mace agreed.

I wasn't sure if I should feel pleased with the compliment or bothered because they were both so surprised I had a sensible idea.

Meghan pulled out her phone. She wrote and sent the quick text to Billy Bob. "So, now what? Do we wait?"

"Once he responds, we can pick a time and place. I'll set up the rest," said Jackson.

We fell into silence, considering our next steps.

"Oh!" The buzzing of her phone surprised Meghan. "He answered already."

"What did he say?" I asked.

"It says, 'You better. Your house tomorrow at 10.' "

Mace gave us a sinister smile. "Maybe he is part of this after all. He just screwed up. Notice he didn't ask where you lived? How would he know unless he was involved in your burglary?"

An equally sinister smile spread across Meghan's face as well before quickly fading. "Maybe he got it from HR since I work there?" Then, the color drained out of her face. "If he knows where I live, what's to stop him from coming after me tonight?"

Mace pursed his lips in concern. "Hmm. Probably best if you aren't there. Just to be safe. Can you stay with a friend tonight?"

Meghan thought out loud, "I don't know many people here and it's really late."

"You could come home with me," I said without thinking. I blushed as they both looked suspiciously at me. "I meant you could stay at my apartment tonight. My nieces are already staying with me. My home office has a futon. The girls are sleeping in the guest room." *At least they're supposed to.*

Meghan paused briefly, considering as she rubbed her face. "Ok, thank you. I'm beat. Even the thought of trying to figure out somewhere else is exhausting."

Jackson eyed me distrustfully before asking her, "Are you sure?" His eyes narrowed.

I avoided any sudden movements so he wouldn't draw his gun.

"Yes, it's ok," pronounced Meghan, raising her chin as she looked me over one more time.

I'd made great strides. Yesterday she'd insisted on meeting me here at Starbucks because she worried I might be dangerous. Now, I had cleared the hurdle of being barely better than staying in her own, hazardous house.

Decision made, Mace shifted into gear. "Ok. Make sure you get back to your house by nine. I'll bring a few officers and we'll set up before Billy Bob arrives."

Meghan and I left Starbucks in her car while Mace stayed behind to make calls to prepare tomorrow morning's sting.

After leaving her car parked outside my apartment building, Meghan and I walked in silence along the hallway to my apartment. It was after midnight and I was wiped. With all of tonight's excitement, I'd forgotten to check in with Mrs. Kim about the girls. Meghan looked drained from the stress of her house break-in, the escape from the Water Agency and the decision to attempt a sting on Billy Bob.

As we approached my apartment, Mrs. Kim opened the door. I nearly jumped back into Meghan, who gasped.

"Good evening, Mr. Marty." Mrs. Kim reached out a hand to Meghan. "Hello dear, I'm Mrs. Kim. Nice to meet you."

Recovering, Meghan introduced herself.

We stepped inside and spoke in hushed tones so we wouldn't wake the girls.

"I'm so sorry I'm back so late. We had a little trouble …" I ran out of steam. I didn't want to explain the last hour with the smoke bomb and Sergeant Jackson. I didn't have the energy to explain the whole crazy situation.

Mrs. Kim, either sensing things were complicated or very tired herself, gave us a small smile. "It no problem. I like the girls. We have good time together. Good night." Without asking for any further explanation, she stepped past us into the hallway and headed to her apartment.

I closed the door behind her. A moment later, I realized I needed to ask her if she could help out in the morning when we had to go to Meghan's house. I opened the door to an empty hallway.

Closing and locking the door again, I said, "I don't get how she does that."

"Does what?" Meghan spoke in a flat voice almost too quiet to hear.

I looked at her. She swayed from side to side and looked ready to collapse. "Never mind. Let's get you settled." I led the way to my office. Carefully, I opened the doors and peeked in. All clear. No Megan lying inside. I gestured Meghan into the room and turned on the light. I pulled out a pillow and blankets from the closet and set them on the futon. In a drawer in the closet, I found some clean sweats and pajamas that Amanda had left here when she last visited.

"The girls are sleeping in the room across the hall. The next door down is the guest bathroom. There should be some new toothbrushes in the drawer. I'll see you in the morning." I stopped myself before telling her to dream about puppies playing ping-pong against ants. I've been spending too much time with my nieces.

———

30

Saturday Early Morning

A scream woke me. Jumping out of bed, I rushed down the hallway. I don't know why people need coffee to wake up. Adrenaline accomplished the same result.

The doors to the office were ajar. Meghan sat on the futon in sweats and Megan, who must have made it into the office sometime last night after I fell asleep, sat on the floor in her pajamas rubbing her eyes.

"You stepped on me," accused Megan with a whine.

"I'm sorry. I didn't mean to. You weren't there when I went to sleep last night and I didn't notice you were on the ground when I got up." Meghan's voice was calm so it must have been Megan whose scream woke me.

Now altogether awake, Megan narrowed her eyes and started to grill my guest. "Does Uncle Marty know you're here? He doesn't like people sleeping in his office."

Meghan kept a straight face as she answered, "Yes, he invited me to stay here because I had a problem at my house."

"No fair." Megan grumbled louder, so I thought it best to jump in.

"Let me introduce you both. Megan, meet Meghan."

"You have my name and you get to sleep in the office? No fair!" Megan jumped up, stomped out of the office, muttering to herself as she went across the hall, and then slammed the door as she went into the guest room. Skye's yell at Megan for waking her up confirmed that Skye was now also awake.

Working hard to keep from laughing out loud, Meghan's smile lit up her eyes. "Perhaps I should go take a shower now." She headed for the bathroom.

With Megan stomping around in the guest room, I felt free to laugh at her display of drama. I walked back to my bedroom and threw on my typical Hawaiian shirt and shorts.

I walked back down the hallway. Outside the girls' room, not yet daring to enter, I announced, "Time for breakfast. Who wants pancakes?"

At least that got a positive reaction so I hustled to the kitchen to get things started.

The girls came out of their bedrooms and sat at the kitchen table. Megan wasn't talking to me, but Skye asked, "Who's the woman?"

"She's a friend who wasn't able to sleep at home last night so she stayed here," I answered, careful to avoid discussion of possible killers who were after both their mother and Meghan.

I walked out of the kitchen. Skye regarded me as a funny expression formed on her face. She pointed at my shirt and gestured with her hand like she was waving me off.

I looked down to check if it had any visible stains. My shirt was clean. "What's wrong with this? I wear it all the time."

Lips pressed together, Skye squinted her eyes and tilted her head to the side and then, with a sad voice, sighed, "No wonder you're not married, Uncle Marty."

I let her comment slide past me. The palm trees and multicolored flowers on my shirt mostly matched the color of my cargo shorts. *I don't understand girls.*

Changing the subject away from my attire, I said, "Hey girls, I have good news."

Megan didn't blink before responding, "I get to sleep in the office tonight?" Her mind was quick, although only seemed to have one-track.

"No, even better. Your mom should be well enough to come home later today." I'd called the hospital last night while Rover drove me to meet Meghan for dinner. "We'll go pick her up from the hospital this afternoon."

Both girls cheered at that happy news. Megan did her happy dance. Although Skye acted too cool for that, she broke out with a wide grin.

I continued, "This morning, I'll see if Mrs. Kim can stay with you again for a little while. I need to go with Meghan somewhere." I didn't want to worry them with all the details. I worried enough for us all.

The girls cheered again. Mrs. Kim had a better reputation in my apartment than I did.

By the time Meghan came down the hallway to the kitchen, I had the pancake batter ready to go on the griddle. I stepped out of the kitchen. "Want pancakes?"

"Sure. Out of clean clothes?" she asked.

"What?"

"Oh. Never mind." Meghan dropped her line of questioning and moved to an open chair at the table.

I don't understand women. I see men wearing Hawaiian shirts all the time out to restaurants or at parties. At least I was sure I would if I went to many parties. I returned to the simpler task of cooking pancakes.

Across the counter that separated the galley kitchen from the kitchen table, I watched Meghan sit down self-consciously at the table, her hair still damp, and look around. Gazing out on my small combination living room/dining room as if I were seeing it for the first time, I tried to assess my place through fresh eyes.

It resembled any number of modern, but not trendy, apartments in the area. A comfortable, beige leather couch, wall-mounted TV, small coffee table and a reclining, leather lounge chair filled most of the living area. Two nice prints bought years ago from local art festivals hung on the walls and some framed pictures of my kids sat on the mantel over the fake fireplace. At least I'd outgrown the forest green, over-stuffed La-Z-Boy recliner from my younger days. Despite fraying at the seams and a few unexplainable holes, that was the most comfortable chair ever. Well, second to Billy Bob's throne. My ex-wife made me get rid of it when we got married. Although I didn't have the most fashion-forward décor, at least I kept the place neat.

Meghan turned back from her brief inspection to look at the girls. "Hi. My name is Meghan." She turned to Skye, "I've already met Megan so you must be Skye."

"How did you know?"

"Marty … your Uncle Marty … told me a little about you. He mentioned you were doing a science fair project on ants. I thought you might be interested to know that I help companies study the impact their new buildings will have on the environment. The project I'm working on right now focuses on a species of endangered ants, with the scientific name of Dorymyrmex insanus."

Skye's eyes almost bugged out of her head as she turned into a human version of the crazy ant. She acted as if she'd been magically transported to a rock concert where the lead singer pulled her up onto the stage. Skye wouldn't let such an opportunity to engage with an ant expert slip by. Both of her arms started shaking as she popped out of her chair and bounced on her toes. She launched into a complicated series of questions where I could practically see the footnotes in the air. Within seconds, the two of them were talking a mile a minute.

They lost me right away. Megan looked at me and then stuck out her tongue to the side of her mouth and made a strangled face that they didn't notice. This didn't appear to the be the first time she had endured her sister geeking out on her. Nor did it look to be her last.

I winked at her and gave my attention to the pancakes cooking on the stove. When the first batch of pancakes finished cooking, I flipped them onto a plate and brought them to the table. After serving everyone, I snagged one for myself as the chef's tax and set the plate with the rest down on the table. I walked back to the stove to get another batch going.

I looked up as the conversation slowed to see a flurry of butter spreading and syrup pouring. Skye and Meghan picked up their forks to take a bite. But Megan picked up an extra pancake from the plate, licked it, and put it down on the plate. Meghan smiled and wrinkled her nose. Before I could react, Meghan picked up a different pancake on the plate, made sure that Megan was watching, then licked it and put it down too.

Skye started laughing. "You're a grown-up, you're not supposed to do that."

"Well, I figured I needed to protect my next pancake too."

Megan leaned forward, now intrigued by this interloper. "Did you have to lick your food too when you were growing up to make sure no one stole it?"

"I have three brothers. I wish I'd thought of that idea, but I don't think it would have mattered to them anyway. If it was food, saliva-coated or not, they would've eaten it."

"Did you have your own room?" asked Megan.

"Sometimes I did, but sometimes I had to share," said a very wise Meghan, sneaking a quick glance at me.

"Did you know the tooth fairy is real?" Megan was pleased that she'd grabbed control of the conversation.

"Oh really?" Meghan kept her tone neutral.

Megan heard doubt. "Betcha?"

"What's 'Betcha'?" Meghan looked to me for an explanation.

"Just go with it," I said.

She turned back to Megan. "Ok. How do you know?" Meghan asked.

"That's not how you play." Megan put her hands on her hips from her seated position and stuck her jaw out in complaint.

In the next instant, her faux frustration disappeared as her excitement bubbled over. Megan reached into her pocket and pulled out a real dollar bill, one of those old-fashioned green paper ones that you seldom see anymore. "See! The tooth fairy gave me a dollar under my pillow last night for my lost tooth." She opened her lips wide to reveal a hole in her mouth from the missing tooth.

"Wow," said a suitably impressed Meghan, "What will you do with it?"

While Megan regaled Meghan with her plans to spend her newfound wealth, Skye slipped out of her chair into the kitchen. She whispered to me, "You owe Mrs. Kim a buck."

I can't win. Even Meghan didn't have to pay up and she had played "Betcha." I settled for bringing out the second batch of pancakes to the table.

"Chocolate chip pancakes?" squealed Megan.

I grinned. *I am the pancake master.* "Yes, I remembered them after I made the first batch and I thought you'd like them."

Everyone took another pancake. I made sure to grab one too before any licking began.

Skye paused and looked at the pancake on her plate before raising her eyebrow at me. "Are you showing off, Uncle Marty?"

Well, maybe a little. A pang of shame struck me as I hadn't remembered I could make pancakes for them earlier in the week. I deftly changed topics. "Megan, I'm sorry I didn't give you an idea for a dream last night. Did you have a good dream anyway?"

Megan's eyes lit up. "Oh, it's okay. Mrs. Kim gave me an awesome idea."

I hadn't expected Mrs. Kim to get called upon for dream duty. "What did she suggest?"

"She told us to dream of pigs and flying around."

"What?"

"She told us it would be super lucky."

"Flying pigs?"

Skye almost choked on her milk as she laughed at this.

Megan crossed her arms against her chest. "No, silly. Us flying around and lots of pigs on the ground. Pigs don't fly." With that clarified, she took another bite of her chocolate chip pancake while Meghan giggled.

As we finished eating, Meghan took her plate to the sink and asked, "Do you have a hairdryer?"

I almost responded "No" before stopping to reconsider. "I'll bet there's one stashed away somewhere under the sink in that bathroom." I didn't justify why a man living alone with short cropped hair had a hairdryer in his apartment, but this didn't seem like the right time to explain that I had a daughter in her junior year in college.

"I'll dry my hair and then I'm ready to go." Meghan's voice trailed off as she remembered our mission to confront Billy Bob this morning.

"Ok, we'll clean up and I'll ask Mrs. Kim to watch the girls."

As Meghan walked back to the bathroom, both girls finished their last bites. While Skye put away the cooking supplies, Megan and I dealt with the dirty dishes. According to Megan, even chocolate chip pancakes had undesirable crusts that she swept into the disposal before loading the dishwasher.

"She's nice. She can stay." Megan had waited until the hairdryer had turned on before making her pronouncement.

"That's sweet, Megan, but she's just a friend who needed a place to sleep last night. She'll be going back home today."

"Then it's my turn to sleep in the office." Megan stomped her foot for emphasis to make sure I understood the plan.

"No, remember you'll be going back home today, too."

"Oh, yeah." Megan's stomping changed into a twirling motion, happy to remember that she'd see her mother soon.

I left the girls to walk down the hallway to Mrs. Kim's apartment. Although I'd always been friendly when we ran into each other in the hallway or outside the building, we'd talked more in the last few days than we had over the last few months. I hated to impose, but I couldn't think of who else to ask to watch the girls this morning.

As I approached her door, Mrs. Kim opened it and greeted me. "Good morning, Mr. Marty. How are the girls this morning? And your new woman friend?"

I took a breath to calm my racing heart. I had no idea how she did it. Perhaps she'd installed motion detectors in the hallway or pressure mats under the carpeting. Deciding this wasn't the time to ask, I plowed ahead. "I hate to bother you again, but my friend and I have to go meet the police this morning and the girls can't —"

She interrupted, "I am very happy to spend time with the girls. They are very good girls." She took a quick step out of her apartment and pulled the door shut behind her. She walked down the hall toward my apartment before I could even close my mouth. Mrs. Kim probably doesn't get a lot of visitors. Once this was over, I'd have to ask her to join me, on occasion, when the girls visited. I caught up with her. "Great. I think I even have a 500-piece puzzle that you might enjoy doing with them."

The girls greeted Mrs. Kim with excitement. When I took out the puzzle, they pulled her over to the table and scattered the pieces.

Meghan and I left the apartment a few minutes later and no one seemed to notice.

"They really seem attached to Mrs. Kim. How long has she babysat for them?" asked Meghan.

"They met on Tuesday night."

"Oh." Meghan glanced at me in surprise. "Well, they all seem to get along wonderfully."

We walked out of the building and turned toward Meghan's car, still parked on the street in the exact spot where we'd left it late last night. I had to admit it was nice to have a car sitting ready for you whenever you wanted to leave, without having to signal for it to come. The only downside was it didn't give me enough time to calm my jitters before launching into the sting.

I slowed, trying to calm down before getting in the car with Meghan. Perhaps Rover should have a new feature to predict when you'd want a car based on your travel habits and personal calendar. Then a Rover car could wait outside for you for a while. Of course, Rover could never have predicted that I'd be leaving this early on a Saturday morning.

I'd bring up the idea of a predictive feature in the product planning meeting with marketing on Monday. It was time that I'd get some credit for a new idea even if marketing would give it a stupid name. After pondering for a few seconds, I broke out with a snort as I came up with my own stupid suggestion for the feature's name. We could call it "W.O.O.F.," standing for "What's Our Outbound Future." I'd sell it to marketing by explaining that customers would tell Rover, "W.O.O.F." or "No W.O.O.F.!" depending on whether or not they wanted the feature activated.

I snorted again. No, even for marketing, that was too far-fetched. *Fetched? Too funny.* I couldn't decide if the marketing team would recognize that I was making fun of them. At least, I wouldn't need to get over-caffeinated like Raj while testing this feature.

"Marty, come on already," yelled Meghan out the window of her car. "It's time to go catch the bad guys."

31

Saturday Morning

Mace and two other cops waited on Meghan's front porch when we pulled up promptly at nine o'clock. Their patrol cars were not in sight so they must have parked around the corner. Or, maybe Mace invoked an invisibility shield around their cars. I wouldn't put it past him. I'm sure it's all the rage for underwear models turned action heroes.

When we reached the porch, Jackson turned to me and spoke without a greeting. "I changed my mind. I don't want you here for this. A stranger in the house could spook Mr. Allen, and I don't want it more dangerous than it already is. Plus, I don't want this screwed up."

"But, ..." I started, unsure what he was implying about me.

"No! He's staying. He can hide in my kitchen or a bedroom if you don't want Billy Bob to see him," said Meghan with an emphatic stomp on the porch.

I kept my mouth shut as beams of invisible power lanced between Meghan and Mace. Their silent, but deadly, struggle of wills lasted but a few seconds while I reminded myself not to get on Meghan's bad side in the future. That made me wonder if we had a future past this morning's excitement. I liked her smile even if her glare made me wonder if I'd need a personal force field for protection.

With one last sharp glance at me, Mace grunted and turned away to pick up his duffel bag of secret police supplies. "Ok, but he has to stay out of it." Either Meghan had won or Mace had decided not to push the point.

"He will," answered Meghan, both of them settling my fate without my participation.

Grateful for Meghan's support so I could see this through to the end, I remained quiet while she unlocked the door to let me and the rest of the strike force into her house.

The other two cops didn't have Mace's good looks or action hero presence. Both stocky, squarely built with close-cropped hair, they wore body armor under their uniform with multiple, official-looking gadgets and gizmos hanging off their uniform belt. Even if I saw them out of uniform, my first thought would be "cop."

"Hi, I'm Marty Golden." I introduced myself and reached out to shake the other cops' hands. Without reciprocating my gesture, they grunted also, leaned over and picked up bulky bags of police supplies and stepped past me into the house.

Yup, we were buds.

Meghan's house resembled an older, smaller version of Laney's. Like most houses in the Bay Area that normal people might possibly afford, it was modest and at least seventy years old on a tiny lot crammed next to its neighbors. A previous owner had updated and modernized Laney's house in recent years while the interior layout of Meghan's home looked untouched from its initial construction as an original California bungalow.

As with many older Bay Area homes, the front door opened straight into the living room. A well-worn, yet comfortable looking couch, two chairs and a few small side tables faced each other in the room. I was surprised not to see any TV screens. She did have some colorful medieval-themed prints on her walls that she'd probably picked up from an artist's booth at a Renaissance Faire.

The dated layout was ideal for today's purpose. Her living room acted as the central passageway for the house with various doors and openings leading off it. Off the back of the room past a pocket, sliding door, a narrow galley kitchen opened to her backyard. Daylight streamed into the kitchen through the glass door to her small backyard.

To the right of the front door was a good-sized coat closet. One of the cops was busy pulling out jackets and clearing room on the closet floor. He'd located his hiding space. The other officer had opened the door to a small bedroom on the right. The left side of the living room had a narrow hallway with yet another pocket, sliding door. It looked like it led to another bedroom and bathroom. The cops would be close enough to protect Meghan in case something went wrong.

The value of a pocket sliding door separating back bedrooms from the living room escaped me. When I was growing up, I'd lived in a small house, too. Hollow sliding doors didn't buffer the sounds from the front room back to my nearby bedroom. When my mother had her friends over for their regular book group, my dad had to set up sleeping palettes in a large closet in their master bedroom on the other side of the house for Laney and me. Despite several closed pocket doors between us, I still couldn't fall asleep until after her friends had left. Their outbursts of alcohol-induced laughter carried through the floorboards and sounded to my young ears as if they stood over me. I'd never understood the appeal. My teachers never made it that much fun to talk about books at school. Maybe if they'd served us alcohol?

I needed a drink now.

Sergeant Jackson leaned in close and spoke in a quiet voice to Meghan before placing something small into her hand. She closed her hand around it, closed her eyes and took a deep breath. She walked out of the living room into the hallway to her back bedroom.

"What was that?" I asked.

"That was the 'wire.' "

"What happens if Billy Bob pats her down or sees the battery pack on her back?"

Mace scoffed. "You've watched too much TV. Modern 'wires' are tiny and wireless. There's enough range for this house and her body heat will keep it charged. She just puts it under her shirt and attaches it with a little piece of tape. It looks and feels like she has a Band-Aid on a cut. Just like you, Princess."

I'd forgotten to pull off my Band-Aid this morning. My paper cut no longer stung even if his nickname for me did.

When Meghan walked back in the room, Mace called everyone together. "Ok, let's just go over a few points to keep everyone safe."

I approved of this idea.

Jackson looked at Meghan. "The three of us will hide all around you. I'll be in the hallway, he'll be in the closet and he'll be in that bedroom." He gestured at the other officers.

"I'll be in the kitchen," I offered since Mace had forgotten the fourth member of his strike team.

Mace ignored me. "You want to make this seem natural, not forced. Just speak normally and the mike will record both of you. Don't give him the folder with the papers right away. Try to ask him some open-ended questions and get him talking first."

"What should I ask?"

"Ask him why he's been trying to coerce you into signing that report you mentioned."

"You should ask him if he tried to kill Laney." I contributed my value-add.

Jackson glared at me, took a deep breath, and then turned his attention back to Meghan. "No. Don't start with that. You could spook him if you start off by talking about someone else. Remember he doesn't know you were there last night. Get him talking first about you. Once he admits to something, then maybe you could mention Laney and see what he says."

"Ok, that makes sense," said Meghan.

Maybe. I didn't want sense. I wanted to know why Billy Bob was trying to kill Laney.

"Finally," Jackson concluded, "there are two code phrases to use. If you want us to hold off on coming in to rescue you, then say 'My Word.' Say 'Bananas' if you want the cavalry to show up immediately."

"What? Bananas?" I was puzzled by that choice.

"Yeah, it's stupid. It's so stupid that people stop to figure out what they just heard. While they're confused, we're bursting into the room."

"I think I have my lines down and know everyone's places." Then, Meghan moved a hand to her chin and ignored us as she began moving her lips silently to get ready for her performance.

I suppressed a smile about Meghan's theatrical approach to the sting. She appeared to have dealt with the stress by thinking of this whole situation as yet another play with her in a lead role. With my character off-stage for this scene, I didn't need to learn any lines. Coding was way less complicated than this monkey business.

Mace made sure to station me in the kitchen first with the door slid all the way closed before he checked that everyone else had settled into their places.

All was quiet well before ten o'clock. With a brief pat on her shoulder for reassurance, I had left Meghan sitting on the couch in her living room pretending to read a book. She had the folder with the environmental data and preliminary report near her, hidden under a pillow on the couch. Standing in her kitchen behind the pocket door with my ear turned to the door to hear better, I heard her foot tapping up a storm on the wood floor. As I'd expected, I heard nothing from Mace or the other two cops in their hiding spots. Now we needed our villain, Billy Bob, to make his appearance so the curtain would open and our performance begin. While I stared at the wall in her kitchen, I started to sweat, hoping that nothing would go wrong.

As if a director had yelled "Action", the doorbell rang. The game was afoot. I heard Meghan walk to the door and open it.

"Mighty fine morning, ain't it?" Billy Bob's voice sounded muffled through the hollow pocket door.

His voice had lost the angry tone from last night with Spike. This morning, he unveiled the voice of a politician, speaking with an overly loud, smooth confidence and noticeable Southern twang. I could imagine him with chest out, striding into the room like he owned the place.

I could barely make out Meghan's initial response.

"Hi." She rallied and spoke louder so the hiding cops could hear and know when to come in. "Why did you try to scare me into signing the impact assessment?" Dispensing with small talk, Meghan got right to the point.

"Well now, I don't know what you're talking about." Billy Bob played the part of a self-righteous politician at a press conference, admitting nothing and pretending that he'd never caught wind of those issues.

Meghan pooh-poohed this answer. "Oh, come on. You had your security people vandalize my car and intimidate me so I'd sign the report without looking closely at the data."

Billy Bob waved this off. "My goodness. You have quite the imagination, my dear. If someone put dog crap on your car in the building parking lot, you should have reported it to the lobby security guard and he'd call the police for you."

"I didn't say it was dog crap." Meghan's voice sounded triumphant.

Billy Bob paused. He'd gotten snagged, but only in a small mistake. When he continued, the Southern accent had disappeared and his voice had turned flat and insistent. "Let's stop playing games. You texted that you have what I'm looking for. Give it to me."

"I've got all the data from the initial environmental study in a folder for you. First, you've got to promise that you and your goons will leave me alone."

"Stop playing dumb. I'm not here for that."

Meghan sounded as confused as I felt. "But then why were you trying to scare me?"

Billy Bob's exasperation was palpable. "I don't care about that now. If you were lying to me last night, I'll leave now. I don't think you'll like it if I do." His voice deepened and slowed as he delivered the vague threat. He'd make a great politician. He knew how to say something without being specific. Although we knew he'd threatened Meghan, I'm sure his lawyers could invent a hundred reasons why we'd misunderstood this poor, saint of an executive.

The sting hadn't followed our script. In cop shows, stings always worked, enticing the bad guys to admit to their crime before the police surged in for the take-down. All cleanly executed and wrapped up before the final commercial break.

Shoulders slumping, I leaned over to touch my forehead to the door. We hadn't outwitted Billy Bob after all. Meghan had asked Billy Bob why he'd directed his goons to harass her. If he'd mentioned something about it, then she might have been able to get him to talk about Laney as well. But, Billy Bob hadn't played his part. He'd gone off script.

I shuddered at how furious Mace must be with me right now for wasting his time and getting nothing they could use on Billy Bob. Last night, everything had seemed so clear. Billy Bob wanted

Laney dead. What if I were wrong and it was all just a set of crazy coincidences?

Something cold and hard tapped my neck.

I turned my head to the left. A gun pointed straight at me, with its cavernous barrel opening looming large enough to swallow me whole. The gun's barrel stretched out almost to infinity back to where a beefy hand gripped the handle. Attached to the hand was the rest of Spike, with a smirking grin on his face.

"Well, looky what we have here." Spike had a sing-song cadence to his voice.

Without taking his eyes away from me, he called out loudly, "Hey Boss, I found something interesting in the kitchen." He nodded his head toward the front and gestured to me with his gun.

I got the point. Sliding the kitchen door open, I shuffled through, with Spike's arm holding the gun pointed at my neck the whole time.

Meghan, startled by our unscripted appearance at stage right, recovered with a speed that dazzled me. "My word," she enunciated clearly, "Spike, I didn't know you were here. Why are you pointing a gun at Marty?"

Meghan must be great at improv. She'd incorporated the code phrase into her first comment even though Spike's appearance had surprised us both. No one wanted the cops jumping out and Spike shooting me, even by accident. Especially me.

"Shut up. I'm the one asking the questions." Billy Bob looked at me. "Who are you?"

My recent experience with the gang at the restaurant helped reduce the stammer in my voice. "I'm Marty." Accurate, although perhaps not complete. I've learned that I'm not at my best with a cold metal barrel pointing at me.

"Ok, Marty." Billy Bob seemed more amused than frustrated. "Why are you here and why were you hiding in the kitchen?" With Spike holding the gun, Billy Bob swaggered around

Meghan's living room, touching her knickknacks, in control of the situation.

"I wanted to find out why you're trying to hurt Meghan ... and Laney."

Laney's name caught Billy Bob's attention and he swung back to me. His fists clenched and he took a step toward me. Through narrowed eyes, he asked, "How do you know Laney?" In a flash, his demeanor had shifted from a confident politician into someone much more sinister.

"She's my sister."

Like a tiger to prey, Billy Bob pounced. "So, you have the paper?"

That confused me. "Meghan has all the papers. She just offered them to you."

Billy Bob scoffed. "I don't care about those."

Meghan must have felt left out of the script. "But they're the proof," she interjected.

Billy Bob turned back to her with a scowl. "Proof of what?"

"They prove you're trying to build a new plant on top of the crazy ants," I said.

"Dorymyrmex insanus," corrected Meghan, with a scientific compulsion.

Billy Bob's head was rotating like a spectator sitting at midcourt of a tennis match. "Insane what?"

I knew the answer to this one. Skye would be proud of me. Despite my nervousness, I started to explain, "They're from Texas. They're known as crazy ants."

Meghan corrected, "Originally South America."

Billy Bob blew up. "Bulletin! I need it. Where is it?"

"What?" Meghan and I both said in unison.

Billy Bob's face grew red with irritation. I had that effect on people on a regular basis. "This is a waste of time. Ok, just give me that folder. Some stupid ants —"

"Crazy ants," I interrupted.

Billy Bob eyed us both carefully, as if worried we were going insane. "Well, I'll take that folder anyway. I don't care if those ants are crazy, stupid, or you've got ants in your pants. They aren't going to stop me from getting that project finished on schedule."

"And getting appointed to run the State Board?" I couldn't resist, although further upsetting him right now didn't seem advisable.

With a frighteningly rapid shift of personality, Billy Bob reverted back to the smarmy politician. His words oozed past me. "I don't know what you're talking about."

Meghan had a sharp eye on the gun still resting against my neck. I hadn't forgotten about it either. "Okay, okay, I'll give the folder to you. Could you please have him put the gun away? We're not a threat to the two of you."

I'd completely forgotten about the cops, hiding around us. Meghan's ability to stay calm and convey helpful information to them impressed me. She'd stuck to the script while managing an improvisation to get us out of this situation without anyone getting shot. With the gun pointing at my head, I appreciated her skill.

Billy Bob shook his head derisively. "Spike, put the gun away. You don't need it. They're too wimpy to try anything."

"Ok, boss." Although Spike pulled the gun away from my neck, it would be a long time before I stopped feeling it resting against my skin. Spike put the gun behind his back into his belt. "Now what, boss?"

Meghan said, "It's time for bananas!"

The house exploded with noise.

"Police! Down! Down on the ground! Hands out. Down!" yelled a cacophony of voices as the three cops burst out of their hiding spots.

Everyone dropped to the ground. Well, Billy Bob, Spike and I all dropped to the ground. Meghan took a step back to make room as the cops rushed in around her.

From the ground, I looked up in time to see Mace rubbing the back of his neck as he cocked his head to the side to observe me with a skeptical raised eyebrow. He shot a questioning look at Meghan before reaching a hand down to me. He pulled me up in one quick jerk. A little rougher than seemed necessary. At least I was off the floor with my dignity restored.

Yeah, that's what I'm going with. I let out a deep breath. After someone puts a gun in your face, or your neck, breathing feels good, shaky or not.

"You're under arrest," said one of the police officers to Billy Bob.

"Why, whatever for?" Billy Bob's Southern drawl had returned, thicker than before.

He had a point. Billy Bob hadn't actually admitted to threatening Meghan or trying to kill Laney.

"Assault with a deadly weapon," said Sergeant Jackson with a police officer's typical bravado.

"Officer, if you will please look closely. I don't have a gun," Billy Bob held his hands up, open and out to his sides. "I'm the CEO of the NorCal Water Agency and I'm just here for a short business meeting with Ms. Emerson." Billy Bob pointed to Spike. "That man has the gun. He put it away when I told him to. If anything, I'm the hero for stopping the assault. I've done nothing wrong. You've got no reason to arrest me."

I had to hand it to Billy Bob. He was cool under pressure. My heart raced and I still shook a little from the gun and then the surprise from the police popping out. And I'd known they were in the house all along.

"Read him his rights and put him in my cruiser. We'll bring them back to the precinct to sort this out." Jackson instructed one of the cops.

The other cop already had handcuffs on Spike and had pulled him to his feet. Spike didn't speak as he was led away. Considering that Billy Bob had thrown him under the bus for the whole episode, his silence was impressive. Billy Bob didn't strike me as the sort of leader that inspired loyalty.

When both men were out of earshot, Mace turned to me. A small vein on his forehead pulsed. "I told you to stay out of this."

"I couldn't help it." It sounded whiny even to me. "Spike had a gun to my head and pushed me into the room."

Mace ignored my comment and spoke to Meghan. "Unfortunately, Billy Bob's probably right. We don't have enough to make more than a misdemeanor assault charge stick, at best. Nothing on bullying you or attacking Laney."

"What do you mean?" Meghan's voice rose. "He's going to get away with threatening me and trying to kill Laney?"

"I'll talk to the prosecutors, but he didn't admit to anything. About either of you. So, it's still his word against yours." Jackson's outstretched arms made patting motions in the air as if he were trying to calm Meghan.

I looked down as I balled my hands into fists in frustration that Billy Bob would get away with it.

Meghan would have none of it. "Are you saying you don't believe me?"

"I believe you." Jackson started sweating. A man with a gun didn't scare him, but Meghan had him on the ropes. "We just don't have enough proof to hold him, let alone win a court case."

A flash of pink from the Band-Aid on my finger caught my eye. Before Meghan could get even more worked up, I said, "Wait. Maybe there is something more."

"I think we've heard quite enough from you. This crazy sting was your idea in the first place." Mace dismissed me with an annoyed grunt and turned back to keep an eye on Meghan.

Ignoring his reaction, I said, "Remember, he used the word 'bulletin' and that he needed it?"

"What bulletin?" Jackson kept his wary attention on Meghan.

I didn't explain, not right away. "When he had his hands up, both his thumbs were normal, weren't they?"

Perhaps intrigued, Mace finally turned to me. He pinched the bridge of his nose and scrunched his eyebrows while one elbow rested on his other wrist. Police get trained to remember details. Engineers were trained to remember equations, but, in general, I was good at remembering odd details. That has proved to be my best talent for uncovering computer bugs.

"Yeah, his hands were normal. Why?" Mace's tone had lost some of its skepticism as he honed in on me.

I kept any pride out of my voice while I explained. "He said 'Bulletin'. As in *The Gonzaga Bulletin*. Remember I told you about those old Gonzaga newspapers in Laney's briefcase. One had a front-page story about how William Robert Allen, editor of the newspaper, had been a hero during the fire at the paper's offices."

"Ok, so what? I can't arrest him for being a hero." Mace had little patience for me.

"The picture showed his hand wrapped in heavy gauze. The caption said that part of his thumb had been cut off, but he was otherwise fine."

Mace caught up. "Wait. Those were two, absolutely normal thumbs he showed us."

Intrigued, Meghan asked, "How does he have normal thumbs now?"

"I don't know. Maybe the police should check it out." Perhaps not the smartest thing to give sarcastic directions to someone carrying a gun, but I felt smug.

Mace just grunted. But, this time it didn't sound annoyed.

32

Sunday Morning

Laney lay on the couch in her family room while I sat nearby resting from a late night and long week. A visiting nurse had only recently left Laney's house and would return tomorrow. Laney's bruises had progressed from red and blue to more of a yellowish-green, along with some multicolored spots. Her face looked like a Jackson Pollock painting come to life, but the nurse had been pleased with her rapid progress.

Although Laney still needed more recovery time before returning to work, she had the strength to get around the house and handle her kids. "Where'd you run off to so quickly last night?"

I blushed. "I went to a play." By the time I got her checked out of the hospital, into the car, and home with the girls, it had been late afternoon. I'd ordered a pizza delivery for them and told the girls to take care of their mother. Then I left, hurrying to the Santa Cruz mountains to catch Meghan's performance at the Renaissance Faire.

"A play?" Doubtful that culture would attract her brother, Laney raised an eyebrow. The prospect of teasing me about doing something cultural energized her. She propped up on an elbow and leaned forward to have a go at me.

I cut her off before she got going. "Did Mace, I mean Sergeant Jackson, call to give you the update?"

"I don't know. I haven't checked my voicemail. What happened?" She settled back on the couch, willing to let me off the hook if I filled her in.

I relished the idea of breaking the news to her. "Well, it looks like the NorCal Water Agency will need a new CEO."

"What happened?" Laney's eyebrows raised slightly as she focused on me.

"Turns out that Spike wasn't as loyal as Billy Bob believed. When the police offered him a deal if he rolled over on Billy Bob, he sang like a canary. He admitted that he'd killed that old woman on your floor."

Laney interjected, "That was so sad."

"Yeah. I met some of her family the morning they found her. Spike told the police that Billy Bob had offered him a bonus to do it. That's conspiracy to commit murder or something like that."

"Why did he want to kill me?" Laney sounded indignant. "Wait, did they crash the drone into my car also?"

"No." My frustration drew a surprised look from Laney. I still couldn't believe that the outrageous drone crash on Monday that started me on this investigation had merely been a slipshod accident. "Some startup trying to crack into DroneTech's market had a bug in their code."

"That bug couldn't fly?" The head injury hadn't affected Laney's wit.

"Funny." I admired her wordplay. Our dad would be proud. He claimed responsibility for our ability, or disability, with puns.

The bug in the startup's system had caused their drone to stop responding to the guidance commands and then veer off course. Eventually, it ran out of power and plummeted to earth. The situation offended my professional pride in my fellow software engineers. This wouldn't have happened if it had been my project. There are effective ways to test your code against unusual scenarios rather than whatever nonsensical approach this company had used.

With the sarcastic tone she'd used since we were kids to drill through the mental fog of my thought processes, Laney said, "Hard to imagine the concept of a startup having trouble getting its code perfect. I'm sure that never happens."

I refocused on her. "You were the lucky bystander, well I guess, unlucky bystander when the drone crashed into that truck at that moment."

Perhaps I could convince DroneTech to pretend my visit to their control center had also been an accident. I needed to ask Daniel to tell the recruiters to treat my earlier visit as a minor misunderstanding that shouldn't affect DroneTech's willingness to hire me.

Laney waved to catch my eye. "Then, why'd Billy Bob want to kill me?"

"Because of that old Gonzaga newspaper article you had in your bag. You know, the one about the fire with the newspaper editor in bandages on the front page?"

Her brow knotted in confusion. "What did that have to do with anything?"

Skye and Megan ran into the room, playing some form of tag with rules known only to them. "Hi, Uncle Marty," they chimed in near unison before racing back to the bedrooms. This morning, I had needed some green tea to get moving without my daily diet of heart-pounding, panic attacks wondering what happened to Megan. Although I appreciated getting my apartment back to myself, I'd been surprised that I missed the noise and energy of having them underfoot.

"Earth to Marty," said Laney, this time with a sigh.

Now I knew where her girls had heard that old-fashioned phrase.

"Sorry. Billy Bob got worried you figured it out last Friday when you mentioned the article and shook his hand at the Water Agency executive meet-and-greet."

Laney scratched her head but winced and quickly lifted her hands when she touched the bandages that still protected her cuts. "I don't understand. I only brought them back with me from last month's trip to Spokane to show them to him. Like a memory of his heroic times."

"How'd you get them?" I was curious how she'd dug up these ancient stories.

"I ran into an old neighbor in Spokane when I stopped at our house." She swallowed, thinking about our recently sold, family home and her years of happiness living in it with her husband and kids. "He'd retired from Gonzaga years ago, a professor of something, I don't know what. He invited me into his house and showed me these stacks of papers from when he'd been the newspaper's faculty advisor. The archives burned down a few years after the newspaper office."

Hmm.

She continued, "I saw Billy Bob's name under that picture. I thought I'd bring him some clippings from his days as the editor as a way to build rapport, you know, to win him over. I had just won the Water Agency business. I thought he might enjoy some reminders of his glory days at Gonzaga." She shifted her position on her pillows. She wouldn't last the day resting that the nurse had recommended. "That made him want to kill me?"

"Yes," I said, smug with anticipation.

"That's bizarre."

"Oh, it gets weirder." I smirked before continuing, "It turns out that Billy Bob and his twin brother both went to college at Gonzaga. One was the school editor, president of his fraternity and a top student. The other barely graduated. He'd been in and out of trouble with the local police ever since their parents died in a car accident during high school. The boys lived with their grandparents, but they were elderly and both passed away during the boys' junior year in college. The boys came into quite a bit of money between the insurance settlement for their parents and their grandparents' estate."

Laney broke in, "That's how Billy Bob got his money?"

I ignored the interruption. "After they graduated from college, the boys took the summer off, traveling around Asia until another tragic accident struck. One brother died in an unusual boating accident in the middle of the ocean near Thailand. His body was never recovered."

Laney's mouth fell open. "Billy Bob's brother died, too?"

"Well ... That's what Sergeant Jackson told me this morning." I kept a close eye on Laney. I wanted to see her reaction. "Turns out that Billy Bob was the school editor who lost part of his thumb in the fire. But the CEO of the NorCal Water Agency has two perfectly good thumbs."

"What?" Her mouth gaped open wider as her palm smacked the couch in exclamation.

I beamed like a Cheshire cat lapping up the reaction. "Yes. Our Billy Bob is actually named Robert Joseph Allen. At least, according to his old, Washington state driver's license fingerprints. Growing up, he was called Bobby Joe." I giggled, despite myself.

She snorted. "How would you ever keep them straight? Remember how Mom used to call me Mar-Laney whenever she'd start to yell at me?"

I did remember. When our mother would get mad, she'd call Laney by Mar-Laney, or M-Laney. Perhaps I got in trouble more often and she got accustomed to yelling my name. I couldn't imagine the chaos in a house with one twin called Billy Bob and the other called Bobby Joe. Would a third son get called Joe Bob or Billy Joe just to complete the silliness?

Something else occurred to me. "You realize what this means, don't you?"

"No, what now?"

"It means the evil twin did it."

"I thought that only happened in soap operas and comic books. Not in real life."

A few moments of laughter ensued before Laney used the neckline of her t-shirt to wipe away her tears of laughter. She shifted her shirt back into place and hesitated. "Do you think Bobby Joe killed his brother in Thailand all those years ago?"

A small shiver ran down my spine. "Maybe. Or maybe he took advantage of the situation when his brother drowned by switching identities without telling anyone. I doubt we'll ever know for sure."

The thought sobered us up.

"How did you know to check him out in the first place?"

I rubbed my unshaven cheek, not quite sure how to tell Laney that I'd investigated all of her recent clients. I decided on the truth and ripped off my metaphorical princess bandage. "I didn't. I, kind of, checked out all of the clients you had scheduled for Monday to see if they did something to you."

She gulped. "Rollag and DroneTech too?"

"Yeah. That's a pretty cool company. I, uh, don't think Rollag wants to talk to you again." *Or me.*

"Thanks a lot." Her lips tightened into a thin line for a moment. Almost as quickly, Laney's mood lightened. "Of course, it's not like they were going to hire me to run their whole HR department. He was such a sexist jerk anyway. I'd wind up having to investigate him for harassment."

"Most definitely," I said, relieved that she wasn't mad and that she already shared my opinion of him. Then I remembered why I needed to call his venture capitalists on Monday and my evil sneer returned to my face.

"What?" She looked a tad worried that an evil doppelgänger of her brother had entered her house.

"Well, we apparently think alike. I called Sierra Smith and pretended to be an IRS agent."

Laney reddened and let out a small giggle. "I know I shouldn't do that. People get so nervous if they think the IRS has called them. Then, when I ask them about someone else, they're so relieved, they blab. It's practically guaranteed."

I tried to pull off a look of haughty disdain while I told her how I'd been a more effective fake agent than her. I explained what I'd learned about Rollag's bribe to Sierra and thus, his subsequent false graduation.

She gasped. "He didn't?"

"He did. He's definitely worse than just a sexist jerk."

Laney surprised me by sitting up, leaning over and grabbing my hand. She pressed my hand to her lips. "You're awesome!"

Why, yes, I am. "Besides saving your life, why now?"

She slapped my hand away. "I wasn't working for Rollag. The VCs hired me. They'll be so happy I found something."

Technically, I found something. But, I gave her this one.

Laney continued, "They put a big bonus in my contract if I found something that fit their reputational clause so they could claw back a bigger portion of the company before it went public. I only asked Sierra if she remembered Rollag or Saunders had been extra flush with money in their senior year. I thought maybe they might have combined the company funds from the VCs with their own money. I never thought to ask about bribery." She trailed off. It must have been in wonderment at my superior detective skills.

Laney swung her feet to the floor, now more alert after my update.

Despite my external show of composure, I couldn't believe what had happened either. "Hard to believe that Bobby Joe could pretend to be Billy Bob for all these years without anyone catching on. Despite looking alike, siblings can be so different. With Megan and Skye, it's hard to believe they're even related."

Laney gained a suspicious glint in her eyes. "Definitely different personalities. What did they do this week?"

Cool Uncle Marty wasn't going to spill the beans on his nieces. "Uh … Nothing. I guess I thought about it this morning when I brought over Skye's science fair project with the stupid ants."

Without thinking, Laney corrected me, "Crazy ants."

"Really, you too?" I spread my arms in a disbelieving shrug.

She grimaced. "Sorry. Skye has me well trained"

I waved it off. "You can't get much more different than feeding ants and tasting different kinds of milkshakes."

"Milkshakes? What are you talking about?"

"Megan's science fair project?" I raised my eyebrows.

Laney raised her eyebrow into a matching quizzical expression. "Megan doesn't have a science fair this year. That doesn't start until next year."

I leaned back, put both hands on my head, and burst out laughing. "Oh, she got me good."

Laney laughed as well at her gullible big brother.

With my update out of the way, Laney leaned forward with a twinkle in her eye. "I've got a few questions of my own for you."

Now I gulped. I checked my watch. I couldn't leave quite yet and didn't see a good way to avoid this. I paused as long as I could, before responding, "What?"

"First, why did I get two messages from the school secretary. Something about the girls having an unexcused absence from school and then about their poor eating choices?"

I reached into my pocket and pulled out my wallet. "There was a little confusion, but the girls went to school every day and I made sure they ate well enough." Taking the two folded slips from my wallet, I handed them to her. "Send these in with the girls on Monday morning."

Laney took them from me without a glance. Before she read them, she continued her interrogation. "Ok. Who is Mrs. Kim and why do I need a tea kettle?"

This one was much easier. "She's my neighbor. You'll like her. The girls really hit it off with her. They stayed with her in the afternoon a few times and one evening while I, uh, had some, uh, work to wrap up." I didn't outright lie to Laney, just stretched reality a bit. I justified this to myself because I didn't want her upset while she recovered.

Laney didn't seem to fully believe me but didn't know what angle to pursue next. Absently, she nodded while she unfolded the slips of paper I'd handed her. Her brows furrowed as she read the Excused Absence Forms. "Who's Dr. Emerson? And while I'm asking you questions, who's this other Meghan and why was she sleeping at your place last night?"

Her doorbell rang. She didn't move as she eyed me while her twinkle disappeared. I felt pinned to the couch. While we both sat there, the doorbell rang again. Skye and Megan raced past us and slammed into the door, neither winning their short, spontaneous race.

They scrambled to unlock the door while Laney uncoiled herself from the couch to control the situation. All three of them stood together as the front door finally swung open. A young man stood on the porch holding a crate. Behind him, a van with a *Pa's Paws* logo sat in Laney's driveway. The young man set the crate down on the ground. Looking up at us, he asked, "Megan Tran?"

"That's me," said an excited Megan, raising her hand high above her head and jumping to make her hand go even higher into the air.

He opened the crate and a large tan streak burst out of the crate and into the house. As the full-grown Labrador's paws clattered on the hardwood floor hallway leading back to the bedrooms, both girls screamed with delight.

They twirled and raced after the dog. As they ran, "Thanks, Uncle Marty!" echoed back down the hallway.

Turned out that the only online, dog delivery service in the whole Bay Area didn't have any puppies available, only a full-grown Labrador rescue dog. I'd figured that would do.

Laney's mouth opened wide as she took a step back to the bedrooms. She couldn't decide whether to go after the girls or argue with the delivery guy.

As if in slow motion, she turned to look at me as their thank-you started to register. "You didn't!?"

"Betcha!" I said and slid out the door, pulling it closed behind me before something could hit me on the way out.

Thank you for reading!

I hope you enjoyed my book. I would really appreciate it if you could leave a review at the Amazon page for Uncle and Ants. Even just a few words would help a lot.

Then turn the page for Chapter 1 of *Chutes and Ladder* (book 2 in the **Silicon Valley Mystery** series).

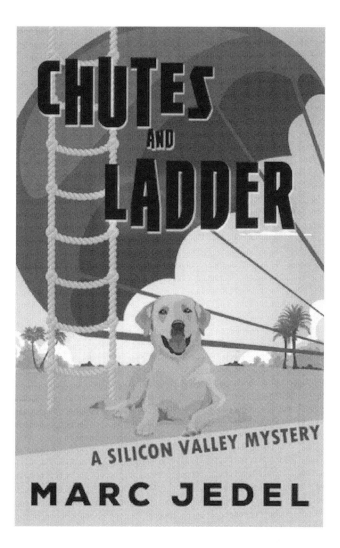

Ready for more adventures of
Marty and company?

Can super-agent (*in his own mind*) Uncle Marty solve not one,
but two mysteries without becoming a victim himself?

Will he ever be forgiven for bringing Buddy, the Labrador, into his sister's house?

All your favorite characters are back in a crazy, new adventure. Plus, introducing a new member of Marty's family!

Get chapter 1 of *Chutes and Ladder* **today** and be the first to hear when it's released by joining my mailing list at: **http://www.marcjedel.com**

Acknowledgements

Love always to my wife! This book would not have been possible without her love, support, editing, and prodding.

To my mother and father for encouraging me to read, write, try new things, as well as for telling me stupid puns and not neglecting the etiquette lessons. Lots of love to my children, sister, and other relatives who encouraged me to write and downplayed their surprise when it turned out well.

Special thanks to the world's best beta readers, especially Bill, Sandy, Andrea, Edgardo, Crystal, Anita, Keith, Ruth, Barnett, and our neighborhood women's book group for their wonderful, early inputs and advice.

One last shout-out to Kristen Weber for her invaluable editorial coaching, assistance, and positivity.

About the Author

In my family, I was born first — a fact my sister never lets me forget, no matter what milestone age she hits.

For most of my life, I've been inventing stories. Some, especially when I was young, involved my sister as the villain. As my sister's brother for her entire life, I'm highly qualified to tell this tale of this evolving, quirky sibling relationship.

My writing skills were honed in years of marketing leadership positions in Silicon Valley. While my high-tech marketing roles involved crafting plenty of fiction, we called these marketing collateral, emails and ads.

Friends would say that Marty's character isn't much of a stretch of the imagination for me, but I proudly resemble that remark.

Like Marty, I live in San Jose, where I write within earshot of the doppler effect of the local ice cream truck. My two kids do live across the country and benefit from what I believe are witty texts from their father. Fortunately, they're too far away for me to hear their groans. Unlike Marty, I have a wonderful wife and a neurotic but sweet, small dog, who much prefers the walks resulting from writer's block than my writing.

Thanks for reading my book! More at **www.marcjedel.com**.

— Marc

Made in the USA
Middletown, DE
28 October 2018